Dirty Truths

RENÉE MILLER

ISBN: 978-0-9878112-6-4

For Carlos, because he's read Dirty Truths more times than I have, and because he's Carlos.

And for Luis, because he's awesome.

CHAPTER 1

Joe McNeil sank onto the stool, his face haunted.

"Rough night?" Wade set a Coors in front of his friend. "Just let me lock up and I'll join you."

"Shit, I forgot you closed early on Wednesdays. I'll finish this and get out of your hair. I just needed somewhere to calm down."

Wade slid the bolt across the door and strode back to the bar. Joe's leg vibrated against the stool as he took a long swig of his beer. Kristina. It had to be. Nothing else rattled Joe.

He lifted a glass from the rack and scooped some ice into it. After grabbing the bottle of Jack Daniels off the shelf, he walked around the bar to join Joe. "Kristina?"

Joe nodded and finished his beer. Wade filled his glass and slid the remaining whiskey to his friend. "Probably not the best idea. I could kill the little fucker."

"Who?"

"Who do you think?"

Daniel Riley. Useless piece of shit.

"When we got there, Kristina said she was carrying the baby and fell down the stairs." Joe's voice broke. He cleared his throat and rolled his shoulders. "I told her she was a piss poor liar. No one gets a fucking shiner from falling down the stairs."

"He hit her?" Rage burned in the bottom of Wade's gut.

"Christ, when isn't he hitting her? This time, he punched

her, kicked her, bit her… fuck. Then he hit the baby. Might have been his worst mistake."

"The baby?" A red haze distorted Wade's vision.

"Well, Kristina says he didn't, but I know when she's lying. Cadence had a bruise on her cheek, but she seems okay. Kristina took the brunt of whatever pissed him off this time. Wait." Joe dug into his jacket and pulled out his cell. He pressed a couple of buttons and passed it to Wade. "There. See for yourself."

Hands unsteady, Wade looked at the images. The eyes, once a bright green and so full of life it made a man ache just to look into them, held hopelessness that broke his heart. He skipped through the pictures, unable to look at them for longer than a moment, before stopping at an image of Kristina's abdomen. The right side was covered by an angry purple bruise, swollen and scraped in spots. "What the fuck, Joe? Did she call the cops?"

"Yeah, after we made her do it."

"You know, I could take care of this. A favor; just between you and me. No one would hear from him again." Wade cracked his knuckles.

"No."

"No?"

"You know what Kristina's like. Just let her do this on her own. I think she's finally had enough. If we do anything, she'll know. She'd never forgive me."

"Joe—"

"No, Wade. I mean it. Leave it be. Please." Joe glanced up.

Christ. "Fine. But if you ever change your mind, you know where to find me."

"I do."

"He hurts her again, I don't make any promises."

"Me neither, my friend."

CHAPTER 2

"I can't do this." Kristina shook her head.

The lawyer touched her hand. "You can."

They sat in a little room awaiting the judge's decision. Although it was to be a place to calm a person's nerves, the pale green walls and old office chairs lent to nausea instead.

Daniel visited the night before, begging her for another chance, insisting he would change. He pleaded with her to stop the divorce proceedings and she'd wavered. In the end, though, she'd stood firm. Their marriage was over.

Now that she had testified against him, the judge sat in his chambers deciding the particulars of their failed marriage. It was all too real. Kristina feared she couldn't handle being alone.

"Look at these and tell me you want to go back." Her lawyer passed the pictures she'd already seen. Images she saw every day in the mirror, every night in her dreams.

They showed a destroyed woman she didn't recognize. It wasn't just on the outside—although the blackened eyes, swollen nose, and bruised body were bad enough. Emptiness reflected in that woman's green gaze, so cold and vast Kristina barely recognized her.

She nodded to her lawyer. "Okay. You're right. I just don't want to fight him anymore."

He smiled, his dark eyes crinkling at the corners.

She didn't want to be the woman in the pictures, the one

who jumped at shadows and trembled at the slightest change in tone.

"You'll fight no matter what you do, because it's what Mr. Riley does. But you have to get him out of your house. He could kill you the next time, and almost did." He squeezed her hand.

She looked away.

"I'm not telling you what to do, but if you were my daughter, I'd urge you to think about the future. What about your baby? What if she grows to be a difficult child? What will he do if she doesn't 'obey' as her mother does?"

Shame burned her throat as she remembered the last time Daniel slept in their home. Cadence had been so still, and the bruise... Daniel didn't look at the photos when they'd passed them to his attorney. Instead, he'd stared at Kristina, his mouth pressed into a firm line. Showing the pictures of her bruises was the only way she'd ensure he couldn't take Cadence, but Daniel would never understand she could have done much worse. If she'd taken pictures of what he did to their daughter, he would be in jail.

Kristina sighed. "I definitely don't want her hurt, but I don't think he—"

"He would."

She looked at her lawyer, a man old enough to be her grandfather and saw the pity in his eyes. God, she was sick of pity. She'd seen it when her parents came to help her, and when they'd taken the pictures. Her dad urged her to tell the police everything, but she didn't want anyone to know what she'd let him do to Cadence. A good mother would never have allowed the situation to become so dangerous. Kristina couldn't bear the thought of losing her daughter, even if she might deserve to.

Everyone in town already knew about her failed marriage. She didn't need them knowing she'd botched motherhood as well.

A small woman dressed in an impossibly tight grey suit opened the door and motioned them outside. They followed her, back to the judge's chambers. She ushered them inside a small dark room. The walls, paneled in a deep brown wood, matched the desk and floor. Three chairs, their metal legs rusted, lined up before the desk. Daniel and his lawyer stood by the door. Kristina shook as she walked past.

Their judge, a thin man who must have forgotten how to smile, sat at a large oak desk covered with papers, most in stacks, a few spread out before him.

He cleared his throat and looked at both of them in turn. "Usually I would decide this differently. I'd send you home and give you a date to return, but given the situation, it's wise to settle matters as quickly as possible."

Daniel's lawyer nudged him forward.

Kristina moved away as he brushed her side. The judge eyed them before putting his glasses on and lifting a thick stack of papers. "I agree for a period of time, Mr. Riley's visits with his daughter should be supervised. I am recommending anger management classes Mr. Riley. You will attend if you hope to see your daughter in your home without supervision. These pictures are disturbing, very disturbing. I know the matter has been dealt with in criminal court already, but I want to make sure you get the help you need so your anger doesn't spiral out of control."

Kristina had trouble hiding a smile. She wouldn't have to leave Cadence alone with him. Whatever else happened today didn't matter. Daniel couldn't take her daughter, and that was all she cared about.

"Mrs. Riley," the judge's dull voice brought her thoughts back to the present and she straightened. "I'm giving you a choice regarding visitation. Mr. Riley may visit your daughter in a designated place with a representative of the court, out of your presence, or in your home with you supervising."

"In my home," she said.

No way would she place her baby in a stranger's care. Daniel could charm anyone. He'd convince them he was a good person and have Cadence on his own within weeks. And if she angered him, he'd make sure Kristina never saw her again.

"Give the decision some consideration. You are under no obligation to supervise these visits, or to ever be alone in Mr. Riley's company again. This is an option, a choice, Mrs. Riley. Please, consider it carefully."

Kristina held her breath. Daniel's gaze turned, his eyes burning into her. Her fear of losing her daughter outweighed her fear of him. "It's better for Cadence to be in her own home."

"Are you sure? This means the restraining order issued previously will be taken away." He lifted a grey brow.

"I—it's okay. He'll be getting help. If he—if Daniel gets angry again, I'll arrange for someone else to handle the visits. I'd like us to be able to get along for Cadence's sake," Kristina said.

"It's settled then. Although I would like you to consider having a non-partial third party present for these visits, at least until Mr. Riley finishes his counseling." The judge rambled on about property, child support and other things related to the divorce. Kristina heard none of it over the roaring in her ears.

Seated on the couch, Kristina stared out the window and waited for Daniel to arrive. Birds chirped and a large blue jay fought with a robin over the seed in the feeder near the window. No matter how valiantly the robins fought, the aggressive jays always won.

The afternoon sun reflected off the neighbor's steel roof. She blinked to clear her vision, her attention moving to two boys walking slowly down the quiet street. Shirtless, towels and fishing poles over their shoulders, they headed toward the river across the road. After climbing over the guardrails next to the old footbridge, they disappeared over the short slope and into the trees. Her mind revisited summers spent with her friends in the muddy water beneath the falls. Maybe next summer she could take Cadence swimming.

Shaded by a tall oak tree, the driveway remained empty; as it had been the last five times she'd looked out. He never came when he said he would. She didn't know why she expected him to.

Kristina stood and turned from the window her gaze drifting once more to the clock. More than two hours late. Cadence had fallen asleep, despite Kristina's efforts to keep her awake. Not that Daniel cared. He paid his daughter little attention when he came, preferring to argue instead.

Hatred burned in his eyes when he looked at her and it soaked every word he said. Even as he pleaded for Kristina's forgiveness, his loathing smoldered in the brown depths of his eyes, through his false tears. It hurt more than she'd ever let on to realize he never loved her.

Gravel crunched outside. A bubble of anxiety grew in her chest. Daniel's black Dodge blocked the window. The sight of the large truck angered her every time she had to look at it. He didn't pay child support, but he bought the new truck only a week after the divorce was final. Of course, Daniel claimed his girlfriend, Desiree, bought it.

She hated herself for it, but every time he mentioned Desiree, jealousy soured Kristina's stomach. Guilt and indecision had plagued her throughout the ordeal of leaving, filing for divorce, and pressing charges against him. She didn't want the marriage they had, but longed for the man she thought he could be. Kristina often wondered what might have been if she could've made him happy. He moved on easily enough, though. So much for dying without her.

The door burst open and Kristina jumped.

"Don't start, I had to meet a client and it ran late," he grumbled.

She looked at his khaki shorts and black polo shirt. "On the golf course?"

"So? It's business. I've told you a million times, but you never listen. Half your problem is your shitty listening skills."

She bit her lip as Daniel crossed the room to Cadence's

playpen.

"She's sleeping," Kristina warned.

He glared and leaned over to pick the baby up. Cadence squirmed, protesting a muffled cry at the audacity of whoever dared to wake her. He straightened her pink dress, holding her in one arm. Opening her eyes, Cadence looked up at her father. She turned her head and, seeing Kristina standing across the room, her lip trembled.

"Fuck, is this all she does? You've got her spoiled."

Daniel bounced her a bit, but it didn't stop the wail that escaped Cadence's mouth. She reached for Kristina but he turned away and walked to the kitchen.

Kristina followed, aching to take her daughter. He held her all wrong. Cadence hated to lie on her back. She preferred to be facing out so she could see everything.

He paced the floor speaking in hushed tones to the squalling infant. Kristina hovered in the doorway. The window above the small table cast little light in the tiny room and the darkness depressed her. She often wished she could knock out the far wall and put a large window in to allow in the morning sun. Instead, she'd settled with painting it a cheery yellow, a color Daniel had forbidden while they were married. If he noticed the change, he didn't comment.

"Here, take her." He pushed Cadence into her arms.

"Shhh," she lifted Cadence against her chest and patted her back. The baby settled at once.

"That's just bullshit. You're turning her against me, just like everyone else."

"I didn't turn anyone against you."

"No?" he leaned against the sink, crossing his arms over his chest.

Kristina backed toward the living room, flinching at his belligerent glare.

"It's been nearly three months. When can I take her on my own?"

"I don't know. It's up to the court."

A muscle in his jaw twitched.

She stared at the bottles lined up on the counter next to his arm. Although she had grown used to the rage, it didn't change the way her body reacted. Cold sweat broke out down the small of her back and she tried to hide the slight tremble of her hands. She didn't want to be afraid, but her body couldn't forget how much Daniel's anger hurt.

"It's not bad enough you tell everyone our personal business and make me look like a monster, you have to make sure I'm miserable too. You like controlling me, making me beg to see my kid?"

"I want you to be happy so both of us can move on." Kristina backed away, trying to put distance between her and the rage that hung in the room like thick smoke.

He snorted, "Right. So you called Desiree because you want me to be happy?"

"She called *me*."

"So she's a liar?" Daniel pushed away from the counter.

Kristina retreated until the playpen dug against her thighs. Skirting around it, not taking her eyes from Daniel, she placed Cadence inside. The baby fussed. Then she noticed the mirror hanging on the side and smiled at her reflection.

"You told her I was sick," Daniel said. "You told her to leave while she had a chance. Right?"

Kristina shook her head. "I didn't say those things. She asked why you couldn't see Cadence and I told her—"

"You had no right to talk to her at all," he roared.

Although she expected the rage, it startled her. Why did it always turn to this?

"You took everything from me and now you're trying to destroy my life."

"Daniel, I just want to forget this nastiness and move on. I don't want your life ruined. Can't we just get along for Cadence's sake? I'm glad you found someone."

"Bullshit! It's okay for you to fuck around and to sleep with whoever shows an interest, but I can't. You want to control my life."

She said nothing. He wouldn't believe her anyway. She'd

told him repeatedly there'd been no one since him, but Daniel preferred to believe the worst about her. Maybe to be able to live with himself he had to make her the villain. The alternative would be unacceptable to someone like Daniel.

He shoved his hands in his pockets and strode across the room.

Kristina stumbled to move out of his way.

He turned, raising an eyebrow a smirk curving his lips. "What are you afraid of?"

"Nothing."

She straightened her shoulders. He couldn't hurt her now. The lawyers and the police said he couldn't.

Daniel strode toward her, his hands still in his pockets. "You're scared."

"It'll be hard to impress clients from a jail cell." She lifted her chin.

"You wouldn't do that to me."

"Yes I would."

He lifted his hand to her hair and twirled an auburn strand between his fingers. "No, I think your boyfriend has your head all turned around, but you still love me."

"You're wrong on both counts."

He lowered his arm and strode to the door. "I know when you're lying."

Daniel opened the door and paused. The sunlight streamed through the screen, giving his blond hair a whitish halo, shadowing his face slightly. He smirked and scratched his head. "I wonder if the court would allow a whore to keep her baby. I think they might reconsider if there was another home—a two-parent home—for her to go to."

He turned, slamming the door behind him as he left.

Kristina sank to the floor, her arm coming to rest on the playpen. She glanced at her daughter, who still cooed happily at her reflection. Kristina had no love left for the angry and hateful monster Daniel had become, but when he'd touched her hair, his eyes softened just a little and her resolve weakened. If only they could go back and do it over. There had been good times. Her heart recalled every moment when he looked at her like that.

Shaking her head, she ran a trembling hand over her face. What had she done to make him so angry? Cadence whined, forcing her back to reality. It didn't matter what she'd done. No amount of regret could put the pieces back together.

RENÉE MILLER

CHAPTER 3

Daniel squealed the truck's tires as he sped down the quiet street.

"What do you think of that, you nosy bastard?" he muttered to the old man who lived next door.

The man shook his bald head and frowned at Daniel, before turning back to his flowers. Every time he came to see Cadence, the prick stood out front watering something. Did he think he fooled anyone? Kristina probably told him all sorts of bullshit about their marriage. She told anyone who would listen.

Cursing, he slammed one fist on the steering wheel and swerved, narrowly avoiding a black sedan parked in the middle of the damn road. These streets were too fucking small. Kristina's always had vehicles lining both sides and no room for anyone to drive. Daniel cranked the wheel, ignoring a stop sign, and careened around the corner. He knew what his wife—ex-wife, was all about. She wanted to ruin him, and she nearly succeeded. His job hung by a thread and his boss had forced him to go to the court-appointed counseling. "To get your temper under control," Carl had said. If Daniel didn't do it, he'd be out of a job.

Arrogant son of a bitch. As if Carl knew anything about anger management. Mr. High and Mighty, Carl Canon, didn't know a thing about hard times or dealing with a bitch. His wife was perfect, wouldn't say shit if her mouth were full of it.

Carl had women on the side and went where he pleased. As long as wifey had enough money to shop and get her hair done, she never said a word. What did he know about Daniel's misery?

Canon Design was as old as this shithole town, just like Carl's family. He'd inherited a fortune and didn't have to work to make a name for himself. Still, as much as he believed the Canon's were white trash with more money than brains, he liked his job. As a sales rep, most of his work consisted of meeting prospective clients and discussing what they wanted Canon to do for their home or business while wining, dining, or playing eighteen holes on a Wednesday. Daniel drafted the plans, got the client's approval, and then sent them Carl's way to sign the contract. He seldom spent time in the office.

Canon was the closest to success he could hope for, at least while staying in this piece of shit community.

He could move to the city, and get the hell out of this area. He'd had enough job offers to know he'd never starve out there. But then he'd be nobody. Daniel had never been nobody.

He slowed as a fat woman with a stroller crossed the road ahead. She wiped her dark hair from her forehead and pulled at her baggy t-shirt. Daniel closed his eyes as she slowly waddled to the other side. Probably one of those welfare cases with ten kids and no husband to whip her back into shape. Did Kristina have any clue how lucky she was to have someone care about her like he had? Christ, he'd busted his ass to make her into the best wife she could be and made sure she didn't turn into a fat piece of trash like that woman. What did he get for giving a damn?

Thanks to him, she lived in a nice house on a quiet street with respectable neighbors. Practically waterfront property. True, no house in Laighton screamed high class, but the one he provided was a damn sight better than the dingy eyesore she came from over on the other side of the river.

Her parents didn't even own a house. Joe, her father, worked in construction and her mother was a cashier. Neither would improve their situation in life. Fuck, Joe could barely read. Because of Daniel, people considered Kristina worth their time and she'd kicked his balls for his trouble. There's gratitude for you.

He squinted through the sun's glare. Turning right again he'd barely accelerated when he had to slow once more. A woman in the car ahead kept touching her brakes, and it pissed him off. The air conditioning, cold as an arctic breeze, blew across his face. Cursing, he switched it off and pushed the button next to his arm to put the window down.

The woman ahead came to a full stop, her right signal light flashing for no fucking reason. He slammed his foot on the brake, clenched his jaw, and tried to breathe. She changed her mind about turning into the lawn to her right and continued forward. He wanted to jump out of the truck and rip her out of the car by her frizzy hair, take her keys and her license, and then find the stupid shit that let her behind the wheel of anything. This is exactly why he never allowed Kristina to get her license: one less idiot woman on the road.

Finally, the woman turned right, no signal this time, leaving the road clear. He slammed his palm on the horn and gave her the finger. She didn't glance his way, but he knew she saw him.

He came to the set of lights across from the grocery store and stopped. The town now boasted two sets of traffic lights as it became apparent more and more of Laighton's residents didn't know what an intersection was or how one should use it. He pulled out his phone while waiting for the light to turn. An old man stood next to the Dollar Store on Daniel's right, staring at the walk sign. Did he expect the flashing man to hop out and help him across the road? Finally, the idiot stepped off the curb and hobbled across the street. Daniel turned his thoughts back to Desiree and dialed her number.

Slim, blonde, and about as bright as a burned out light bulb. But she had potential because she made it her mission in life to please him. As Desiree's phone rang, he thought back to the day he met her. It always made him smile.

Kristina had been at the doctor's, having an ultrasound

done to determine the sex of their baby. Turns out they'd driven all the way to Salach for nothing. At the time, she said they couldn't tell because the baby wouldn't turn. She lied. He didn't want a girl and she tried to cover it up so he wouldn't be angry. Kristina learned that day no one lied to him.

Desiree had been sitting in triage, her arm in a sling. Holding a copy of some women's magazine, she chewed on a manicured nail and flipped the pages idly. He'd paused. Just looking at her he could tell she was a woman who didn't go anywhere looking frumpy, not even to the hospital with a bum arm. Her hair fell over her shoulders in carefully constructed honey-colored waves, and she wore a pink cotton dress and strappy shoes that looked as though the slightest stumble would break them. Carefully applied makeup accentuated her large brown eyes.

Daniel tried to impress upon Kristina the importance of always looking her best. She represented him when she went out, but she never paid attention. Hell, he couldn't remember the last time she'd put makeup on or wore anything but a sloppy ponytail. He preferred blondes too, not brunettes. He'd told Kristina numerous times she should dye her red mess a more attractive color.

Daniel had sat in the chair next to Desiree and picked up a magazine. People coughed and moaned in the chairs around him. He'd glared. Normally he'd have returned to his truck after making sure Kristina went to her appointment, but the sight of Desiree intrigued him enough to risk the germs of the degenerates and hypochondriacs filling the hospital's emergency department. Desiree glanced at him a couple of times before he gifted her with his smile.

She looked away blushing.

He took a chance. "I'm Daniel."

"Desiree. Um…I think I broke my wrist."

He looked at the sling, noting her swollen hand. "How did you manage that?"

She blushed again.

He set the magazine down.

"I tripped over my cat."

Daniel laughed. How stupid. Tripping over a cat? Daniel didn't like pets. Stinking, stupid wastes of space. There was a reason man stood at the top of the food chain. "When you're done, do you want to get a drink or something?" he asked.

"I'm going to be a while. But maybe another time."

Daniel didn't pause to think about it. He took out his wallet and searched for a business card. "Here, call me when you're done."

She took it. "Are you sure?"

"Yeah, I'm not busy tonight. I'm waiting for a friend, but once I take her home, I'm free."

"Her?"

"It's complicated." Daniel waited as she digested this. He made no move to cover his wedding band when she looked at his hand.

She smiled and nodded after a moment. "You can explain over drinks."

He'd worked on molding Desiree into what he needed her to be for months. Too bad she couldn't retain simple instructions.

Desiree's phone went to voicemail. Daniel jolted out of his thoughts and snapped his phone shut. Where the hell was she? He specifically told her to be around. She knew he hated when she didn't answer her phone. It made it seem like she had something to hide.

The light changed and a blonde in tight spandex shorts and a bra-like shirt darted across. He mumbled under his breath, waiting for her to clear the front of the truck before turning left, the bumper a breath away from her fat ass.

She glared.

He smiled. *Bitch.*

He hadn't yet committed to keeping Desiree. Sure, she was manageable, but he had so much work yet to do with her. Kristina had been so close; he hated to give her up. He shouldn't have hit Cadence, and he wouldn't do it again, but he'd been angry. He felt terrible when he'd seen his daughter the next day. Kristina's father stood in the window holding Cadence while the cops informed him he could no longer go into his own house. But if Kristina hadn't behaved so stupidly, he wouldn't have lost control. He prided himself on always being in control.

After rescuing the phone from the passenger seat, Daniel hit redial and waited. As he sped out of Laighton, past the cottages along the lake where he used to meet Desiree, it went to voicemail once more. He punched 'end' and then hit redial again. She better pick up before he reached Salach or she would be in more shit than she'd ever known.

Maybe his mistake was allowing Desiree to keep her cell phone. It had only taken one mistake for Kristina to learn never to leave the house when he told her he'd call. A cell phone was out of the question, and she never questioned his decision. Desiree couldn't seem to get it through her thick head. She needed to put him ahead of everyone else, and that included work. Waitressing didn't demand a lot of brainpower. She should check her phone on breaks, every break, in case he needed her for something. Just because she had to turn it off didn't mean she could ignore his calls. She'd have to give up her job. It wasn't like she contributed anything anyway.

Daniel took very little in as he sped home, hitting redial several times and still getting her voicemail. A car passed him, red with a cracked rear window and rust along the passenger door. He cursed. If he didn't have to worry about her bullshit, the asshole would have been eating his dust. He could barely keep the damn truck on the road he was so pissed. When Desiree's voice filtered to his brain, Daniel tightened his grip on the phone and stepped down on the gas.

"Where the hell were you?" he yelled.

"I'm at work. I had to shut my phone off; you know they don't like it ringing when we're busy," her voice shook. She knew she'd screwed up.

"So busy you don't have time for me?"

"Dan, come on. You know that's not true. There's a big golf tournament today, and we've got a party of twelve in my section. How am I supposed to check my phone when I haven't had a break all day?"

"That's some attitude you've developed. All those guys flirting with you got you feeling like someone important, eh? You think any of them will give a shit about you like I do?"

"This is stupid. Were you just at your wife's?"

"What does she have to do with you and me?"

Daniel slowed the truck as he approached the 'Welcome to Salach' sign and turned off the highway. A large truck stopped suddenly and Daniel had to slam on the brakes to avoid hitting it. He dropped the phone and cursed.

"Dan? You okay?" Desiree's voice came from under the seat.

Daniel reached under and picked the phone up, fury smoldering in his chest. If she wasn't so goddamn stupid... he'd almost wrecked his new truck.

He glanced through the windshield and caught the grinning face of Wade Bowen in the mirror of the truck ahead of him.

Fucking asshole.

"Dan?" Desiree's voice held a note of panic.

Daniel put the phone to his ear, and lifted his other hand to give Bowen the finger. The other truck sped away. "Listen, Kristina is none of your fucking business. You got me?"

Desiree murmured something unintelligible.

"She might have her head screwed on crooked, but she damn well listens when I tell her to do something. If I needed her, she was there. Every time," he continued.

"I know. I'm sorry, Dan. Really. I just got busy and I forgot you had to go there today. Was it terrible?"

Daniel's anger subsided; she knew she was wrong. He'd deal with her tonight. "Yeah, she's turned Cadence against me. I can't even pick the kid up without her crying for her mother."

"That's awful. How could she? I'd never do that to you, no matter what happened between us."

"Yes, you would. Women are all the same." He stopped at a red light just past the arena.

19

The Stingray van parked outside and kids swarmed it. Damn, he meant to sign up for the summer hockey camp. Carl liked them to be involved in shit like that.

"She just needs to remember how lucky she was to have me there to guide her and then we could straighten this shit out."

"You don't need her. We can have more children." Desiree's voice raised a notch, as it always did when he talked about going back to Kristina.

The light changed to green. Daniel turned right and followed the heavy traffic slowly inching his way to Front Street and their apartment. He made a mental note to call about getting in on the hockey camp.

"It's the principle of the whole thing, don't you get it? She fucked me over and that can't be ignored. I *own* her. Marriage means something to me."

"But what about us? You guys are divorced, Dan. How much more over does a marriage get?"

"Shit, I don't have time for this. I told you before. Things don't have to change between us. I love you, but you've got a lot to learn before I'd consider getting serious. If you'd just listen to me then I could give you what you want. But I don't settle."

"I know. I'm sorry." A loud crash and Desiree's muffled voice as she covered the phone. Of course, now she'd have to go.

"Listen hon, I have to get back. I'll see you at home."

"Yeah, we'll talk about this later. You make sure you go straight home. I don't want to come looking for you."

"I will. If I run late I'll call."

"You won't run late." Daniel shut the phone and tossed it back on the seat.

He saw his apartment building but drove past.

He needed a drink.

Desiree arrived home one hour late, excuses running out of her mouth before she'd even closed the door.

"Sorry. I called, but you didn't answer and I thought you'd gone out. We had a table come in ten minutes before closing and Mike sent Laura home early so I had no choice." She set her purse on the counter.

Daniel sat in the darkened living room, his feet up on the coffee table. "I told you what would happen if you didn't come home when I asked you to. I specifically said you were not to be late. Not tonight. It doesn't matter whether I answered the phone or not. My instructions didn't include doing what you fucking pleased if I happened to step out for a minute. When are you going to learn?"

He moved his feet off the table and stood. The room spun, and he closed his eyes to steady himself.

Women. God put them on this earth with a purpose, but not the one most women nowadays believed. *No one reads the Bible anymore, that's the problem.* Daniel seethed as Desiree wrung her hands in front of her. She should be worried.

In the Book of Daniel, which was written by his father, if you couldn't manage one woman, you were shit, not a man at all. They existed simply to ease the empty hours, and to make babies. They weren't supposed to think. He didn't enjoy punishing Desiree or Kristina; not the way his dad enjoyed knocking his mom around. Sure his mom deserved it most times, but his dad sometimes looked for reasons to punish her, which was wrong. It was different for Daniel. He cared about making them the best they could be, but the pair of them insisted on trying to emasculate him and he had to act accordingly. He could let some things go, but being too lenient led to trouble. Give them an inch and they'd take a mile. His mother had taught him better than that. His dad let her off easy just once and the traitorous bitch abandoned all of them.

"Please Dan, I tried," Desiree's voice broke the silence and her brown eyes filled with tears. She did this every time he had to correct her. He didn't give a shit about her tears.

"Not hard enough. What am I supposed to think? I didn't

know where you were or who you were with. You could have been doing anything, like fucking Mike for all I know."

"No." She shook her head. She'd piled her hair into the same sloppy ponytail Kristina was so fond of.

The sight of it made his blood boil. He reached up, ripped the elastic out and tossed it aside. She flinched as he pulled out a chunk of hair with it. "I told you I hate your hair like that."

"I was going to take it down when I got home."

"Shut up—just stop with your stupid excuses. I think you're trying to piss me off."

She shook her head and moved around the table, as if it would stop her punishment.

He followed her, stumbling slightly. "Don't make me chase you."

She stopped and brought her hands to her chest. Kristina would have stood there without a word and taken what she deserved. Desiree would learn, but he was sick of having to teach her the same thing repeatedly. The problem with trying to teach anything to an airhead is they learn about as fast as a retarded dog, and their memories were as short. Kristina rarely had to be told twice, and never more than that.

Desiree's boss, Mike Connors, always had his eye on her. He gave Desiree special treatment, and made her stay late so he could try to get her into bed. Desiree encouraged him. Daniel had seen it himself. She batted her eyes and swung her ass, inviting Mike to look at her. Sickening.

"Who was it? Was it Mike?"

"No, Mike has a girlfriend. He—"

The slap echoed in the stillness of the apartment. Desiree gasped, holding her face.

Daniel grabbed her hair and dragged her toward the hall. "Don't lie to me. I see I need to remind you of a few things. I wish you'd stop making me do this."

"Please Dan, not like this. I love you. I don't want to do this with you angry at me."

"Shut up."

Desiree's body shook with sobs and he shoved her through

the bedroom door. She stumbled and fell against the dresser. Tears streamed down her cheeks but she choked down the whimpers allowing only a couple of sniffles out.

"Get your clothes off. I bet Mike can't make you scream like I can." He unbuckled his belt as he spoke.

"Dan—"

"Do it!"

Her hand flew to her blouse. With trembling fingers, she undid the tiny buttons and slipped it off her shoulders. Daniel smiled. She stepped out of her skirt but he shook his head when she reached for her stockings. "Leave them."

She stood before him, her body tense, and he sighed. She knew what came next, but every time he had to remind her.

"Get on the bed."

"I don't want you mad at me. Can't we talk about this?"

Daniel grabbed her arm and dragged her to the bed, shoving her onto her stomach. She cried softly as he stood over her. His mind clouded, Desiree's blond head blurred and he thought of Kristina. He wished it was her lying there. Someday it would be.

Daniel sat on the balcony in the dark, phone in his hand. Desiree was inside, crying herself to sleep. He hated how she made him do this to her. She knew there were rules. He only asked her to respect them and do as told. Fuck, he shouldn't feel guilty for her tears. He needed to get Kristina back. His life would have some normalcy then. He'd have to give her enough time to realize their divorce was a mistake.

Daniel didn't want to waste his time fixing Desiree when he already had a woman who knew what he liked and what he needed. Desiree was fine on the side, but living with her day in and day out wore on his nerves. Staring at the phone in his hand, he frowned. He'd been too patient with Kristina, it was time to turn up the heat and get his wife back.

CHAPTER 4

The alarm clock's buzz shocked Kristina awake. She reached for the nightstand. After fumbling for the snooze button, she rolled over. Cadence lay next to her, blue eyes wide, also startled by the noise, then she offered a dimpled grin and reached out to yank Kristina's hair.

"Well thank you." Pulling a slobbery fist away and picking out the bits of hair she managed to keep, Kristina tickled her daughter's belly. "Let's get you ready for Nana."

She rolled off the bed and leaned down to pick up Cadence.

She squirmed and wriggled trying to escape her mother's grasp.

Kristina sighed at the wet spot on the sheet; Cadence's diaper had leaked. Warm moisture seeped through her shirt. Cadence bounced in her arms, as though pleased with herself.

"Yeah, you got me," Kristina grumbled and walked to the door.

She tripped over the doorstop, as she did every morning in semi-darkness, and bit her tongue to choke a curse. "Mornings are for the birds and lunatics. Since you aren't a bird, dear daughter, I'm afraid you're one of the lunatics."

Cadence stared, chewing on her fist.

Kristina carried her to the small room adjacent to her own. She laid the baby on the change table and peeled off her sodden pajamas, then reached down to the shelf below to feel around for clean clothes and diapers. Balancing the naked baby in one arm, Kristina carted her into the bathroom for a bath before dressing her, and then carried a dry Cadence downstairs. She leaned across the end table near the living room's door to switch on the light before dragging the pink and yellow swing out of the corner near the couch and set the baby in its seat. Cadence's eyes lit up as she spied the spinning ball on top. She gurgled happily.

Yawning, Kristina turned toward the kitchen and paused at the blinking light on the answering machine. She didn't remember hearing the phone ringing, but she'd been tired. *Daniel.* She pressed a button, waited, and regretted it as soon as his first words issued from the tiny speaker.

"Kris, pick up the phone," Daniel's voice sounded hoarse, as though he'd been crying.

Her chest tightened.

"Please, I need you. I'm so sorry I hurt you, but I can make it up. We can fix this, baby, I know we can. I feel like I'm falling apart," Daniel's voice broke. He sobbed.

Kristina covered her mouth and took a breath. She couldn't stand hearing his pain, no matter what he did to her. She could handle angry Daniel, but this she didn't know how to ignore.

"I love you so much and I'm miserable without you. I'd rather die than never hold you again. Do you hear me, Kris? I'd rather die. Why do you hate me so much? I only tried to love you." A choking sound and the line went dead.

Kristina stared at the machine, her body trembling. Why did he do this? One minute he hurled insults and punches, and the next he was pouring his heart out and begging her to understand his messed up head. She'd tried, God how she'd tried, but Kristina couldn't fathom how someone who loved you could even think about hurting you. She knew he had issues, that he'd been damaged long before he met her, but should she and Cadence pay for her mistakes forever? She reached out to press the delete button.

Jackie's blue Taurus pulled into the gas station an hour late, leaving Kristina only thirty minutes to balance her till, close out her cash and get to the store. She wouldn't have time to run home and see Cadence.

"I'm so sorry," Jackie called as she ran to the booth. "Tim didn't get off work until just now, and I had no sitter."

Kristina smiled and finished recording the balances from the pumps. Though the sky dulled from a brilliant blue to a hazy grey, the air remained humid. Jackie wore short denim cutoffs and a pink tank top. She'd pulled her blond hair into a ponytail and applied way too much makeup, which was likely what made her late, not her husband. Jackie had only worked at the gas station for a month and half the time she arrived late. Kristina hadn't told their boss. It wasn't as if Jackie did it because she was lazy. She just couldn't get her shit together.

"You want me to do your cash?" Jackie asked, joining her at the gas pumps.

"No, I've almost got everything done. I've just got to count it and put it in the safe."

"I'm really sorry."

"It's okay; I'm just going to work again anyway." Kristina closed the clipboard and entered the small store next to the pumps. She cleared Jackie's purse and her book off the desk.

If she worked nights at the station, Kristina could relax while reading about how the warrior won the heart of the fair maiden too. Fairy tales, love transcending everything bad in the world like they claimed in those books didn't exist in the real world.

Her mind replayed Daniel's message and her chest tightened. It would be so easy to give up and go back. But he would never change. She was tired of fighting and he'd never stop.

After counting the cash, she made entries in the ledger under the desk and then stuffed it in the small safe behind her.

Outside, Jackie leaned into the window of a red Chevy.

Kristina shook her head and reached to her right, next to the door, to switch on the pod lights that lit up the pumps.

Jackie glanced back and waved, then turned to the man in the truck. She ran a finger along the driver's door, tilting her head and laughing at something he said.

The Chevy had been through nearly every night Jackie worked, yet never when Kristina worked alone. She hoped Tim didn't catch on, or Jackie would have some explaining to do. She couldn't imagine anyone worth lying for. Love wasn't about sneaking around. Passion and lust could be good reasons for acting like a fool when you had the excuse of being young and stupid. But not love. If you loved someone, you didn't hide it. In Jackie's case, a divorce would be logical, but Kristina doubted the guy in the truck inspired feelings of love for Jackie.

She opened the door and stepped down to the curb. What did she know about love? Only that it hurt. Kristina didn't recall ever being passionate about anything to the point of obsession. Once a long time ago, she'd thought she was passionate about art. She sketched and dabbled in watercolors, but after marrying Daniel she'd given it up. He didn't like her doing anything that took her attention from him and his needs. As she crossed the street Kristina marveled at how totally brainwashed she'd been, before heading toward the second job of the day.

Glancing up at the big clock on the wall above the cash register, Kristina sighed. Eleven o'clock. Almost done.

It had been busy all night, the floor now covered in mud from the rain that fell early in the afternoon. They were supposed to mop the back and front sections of the store before leaving and John, who had worked the previous shift, hadn't bothered. He never cleaned but she'd hardly go around correcting the boss. Earlier in her shift Kristina had cursed him silently as she cleaned up the milk crates strewn everywhere and the empty pop cases stacked against the cooler door. She'd had a full two hours of cleaning at the beginning of her shift and now she'd have to do it all again. At least the work kept her mind from straying to darker thoughts.

Although she'd sat on pins and needles all day expecting Daniel to call again, he hadn't. Obviously, he didn't miss her as much as he professed, or he'd have at least called to see if she got his message. Stuffing a pile of redeemed lottery tickets into the bin under the cash register Kristina snorted at the thought. Knowing Daniel, he'd been drunk and didn't remember the call.

She walked to the storeroom to the left of the counter and pulled the yellow mop bucket from behind the door. It tipped. Murky water left from last night's shift sloshed over the cement floor and under the metal shelves that ran the length of the narrow room. Cursing, she righted it and grabbed the mop from its spot against the wall, attempting to catch most of the water before it was lost forever behind the shelves. The smell of the storeroom was bad enough without adding dampness and mold to it. John, her boss, smoked like a chimney too, so the smell of stale cigarettes and rotting food burned her nose every time she entered the room.

She set the mop against the wall and dragged the bucket to the door, careful to lift it over the step to the opposite side of the counter where the bathroom and a big sink sat. It would have made more sense to keep the bucket next to the sink, but John said it took too much room. If he actually used the bucket, he might see things differently. The bell over the door jingled as she upended the water over the sink. Kristina set the bucket down and stepped out from the small room.

Wade Bowen, a friend of her dad's, stood at the counter in his usual black t-shirt and jeans, both fitting his body like a glove. His presence always triggered a jittery feeling in her stomach. Silly. It's not as though she'd ever entertained anything more than a passing acquaintance with him and he definitely never hinted at anything inappropriate.

He smiled. Dark eyes sparkled with mischief, and her heart fluttered. No matter how engaging Wade's smile might be, a darkness around him set her on edge. Kristina kept a safe distance from Wade and his wife, Amy. Everyone knew Wade was the man to go to if one needed anything not available through legal channels. He'd even killed men, so the gossip went, but she doubted there was much truth to most of those tales. Wade may have done some dishonest things, and she could imagine him roughing someone up a little, but never murder. Wade and her dad had been friends since she was twelve years old. Her dad wouldn't be friends with a killer.

Still, her breath quickened at the sight of him. Maybe it was because he always looked at her as though stripping away the outer layers of her being to reveal her soul and the secrets she hid from the world. What girl wouldn't like having someone look at them the way Wade did?

He leaned on the counter, his elbow brushing the lottery ticket display, causing a couple to shift out of their slots. His smile deepened.

Her cheeks burned.

"And how is Kristina?"

"Okay, I guess. And you?"

"Couldn't be better. How's Cadence? She must be growing like a weed."

Kristina laughed. The few times Wade had seen Cadence, he'd scooped the baby up as though it were perfectly natural for a six foot four giant with tattoos on his arms and a scarred jaw to cradle a cooing infant.

Averting her gaze, she focused on an imaginary speck of dirt on the counter. She could never look into his eyes for long. "I can barely keep her in clothes. How's Amy? She was talking about going back to school the last time I saw her."

His silence forced Kristina to glance up.

He frowned and shook his head. "No, she never bothered with school. She found something else to do. Rather, she found *someone* else to do."

"Oh," Kristina didn't know what else to say.

"It's okay. Except for the paperwork, we're as good as divorced. Maybe someday it'll be official."

"I guess." Kristina said. Amy had always been nice, but she ran around on Wade. Everyone knew about it. Most people in town were astonished he let her get away with it. Kristina's dad said he had no choice; Amy had too much on him. If he left her, she'd rat him out and he'd do serious jail time. She couldn't imagine why Amy would want to stay if she didn't want Wade anymore, but then Kristina wasn't a good judge of relationships. She'd definitely failed on that front.

"How many jobs do you have anyway? I saw you last week at the gas station. Your dad said you still work weekends at Maude's. I haven't had their bacon and eggs in a while, I should stop by soon. Maybe my favorite waitress will be on," as he spoke, Wade fiddled with the lock on the ticket box.

"I have three, but only this one is full time. I only work three days at the Petro and the breakfast shift on Saturday and Sunday at Maude's."

"Is that all?" Wade tilted his head, then reached across the counter and brushed her bangs from her eyes.

She wasn't sure how to handle the intimate gesture so she did nothing.

"What if you didn't have to work every day and night?" he asked, and lowered his hand.

"I'd have to win the lottery, unless you know something I don't. Is there a money tree hidden away somewhere?"

"Doesn't he help you out?"

"Who?"

"The asshole you just divorced."

"Oh—Daniel. He let me have the house, so I don't have to worry about rent. He's pretty strapped right now since he's paying the taxes and the mortgage on the house, so I don't bother him about the child support. He'll help when he can."

A lump formed in her throat at Wade's snort. Her dad had the same reaction when she tried to defend Daniel. Excusing his actions was a habit. "He's not entirely bad, you know. I don't want people to hate him."

Wade's face reddened. He tapped the counter with his keys, staring.

The thought of having angered him confused her. Why did he care whether she made excuses for Daniel? He barely knew him. Why was he there anyway? Did he plan to buy something?

"I won't bother telling you what I think of Daniel. You've got enough on your plate without my lecture." He stood and put his hands in his pockets.

Kristina's gaze traveled to his jeans, horrified when heat spread from her stomach down to her thighs, to areas it had no right warming up. Embarrassed, she looked away, her cheeks on fire. Obviously, the stress of the past few months wreaked havoc on her senses. Wade was at least fifteen years older, and not someone she should even consider thinking of that way. She risked a glance at his face. He smiled, furthering her humiliation. His eyes darkened just a little and Kristina cursed herself for being such a child. Damn, she wished she didn't wear her thoughts on her face for everyone to read.

"Have you ever bartended?"

"No."

"Would you consider it?"

"I don't know." Kristina knew where this was going. Wade was going to offer her a job at his bar. He was right, the money would be better than she earned working the jobs she currently held, but anyone who did risked being looked down their noses by the town's elite and she'd had enough of feeding the gossip mill. Besides, Daniel would freak out. Only trash worked in a bar, not mothers with responsibilities and self-respect. Daniel expected her to present herself with dignity. Funny, he didn't think it was necessary when it pertained to his treatment of her.

Wade shrugged. "It's up to you, but at least give it some thought. You could quit at least two of these jobs. I'd bet the tips you'd make with those eyes and your cute little ass would be enough to quit all three."

"Wade, stop it."

"I'm sorry. You're just fun to tease; the way you blush at just a thought is fascinating. Makes me wonder if it's just your cheeks that get all flushed."

Kristina smiled.

"Oh and dimples too." He clutched his chest dramatically.

She laughed.

"Seriously, though, at least consider it. You shouldn't be working yourself ragged like this. Your daughter deserves more than just a piece of you."

He was right. "I'll think about it."

"Good, I'll come in again in a couple of days." He turned and walked to the door, pausing before he opened it. "I hope you change your mind. It'd be nice to see you smile again." He pushed the door and walked out.

Kristina stood for a moment, staring after him.

Wade got into his car and although the lights shone in the window, he didn't pull out .

She walked to the sink and filled the mop bucket. When she emerged into the main section of the store, he was gone. As she dipped the mop into the water, she realized he hadn't bought anything.

Walking through the darkened street to her mother's apartment building Kristina hugged her purse close to her body. No one roamed the sidewalks, not even a car traveled the main roads. Midnight in Laighton was quiet, but in a couple of hours when the bar let out there would be a few people stumbling home. Now she had the town to herself. It made her nervous and she glanced around before stepping toward her parents' apartment building at the end of Jamieson Street.

Earlier, while she cleaned the store and tallied her cash, she had mulled over Wade's words. Now, as she rushed past darkened homes, jumping at imagined noises and hallucinated shadows—never able to shake the feeling of being watched—she was tempted to take his offer. She fished her key out of her pocket to unlock the main door. Maybe she'd run it by her mother.

As she climbed the two flights of stairs to her parents' door she continued to think about Wade's offer, wavering once more. As it was, she hated how people talked about her and Daniel. Could she handle more gossip?

When her mother opened the door, Kristina realized she'd forgotten to call. "Sorry Mom, I forgot."

"It's okay. I called and Carrie said you were on your way." Her mother wore her favorite housecoat, muted pink with tattered sleeves, and held it closed with her arms. "You look tired."

"I am." Kristina sighed.

Her mother backed into the apartment. "I'll wake your dad while you get Cadence ready."

"Wait, I want to ask you something."

In the small kitchen next to the hallway, Kristina set her purse on the counter, then walked to the living room and flopped down into the couch. She loved her mom's couch. Although it was probably fifteen years old it felt like sinking into giant fuzzy arms.

Her mom sat in a mismatched leather chair opposite, her body stiff, perhaps worried she would hear more bad news. Shame warmed Kristina's cheeks. She'd put her parents through hell and she could never make it up to them.

Kristina offered her mom a smile. "Wade came in tonight and offered me a job."

Her mom relaxed, and brushed a hand over her red curls. "Oh, I thought you had bad news. That's great."

"You don't think it'd be kind of trashy? I mean, they wear those little shirts and I'd have to buy some black pants. I don't have any. And I'm not sure I could wear them quite as snug as the rest of the girls. He might not like it."

"I don't think Wade would make you wear anything you're uncomfortable with. The tips there are really good. I heard they make more than a hundred a night. Add your regular wage and you'd be able to quit all these shitty jobs."

"But I'd have to work until three in the morning. It's going to be rough," Kristina argued.

"So? You'd have all day with Cadence. You wouldn't have to work all week either. Imagine spending whole days at home. You're crazy not to do it."

Kristina stared at her hands. Her mom was right. She had one day off each week and spent it cleaning and running errands. Poor Cadence received very little attention unless she was crying or hungry. "So you think I should do it? People are going to talk. Wade's not exactly a squeaky clean kind of character."

Her mother waved her hand and Kristina smiled at her scrunched nose. "Screw them. They talk anyway; it's a small town. Wade is a good man; he's been a loyal friend to your dad and helped us out of trouble more times than I can count. He keeps his private business separate from the bar and besides, he's not asking you to do anything other than serve drinks. He's offering you a chance to change things and I think you should take it. Besides, Amy looks after the bar too. It's not like it's going to be just you and Wade there. No reason for rumors at all. Find out how many shifts you have, keep the gas station until you know what kind of money you'll make or stay at Maude's, and quit the other two. I'll keep Cadence overnight when you work at the bar."

"Oh Mom, I can't ask you to do that. You have to work too."

Her mom leaned forward and smiled. "Stop it. This is easier for me. I work afternoons, remember? Cadence can come here, go straight to bed and I can sleep. I don't have to wait for you and your dad doesn't have to get up to take you home. It's better for all of us."

"Okay, I'll tell him when he comes in again."

"Good, it's a smart move. I'm sure of it." She stood and walked to the bedroom to wake her husband.

Kristina smiled. She hoped she was right in doing this. It would be nice to work a regular week like everyone else. She even dared to hope her life was turning around.

CHAPTER 5

Kristina pulled the mop bucket through the small door. She bumped her hip on to the ice cream freeze and grunted as burning pain shot down her thigh. Two customers roamed the aisles, which meant she'd have to wait to begin cleaning up. As she turned to step behind the counter, the bell above the door jingled. Stomach fluttering, she surprised herself by hoping it would be Wade. She glanced over her shoulder to meet his gaze. He smiled and Kristina rushed through the little door and to the safety of the cash register.

"So?" He came to lean on the counter as he'd done the night before.

"Yeah, I think I'll try it if the job's still available." Kristina's cheeks burned.

A chip bag crinkled.

Kristina turned.

Katherine Morton paused in her perusal of the chips to stare openly.

Anger rose to sting Kristina's throat.

Katherine, or Kat as she preferred to be called, a short round woman in her forties and one of the worst gossips in Laighton, could be sweet as honey to your face—until she ferreted out the information she wanted. Then she'd turn it around to make it more interesting before telling whoever would listen. Kristina could imagine where she'd take this little scene.

Wade followed Kristina's gaze and nodded at Katherine. "Hey Kat, nice to see you recovered from last weekend. Harold ever find you? Or was Matty taking you home when you guys left out the back door?"

Kat reddened.

Kristina felt a sense of pride at Wade's subtle way of putting the bitch in her place.

"Of course he found me. You know I went straight home. I don't often drink so much, but it was a birthday party. Matt was getting me a cab."

"Of course. Hope to see you in again soon. I'm sure Harold would love to come with you next time."

"Yeah, probably," she muttered and walked to the coolers at the back.

Wade turned to Kristina and winked. "You won't regret it, I promise. It's better than running around like you have been. I'll call you with your hours."

"Sure, but I'll have to give notice so they can cover my shifts here. I'm not worried about the gas station. They just hired a student so they'll be fine."

"We'll work it all out. Dirty Truths will be a brighter place with you in it." He smiled.

Distracted by Katherine and an older man bringing their purchases to the counter, Kristina didn't reply. Wade moved to the side and she wondered why he didn't just leave. She grew more flustered. Her hands trembled as she scanned Katherine's items through the register.

Katherine must have noticed too and smirked as she closed manicured nails over her change. She flipped dark hair streaked with platinum over her shoulder. "You look tired, dear. I guess single parenting doesn't agree with you. Say hello to Daniel for me, would you? I haven't seen him in ages."

Kristina bit her lip. To reply would only make Katherine worse.

The woman gathered her things. "Have a good night, Wade."

He nodded, his gaze never leaving Kristina. He tapped his

keys on the wall and then ran a finger along the magazine rack hanging below the counter.

Kristina rang the old man's purchases through.

He smiled a toothless grin and took his bag. "She's just jealous because all the chemicals and tools on the planet won't give her a gorgeous face like yours. You have a good night Sweetie." He nodded to Wade.

Kristina felt the heat of another blush. "Thank you. You too."

"Oh I will now that I've seen your pretty smile," he chuckled, and winked as he walked to the door.

Kristina never knew how to react to customers who flirted. They were only being nice but it unnerved her every time.

Wade stood grinning, his hands again tucked into his pockets. "I need your number."

"Oh shit," Kristina laughed and pulled a slip of paper from the receipt feed. "I'm sorry. Of course you do."

He took the paper, his fingers closing over hers.

Perhaps he lingered just a little before pulling away but then she scolded herself for being silly. Her hand tingled where his fingers ran over her knuckles as he drew away.

"I'll be talking to you. Make sure you do have a good night, sweetheart, like the old guy said."

Kristina nodded and he left. Sighing she moved away from the register, and pushed the mop bucket to the middle of the store. She ignored the voice in her head warning she'd regret it.

Wade clutched the paper she'd given him, opened the car's door, and climbed in. The light from a large white sign on the front of the building lit up the empty parking lot directly below. He'd parked to the side, just out of the pool of light. Hidden in the shadows, he waited.

Kristina lugged a yellow bucket out and began mopping.

He slipped the key into the ignition but didn't turn it, his gaze on her face.

She bit her lower lip as she mopped, her brow furrowed in concentration.

If he didn't know her better, he'd think she was searching for the secret to life under the dirty floor. But he knew she mulled over her decision, probably regretting it already. By morning, she'll have worried herself sick, and if he didn't act before she did too much thinking, she'd change her mind.

She heaved the mop over the bucket again and wrung it out.

He remembered the day he met her at a barbeque held at a friend's house. She'd been so young; a little chubby, with fuzzy strawberry blonde hair, and a tendency to slouch. She'd turned and smiled at him and a little shiver had coursed down his spine. Her dimpled smile and pale green eyes boldly appraised him. The look had stuck in his mind, haunting his dreams and causing him a few sleepless nights.

Being drawn to her had disgusted him. Christ the girl wasn't even sixteen. A child. But over the years—as he and her father, Joe, became good friends—he'd watched the gawky child grow into a beautiful woman. The brassy hair had darkened to a deep brown and she'd slimmed out a little, but the innocence stayed there for a long time. He'd been sad when it disappeared, as though part of her had been stolen from him. Although, he didn't know why he thought it belonged to him in the first place.

Kristina pushed the bucket toward the back of the store. She straightened, rubbed her lower back, and turned.

Wade froze, certain her gaze met his, but she turned away and leaned over the mop again. As she moved across the floor, he relaxed. Her mouth was set in the frown that marred her beautiful face too often.

When Joe had lamented over the man she'd begun dating a few years ago, Wade checked him out. He hadn't liked what he'd found.

Daniel Riley had been accused of several assaults, but the accusations never amounted to any real charges. His high school sweetheart left town before she finished her senior year. Those who knew her said she'd left a complete mess, with a broken arm and wounds on her face that would stay with her for life. She didn't go to the police though. Wade figured Daddy Riley had something to do with her sudden silence. He would bet if the old man lived today, Kristina wouldn't have gone to the police either. The old man's wife had disappeared years ago, and no one could explain what happened to her.

At the time, Wade advised Joe to stop the relationship before it progressed too far, but Kristina had proven too stubborn. The more her poor father objected, the more she fell in love with the miserable prick. She had been impressed by Riley's name and his charm, a trait Wade grudgingly admitted he had.

Daniel used to be respected around town, rather his family's name was respected; the man himself was a loser. His connections and his bad boy reputation made his slow manipulation of an innocent girl much easier. Nice girls always fell for the tormented soul, the one no one understood, believing their love could tame the beast within. Men like Riley made sure they played up the fantasy too. If the girl could just make herself good enough, she could make him happy, and then she'd earn scraps of his affection. Although Wade thought it sick and ridiculous, he understood how a girl could fall for it. Especially a gentle soul like Kristina. In his youth, Wade had used a similar ploy, but unlike Daniel he'd never wanted to control or abuse them. He'd just wanted to get in their pants. Wade smiled at the memories.

When he heard Kristina agreed to marry Riley, Wade could do nothing. He couldn't even tell her how he felt; a married man, friend of her father, and far too old to offer her anything more than sex. She'd have laughed in his face. Amy didn't care if he slept around. He had done that more than he cared to admit. But he knew she'd have a problem if she found out his feelings for Kristina went beyond sex.

Remembering how Kristina had been at her wedding made his stomach burn, his hands tightening into fists. He didn't want to go but Amy had insisted. She made a fuss about appearances. In the end he went just to shut her up. He hadn't seen Kristina in nearly a year. The difference between the woman in white satin and lace and the girl he knew before had been startling and sad.

She should have been radiant and hopeful. Instead, her voice was empty, and her skin so pale. When Daniel's voice turned sharp, she flinched and kept her eyes downcast. How did the guests miss the misery written in every move she made? They'd laughed, danced, and made jokes to the newlyweds. Everyone, except Wade and her parents, behaved as though the couple were normal and happy.

As the night wound down Wade had hugged her and leaned in close to her ear. "You deserve better than this jackass. Promise me you'll ask for help if you need it."

She'd pulled away, flashed a startled gaze and quickly pasted a false smile on her face. "It was good to see you and Amy. Thanks for coming." Then she'd turned away.

After the wedding, the light in those beautiful eyes had gone out completely under a myriad of bruises and insults. He knew what Daniel had done, and he often reminded Joe he could get rid of her problem once and for all. But Joe asked him to stay out of it.

Wade stayed away from her for months so he wouldn't have to endure the evidence of Daniel's cruelty; although Amy loved to tell him everything she heard. He ignored his wife's gleeful reports as much as he could.

He'd pushed the fantasy of Kristina away the second she got married, not allowing himself to think about her. Then, a few months ago, Joe mentioned she'd left Daniel. Wade had thought of little else but his old fantasy—and how much he wanted out of his marriage.

His obsession began in earnest when she went through with the divorce. He stopped by the gas station while she worked, observing her secretly. A few times, he'd waited in the parking lot behind a hedgerow that divided it from the house nestled between a lumber yard and the convenience store. At the end of her shift, he would walk behind her to make sure she made it to her parents' house safely. She'd looked around a few times, as though aware someone followed her. She never saw him. He was too good, though Kristina was far from his regular prey.

Who was he trying to kid? No matter how much he wanted her, he'd never have Kristina. Not the way he wanted to. Amy would be around until she died. She knew far too much, and the Brotherhood wouldn't allow her to keep breathing if she got too far away. He couldn't sign her death warrant just because he didn't love her anymore. Amy wasn't a bad person, not all the time. They just weren't meant to be. Kristina would only see Wade was a married man.

When she glanced at the window again Wade turned the key, the paper still in his hand. He had to stop thinking of her in that way. She would never allow what he desperately wanted to happen. Although the way her hand trembled tonight and the flush of her cheeks told him she would like to.

He backed out of the empty parking lot and turned toward home. Opportunities arose for a reason and only a fool would let them pass by unnoticed. He'd see her eyes light up again, if only for a moment, before he let this silly fantasy go. Maybe he'd see more. As he stopped at the red light at the end of town, he shifted uncomfortably in his seat. Damn if his pants didn't grow tighter at the thought. Wade imagined her whispering his name and groaned. If things were different, if Kristina were different, he'd have had her by now.

Kristina set her keys on the counter and carried Cadence to the living room. In the playpen, she covered the baby with her favorite pink blanket. Cadence stirred, curled one corner of the soft cover into her fist, and rubbed it against her cheek. Kristina smiled and turned to check the phone. The light on the answering machine next to it flashed. Her stomach ached.

Probably Daniel, calling to confuse her some more.

Sighing, she pressed the play button and waited. Wade's deep voice startled her. The sound released a strange feeling, like tiny bubbles bursting around her heart. She replayed the message to hear his voice again.

"Hey Kristina, it's Wade. Bet you didn't think I'd call so fast. I had to make sure you didn't have time to back out," he chuckled.

Her breath caught.

"Could you come in Friday and Saturday around eight? I'll have a shirt for you. I think I have one to fit, but if not we'll figure something out."

Kristina smiled at the thought of the slinky shirts.

"Oh, and don't worry about pants. Just find something dark, even blue is fine and once I have your size I'll pick some up for you. No arguments."

The machine stopped and Kristina reached to delete the message, her finger pausing over the button. She knew it was silly but she didn't want to erase his voice. Except for her father's, it had been a while since she'd heard a male voice filled with warmth. She pulled her hand back and walked to the stairs to shower and change. She'd leave it just until tomorrow, in case she forgot when she was supposed to work.

She climbed the stairs and pulled her shirt over her head. When Kristina reached the landing, she tossed it in the hamper next to the bathroom feeling silly for keeping the message. She scowled at her reflection in the mirror. It's not like Wade would want her anyway. He offered the job because he and her dad were friends and he wanted to help her out. Wade could have any woman in town. It wasn't just that he was attractive, although it definitely helped. He had an aura about him, a way of making a woman feel special that was hard to resist.

Kristina turned on the water and slipped her pants over her hips. She glanced at her body in the mirror and snorted. No, Wade would never want her and she was being ridiculous just thinking about it.

CHAPTER 6

Kristina pushed through the steel door and walked the short hallway into the bar. The smells of beer and stale cigarette smoke clung to the narrow space, although no one had smoked in Dirty Truths for years. She cringed at the stained red carpet; it had probably been there from the day they erected the building.

Tugging her pants away from her legs, Kristina tried to breathe slowly. Despite Wade's orders not to, she'd gone shopping with her mother and bought the low-rise black jeans similar to the other girls' at the bar. Kristina refused to come out of the changing room and only relented when her mother enlisted the sales girl to bully her out. She'd never worn pants quite so tight, or so low. The waist just covered her hips. Giving them another little tug before entering the bar, knowing they wouldn't go higher no matter how many times she hiked them up. A girl with short dark hair waited on the customers, most of them men, running back and forth carrying bottles, money and glasses, smiling and joking the entire time.

Shit. Kristina stared after her, despair eating away at her stomach. She couldn't do it. Carrying dinner plates, writing down orders for food, sure, but this was a different ballgame.

"Kristina," Wade's deep voice startled her. He emerged from a little door to the far right of the bar and neared.

She smiled. "Hey."

"You went shopping I see. Nice to see you haven't learned

to do as you're told. Let's get you suited up and Sheila will give you the rundown."

She jumped when he placed a large hand on her lower back.

He frowned. She looked away, embarrassed, but he didn't remove his hand. Instead, he pushed her toward the door he'd just exited. They passed the bar, full of curious stares. She avoided their eyes, but their gaze burned into her back as Wade ushered her into a little room, his office.

She looked around, shocked at the chaos. "This is your office?"

"Yeah, when they're not trying to turn it into a closet." He pushed a pile of paper off a metal folding chair in front of what she assumed would be a desk, if one could find it beneath the liquor bottles and paper.

"I don't know about this—" she started.

He turned and shook his head, stopping the words before she could get them out. "Don't say no until you've tried it. Here, your shirt."

Kristina took the white shirt, holding it up in front of her. It would cover, but only just. It looked impossibly skinny. "What size is this?"

"The only one there is. It'll look fine. I'll leave so you can change, and then come on out to the bar and you can start."

Kristina set her purse on the chair, and then waited for the door to click shut before removing her t-shirt. She struggled into the one Wade had just given her. Tight was an understatement. It clung to her, leaving nothing to the imagination. She looked down the low-scooped neck, with "Dirty Truths" written in red across her left breast. She smoothed the soft cotton down, tugging from the bottom to stretch the material. It sprung back, hugging her body like a glove.

The hem just touched the top of her jeans and when she moved, about an inch of flesh peeked through. God, she could not go out there in this. She hadn't put a bathing suit on since getting married and only started wearing tank tops after leaving Daniel. Although this covered more than the strappy shirts, she felt exposed. None of her clothes fit her like a second skin.

A knock at the door made her jump. She leaned over and opened it to the smiling woman from the bar.

"You ready?"

"Um, I don't know." She backed away.

The woman entered, her eyes running down Kristina's body. She let out a low whistle. "Shit, I wish I filled out my clothes so well. Look at your tiny little waist." She reached over and poked Kristina's stomach. "You just had a kid?"

"Almost a year ago,"

"Damn. I'm jealous."

Jealous? Kristina stared at the woman, unsure whether she was making fun of her or not. "I think I made a mistake. I'm not really made for this."

"Don't be silly, we're all made for this. It's fun. I'm Sheila by the way. I know you're Kristina. Wade's talked of nothing else since he hired you."

"I just don't want you to think I know what I'm doing, because I don't. I'm terrified actually."

"Of course you don't know what you're doing. That's why I'm training you. Come on. Let's show those rednecks what a real woman looks like. I think I'll be losing some of my best tippers."

Kristina let Sheila drag her into the bar. If the stares were unsettling when she entered, nothing compared to the heat in Wade's gaze when she walked behind the bar.

Wade struggled to focus on making drinks and taking money from his customers, but Kristina's presence made it almost impossible. She looked like a frightened deer, ready to bolt at the first opportunity. Twice she'd caught him staring, and both times caused her to drop the drinks in her hands.

"Earth to Wade," Thomas's voice. What was Thomas doing in his bar?

Wade tore his gaze from Kristina's back and met the unsettling dark eyes of his boss. He forced what he hoped was a friendly smile to his face. "Fancy seeing you here."

"A guy needs a drink now and then," Thomas smiled. "New girl?"

"Yeah," Wade grabbed the bottle of bourbon beneath the counter, Thomas's bottle, of course. It was an effort not to look back to Kristina. If he had any luck, she'd stay at the far end of the bar until Thomas left.

"She's cute," Thomas said. "Young… but cute."

"Daughter of a friend," Wade set Thomas's drink in front of him and picked up a towel to occupy his hands. While Thomas was Wade's boss, they were friends first. Thomas would never hurt anyone who didn't threaten the Brotherhood. If Thomas suspected his feelings for Kristina, it could cause problems.

"This isn't the girl who was married to the Riley, is it?"

As if he didn't know. Wade's gut tightened. Thomas didn't associate with many people, and yet he seemed to know everything about everyone in town. "It is."

"Arrogant prick. I never liked the guy."

"No arguments from me." Wade smiled. "So why are you really here?"

Thomas lifted his glass and drained the contents. He opened his mouth to speak, but a crash turned their attention to the pool tables.

Kristina stood in the middle of her mess. Bottles and broken glass littered the puddle of liquid at her feet. Her lip trembled as she knelt to pick up the pieces.

Thomas chuckled. "Might be more trouble than she's worth."

"She just started the other night. Still a little nervous."

"Never pegged you as a sucker for a pretty face."

"She needed a job, so I gave her a shot. Sheila breaks shit all the time and I haven't fired her yet. I should help her get that cleaned up."

Thomas nodded. "Of course you should. I scheduled a meeting. Usual place, usual time, tomorrow night. I expect to see you there."

"Something up?" Wade hated Thomas's meetings. They always ended in Wade doing something nasty.

"Not really. This is just precautionary."

"I'll be there."

Thomas stood, his gaze traveling once more to Kristina. She turned, catching the two of them staring. Wade looked away first, but Thomas didn't care if he made the poor girl uncomfortable.

"Is that it?" Wade asked.

"This better not become a problem." Thomas pointed to Kristina. "Don't make me do something unpleasant, Wade."

"She's just an employee." Wade lied.

"Keep it that way. You've got enough complications in your life."

Near the coat racks, Kristina paused to catch her breath and stare at the crowd filling the dimly lit barroom. She stood at the back by a polished wood counter that ran nearly the entire width of the space, filled tonight with players from a local golf tournament. Maybe Wade wouldn't notice she still struggled after two weeks of training.

Toward the small stage and dance floor, on the left side of the bar, patrons sat at tables pushed close to take advantage of every inch of space. The right side held four pool tables and little else. Smaller versions of the main bar divided the room; pine-topped islands surrounded by stools. The rest of the furnishings were of the same pale finish as the main bar, with green leather seats on the chairs. They had tiled the floor in a black and white checkerboard pattern. Kristina found it dizzying to look at, but Amy said it made the old bar look modern. She didn't have the heart to tell her nothing could make the place modern.

One waitress had to cover the entire room and it took

Kristina a few nights to figure out a pattern that worked for her. She took orders on the right side as she cleared empties. Then after delivering those drinks, she worked her way up the left.

Wade had been patient after she messed up horribly the first night and dropped more drinks than she managed to sell. He told her to come in the next afternoon when she finished her shift at Maude's so he could go over everything slowly. Serving didn't put her on edge, though. It was the customers.

More than once on her first night, she felt a pinch on her ass or a hand running down her back. Horrified, she forgot orders and spilled drinks. Wade told her to let the guy working the door know if anyone crossed the line. But Kristina didn't like the way Wade's eyes darkened as he said it. She learned to deal with it her own way, making jokes or avoiding the groping hands altogether. If Daniel knew even half of what happened at Dirty Truths, he'd have killed her.

By her third shift at Dirty Truths she'd stopped working at the convenience store, and worked her last shift at the restaurant the next morning. She couldn't wait to be down to just one job. Two weeks of juggling had left her exhausted and relieved she'd quit the gas station before starting at the bar.

She surveyed the room. The bar held more people than she imagined it could and they drank a lot. She was glad her mother kept Cadence so she could crash when she went home. The tips made the stress bearable. Even with the errors she'd taken home close to two hundred dollars each night so far, she could never make as much with her other jobs. Leaning against the wall, her legs and feet screaming in protest at the thought of one more step, she longed to climb into bed for a couple of days and just sleep.

The band bustled around on the tiny little stage setting up for their second set, and she took advantage of the distraction to gather her thoughts. The men from the golf tournament had proven a rowdy bunch, with lewd comments and propositions ready each time she passed their table. She considered asking the girl working the bar to trade with her. But the tips were better on the floor and Kristina didn't want Wade to know they'd given her a hard time. In the end, she endured the men's unwanted advances and prayed the night ended soon so she could go home.

Taking a deep breath and gathering the drinks for the group at the farthest pool table, she set them on her tray. Balancing it on one hand she moved out from behind the bar. The thought of passing the golfers' table made her nervous, but she had no choice.

Kristina lifted the tray above her shoulder and passed the table, letting out the breath she held as she made it past the worst of them. Then a hand on her free arm forced her to stop.

"Hey, sweetheart. Where do you think you're going?"

Kristina closed her eyes and squared her shoulders before turning. "I have to take these drinks to the front, but I'll be back in a minute."

She tried to pull her arm from his grasp but his other arm snaked around her waist and he laughed. "Don't be like that. I just want a little sugar."

The tray tipped and Kristina struggled to right it, allowing him to pull her into his lap in the process. Her free arm became wedged between his body and hers. She felt him growing hard. Of all the bad luck in the world, she must have most of it. Sam was a big man, arms like steel, and her attempts to push away while still holding her tray only made the situation worse, as she unintentionally ground her bottom against his groin.

"That's what I'm talking about," he slipped his hand into the waistband of her jeans.

Kristina jumped.

The drinks came crashing down on them.

The man leapt out of his chair, dumping Kristina on the floor. "You stupid bitch," he yelled.

"I told you—"

He stepped toward her. Shocked at his fury she closed her mouth and cowered. He raised his arm and Kristina prepared for the blow.

Wade sighed at the crash, but smiled as he pictured Kristina tripping over her feet again. He stood and walked out of the office into the bar. As he emerged, his gaze found the reason for the noise. In a rage, he strode toward the table near the bar.

"You stupid bitch," Sam Thompson yelled.

Kristina sat in a heap on the floor, her shirt soaked and her eyes wide. She flinched as Sam raised his fist.

"What the hell is going on here?" Wade kept his voice low and even.

"She spilled the tray—"

"Why?"

Sam paused, his face reddened and he opened his mouth but nothing came out.

Wade turned to Kristina. "What happened?"

"He g-grabbed me and I told him I'd come back, then he put his hand in my pants and I forgot about the tray. I didn't mean to spill it." Kristina's voice trembled forcing a lump to Wade's throat.

Wade held out his hand.

She took it and stood.

He squeezed her fingers, relieved to see color flood her cheeks again. "Go get a clean shirt. It's okay. You did nothing wrong. Come on Sam, you and I need to have words."

He grabbed Sam by the collar; the fool proved wise enough not to struggle. Wade half-dragged him out the door and around the building to the dumpsters. When they were out of sight, he threw him against the brick wall of the building. Wade's shirt clung to his back. The night was still humid and the small effort it took to drag Sam outside had him sweating. "Who do you think you are coming into my bar and treating my staff like that?"

"I didn't know—"

Wade swung, his fist connecting with Sam's nose.

A sickening crack and Sam fell to his knees. "Fuck, Wade."

Wade allowed him to regain his footing. Blood covered Sam's chin and the front of his white polo shirt. "You think you can just treat women like garbage?"

"Fuck you. You're nothing without your friends around. I'm not scared of you." Sam spat, bringing his arms up.

Wade stepped forward. "Let's see about that."

Kristina stood at the sink behind the bar rinsing the towels she used to clean up her mess. The door opened and she looked up. Wade strolled in alone. Was that blood on his hands? He walked to the bathroom, emerging a few minutes later, his hands clean and his shirt tucked in once more.

Coming around the bar, he paused behind her. Kristina shivered as the warmth of his breath reached the back of her neck. "Don't worry, he won't be back. You better tell me next time you have a problem, before it comes to that."

Kristina dropped the damp towel and turned to face him. She paused startled at the force of his gaze, his eyes so dark they appeared almost black. "I can't do this Wade. I'm sorry, but I'm going to see if I can get my job back—"

"What? No fucking way."

"I can't do this and I keep screwing things up. I'm just not cut out for this place."

"The customers love you, although a bit too much some-times. You take home more in tips than anyone I've seen yet." Wade reached out and brushed her bangs from her eyes, his gaze softened and he smiled. "You're our comic relief. What am I going to do without you? I can't spill the drinks myself."

"Funny." Kristina looked at her hands, noticing for the first time she still wore her wedding rings. She covered her left hand with her right. "Seriously, Wade, why would you keep someone who is terrible at their job?"

He sighed, glancing at her hands. He frowned and shook

his head, then looked at her with a crooked grin. "You aren't terrible. Your drink to table to floor ratio is improving. Don't let one bad incident make you give up. That's not the girl I remember."

Kristina stared at him, trying not to laugh. He was right. She had improved. A bit. But the fear Sam forced to the surface made her remember Daniel and all she wanted to run away from. She hated that she could go back to a spineless coward so easily.

"I guess if I quit then guys like him win."

Wade put his hand on her shoulder and squeezed. "Exactly, and I will never let it happen again. So? You'll stick it out? I'd hate to have to drag you in here kicking and screaming every night. It's bad for business."

"I guess so, as long as you can afford the damage."

"For you, I'd pay any amount." Wade grinned and walked toward the office.

Kristina stood for a moment, her breath caught in her throat.

For you, I'd pay any amount.

She picked up the towel, draped it over the little sink under the bar and picked up her tray. If only it were true.

CHAPTER 7

"Did you see Sammy yesterday?"

Two men sat at the end of the bar nursing their beers. Jimmy and Mark, or Ren and Stimpy—as the bar staff affectionately called them—were like fixtures. Wade might as well have nailed them to the stools and give them a fresh coat of paint now and then.

Kristina wiped the counter. The bar wouldn't fill for at least another hour but these two arrived at the same time each night, gossiping like old women until the wee hours. She wondered how they did it day in and day out. How they could afford it.

"Yeah, Wade adjusted his attitude, didn't he?" Mark raised the glass to his mouth.

At the mention of Wade's name, she moved closer.

"Sam always did think he was hot shit. Fuck, Tommy said he came into work with a broken nose and his arm in a sling. He walked with quite a limp too. Told the boss he had a car accident and needed a couple weeks off."

Kristina paused, dismayed at the memory of Wade's bloodied hands and disheveled shirt. Did he break the man's nose? Two weeks off work?

"I heard he broke some ribs too," Jimmy said.

Kristina looked up.

Eyes wide, Jimmy grinned. "You don't fuck around with guys like Wade. He doesn't take shit from anyone. Good way to find yourself in a ditch bleeding out. Remember the guy who ratted on the Brotherhood? They found him on the highway, right outside the cop station so messed up they put him in a nursing home. I heard it was Wade who put him there. Guy's got fucking balls I tell you."

"Yeah, Sam's lucky Wade wasn't doing a hit. Still, I don't think we'll see him around for a while. I could have told him to keep his hands to himself. Wade's soft on that one."

Kristina's cheeks warmed when Mark pointed a stubby finger in her direction.

They continued to talk, as though the bar between them provided a sound barrier.

She moved away, heart pounding, pressure building in her chest. After a glance at the clock, she walked to the door and flipped a light switch to turn off the overhead lights. The dim pot fixtures that ran down the center of the bar lent a pale yellow glow to the room.

"Hey! Why'd you shut the lights off? Now we can't see those pretty eyes," Jimmy called.

Kristina smiled. Every night she worked Jimmy said the same thing when she turned off the lights at nine o'clock. "Sorry Jim, you'll have to look closer I guess."

"Tease. Where's Wade? Isn't he supposed to be here by now? Lazy prick."

The door clicked shut. "Lazy what?"

Kristina turned on her way back to the bar.

Wade stood, hands on his hips, a mock scowl on his face.

Jimmy held up his hands defensively. "Uh, you must have heard me wrong. I said you were a nice guy who deserved a little holiday."

"Oh is that what you said?" Wade laughed and pulled out the stool next to them. He nodded to Kristina and she grabbed a tumbler from below the sink to get him his usual rye and Coke.

"I hear Sammy had an accident last night," Mark said, and paused to tip the bottle to his mouth.

Kristina had to smile at his audacity.

"He had to take time off work."

"Really?" Wade murmured.

Kristina kept her gaze on the bar as she handed Wade his glass. She shivered when his long fingers brushed hers.

"I can't imagine what happened to him. He was fine when he left here."

Mark snorted.

Kristina looked up from the sink, to catch Wade's gaze. He winked and she turned away.

When the door opened and a group of girls filed in, Wade got up from his stool, said his goodbyes to Mark and Jimmy and walked into his office behind the bar.

Most of the night Kristina worked in a haze; her mind distracted by what Wade had done. She should have been upset, at least unsettled by it, but no one had ever stood up for her like that. Although she didn't like violence, it didn't stop the giddiness that took over as she remembered the intensity of his gaze when he helped her off the floor. Wade cared for her, not the way her body wanted him to, but enough to defend her.

Her gaze wandered to him as she wiped tables, while taking orders, and when she cleaned glasses at the end of the night. No longer did she see her dad's friend, but a man. Someone she knew nothing about. Now and then, he caught her staring and winked. Then, she would look away, embarrassed, but her gaze would drift back for another glimpse of his crooked smile.

She had to stop. Kristina scolded herself for her silliness while walking home. Wade had a wife and he was almost old enough to be her father. He wouldn't ever cross the invisible barrier between them. Although she knew it was stupid she wished things could be different. With Daniel around, a relationship with any man was impossible. Daniel wouldn't allow it. Yet, the thought of Daniel tangling with Wade made her laugh just a little. There was a fight Daniel wouldn't win.

Kristina opened her eyes to sunlight and rolled over to look at the clock. "Shit."

She jumped out of bed. With her mom and Cadence due any minute, she wouldn't even have time for a shower.

A knock on the front door and her mother entered. "Hello? Kristina?"

"I'll be down in a minute. I slept in, sorry." Grabbing a T-shirt from the basket next to the door Kristina promised herself she would put the laundry away at some point, although it never seemed to happen.

When footsteps sounded on the stairs, she picked up the jeans she'd worn to work and struggled into them but gazed longingly at the blue track pants folded neatly on top of the basket. Her plan for the day included going out, and she made it a point not to look like a bum anymore if she could help it.

"Sorry hon, but I'm late for work." Her mother pushed the door open and entered the bedroom, Cadence resting on her hip. The baby grinned and held her arms out.

"Hey Monkey," Kristina took her after giving her mom a hug. "I know, sorry."

"Don't be. I kept her longer this morning because your dad decided to feed her ice cream last night and she was up so late. I let her sleep longer so she wouldn't be grumpy for you."

"That's okay, she probably loved it. I've been trying new stuff. But I do it early, in case it doesn't agree with her."

Her mom rolled her eyes and kissed Cadence before heading down. Kristina followed making faces at her daughter as they descended the stairs. Cadence giggled and clapped her hands.

With Cadence settled into her highchair a few minutes later, the smell of brewing coffee teasing her nose, Kristina leaned on the counter and gazed out the window. Another sunny day, maybe they'd walk across the road to the river and test the water.

Another knock at the door and Kristina rolled her eyes. She glanced around the living room hoping to see what her mother could have left behind. Finding nothing, she opened the door.

Her smile faded and she moved back. Daniel stood with his arms crossed, a scowl on his face.

"Well?" he asked.

"Well what? I don't know why you're here."

"Um, I think I still have a daughter who lives here, unless you've managed to take that from me too."

Kristina stepped aside, her good mood chased away by Daniel's darkness. "You do know tomorrow is your day, don't you?" She followed him into the living room.

He spun around forcing her to skid to a halt. "What's this about the bar?"

"I—what do you mean?"

"What do I mean? You are working there aren't you?"

Kristina's cheeks burned. She knew he'd be pissed but dared to hope after she'd worked the first week without comment, he'd decided it wasn't worth arguing about. She couldn't be so lucky. "I don't have much choice. I make more money there in three days than I did working two jobs for seven. I can spend more time with Cadence."

Something clattered in the kitchen; Cadence had thrown her plastic keys to the floor.

Kristina walked around him to pick them up. "I'm not bugging you to pay the support you never give me, so I don't see why it should bother you."

His footsteps sounded on the carpet behind her, then on the kitchen floor. Dizzy with fear, Kristina bent over and picked up the keys, setting them back on Cadence's tray before turning around.

Fury clouded his eyes.

She'd sworn not to let him do this to her anymore but stepped back anyway.

He smirked and moved closer. "So tell me, how much does a blowjob next to the dumpster pay nowadays? Forty, fifty bucks?"

Kristina opened her mouth and then closed it, unable to speak. Her body shook, but rather than allow him to draw her into a fight she spun around and walked to the sink. "You came to see your daughter, there she is. Have your visit and get out of my house."

Her head jerked back as he grabbed her hair and she stumbled against him.

"Whose house? The paperwork says it's mine. Don't forget that. You think you can just do whatever you want without consequences?"

She closed her eyes, his breath hot against her cheek as he held her against him, one hand in her hair the other around her waist.

"I won't have a slut raising my kid. We'll see what the judge thinks of a mother acting like a common hooker."

He released her, shoving her into the counter.

Kristina stood for a minute, her hands on the white laminate, and stared at the steak knife lying next to her thumb. If only she had the guts. Instead of picking up the knife and making a fool of herself she turned to face him.

Skirting the chair she'd moved to make room for Cadence's highchair earlier, she walked toward him. "No judge would take her from me just because I work at a bar. There's nothing wrong with it. We're not married anymore, so you can't order me around like I'm your slave. I'm not scared of you, Daniel, so if you only came to bully me, you can leave."

Daniel grabbed her arms. His fingers bit into her skin.

She winced as he squeezed, his arms shaking from the force of his anger. Her fingers tingled, and she struggled to break his hold. Daniel shoved her away from him and Kristina, startled by the sudden push, stumbled backward over the chair. It toppled with her, the legs catching her shin. Her head smashed against the stove.

"I'm visiting my daughter and I'll leave when I'm ready to leave. This is still my house." Daniel pulled Cadence out of the highchair and walked to the living room.

Kristina sat stunned, rubbing her shin. She moved when Cadence cried out, stumbling to her feet and wincing at the stabbing pain in her leg. She rubbed a small bump forming on the back of her head and gritted her teeth. Although she knew the rumors about Wade being a murderer weren't true, she wished they were just long enough to get rid of her ex-husband.

Daniel stood at the window in the living room, staring out at the empty street. Cadence sat in her bouncy chair, her face scrunched into a scowl. Kristina walked to her before she let out the wail she was forming and picked her up.

"You'll quit the bar tomorrow. I will not have a whore raising my daughter."

"I'm not quitting."

"Yes, you are." He didn't wait for her answer, turning on his heel and walking to the door.

The house shook when he slammed it shut behind him. Cadence jumped at the noise and cried out. Kristina shushed her and held her close, swaying back and forth to soothe her.

Outside Daniel's truck roared to life, tires squealing as he pulled out of the driveway and sped down the street. Kristina walked to the window, her gaze on the skid marks his tires left behind.

This had gone on long enough. They weren't married anymore and Daniel had no control over her. If she continued to let him dictate her life, she might as well walk down the aisle again and paste a sign declaring she was a doormat where everyone should feel free to wipe their feet on. No, she wouldn't do it. She would not quit.

CHAPTER 8

The Sunday crowd usually had the girls running off their feet until at least midnight, but this week was quiet. Wade stood at the cabinet behind the office door, searching for the next month's schedule he was certain he'd put in there. He had to post it soon or they'd be nagging him about it.

His office looked like a bomb exploded; papers covered the desk and no amount of organizing seemed to clear it. Cases of booze lined the right wall, stacked five or six high. Wade often stared at them and wondered when they'd topple over on him. One day they had to. The opposite wall held a large bulletin board with pictures of staff parties, a calendar with everyone's hours scribbled in his hand and flyers announcing the current month's bands playing. Somehow, he'd managed to fit a computer and keyboard on the cramped desk, but papers managed to slip under and on top. It never stayed in the same place. He'd lift the keyboard to search for something and never put it back in its original spot when he found what he'd been looking for.

He'd had a desk lamp, but didn't know where it ended up. It disappeared in the chaos soon after he brought it in. The filing cabinet he'd forced behind the door, with several hooks screwed in the wall above for everyone's coats, aprons, and purses. Often when he had to look in the old beast he wrestled with the clothing hanging above just to open and close the drawers.

Kristina's voice drifted to his ears; she murmured something he couldn't make out. He paused to peek around the door. Sheila stood beside her, smoking a cigarette and gazing at a small group of customers playing pool.

"I think this is all we're getting tonight," Sheila said, examining her nails.

She had them done at the salon although Wade thought any five year old could paint them purple with pink hearts on the tips. But he didn't voice his opinion. Women were strange about those things.

Sheila was a nice girl, he'd even been attracted enough to take her home when she started working for him a couple of years ago. They agreed—after Amy raised a stink and Wade realized he had nothing in common with her—they'd be better as friends. He paired her with Kristina because they seemed to fit. He trusted Sheila too. She would look out for Kristina like a mother hen. The other servers—two women in their forties—preferred working afternoon shifts alone, so Wade left the busier shifts to Kristina and Sheila. His wife opened the bar Monday through Thursday although Amy made sure he knew how much she hated it.

"Hey, what's that?" Sheila touched Kristina's left arm.

Wade drifted closer to the door. An angry looking bruise, deep purple lines, four of them—fingers—marked Kristina's upper arm.

"How did you get that?" Sheila asked.

"I—" Kristina paused, and pressed her lips together.

Wade waited for her to explain, his gut tightening when she flushed and clasped one hand over it. "My ex-husband got a little angry the other day. I bruise really easily. He just grabbed me. Nothing major."

Gripping the door, Wade barely noticed the rough wood biting into his palm. The image of the prick tossing Kristina around triggered a red haze in his brain. Even if she bruised easily, it would take a lot of force to leave marks like those.

"His temper just got the better of him." Kristina continued to defend Daniel. "He's not nearly as bad as he used to be.

Barely touches me now and he's really trying to manage his anger."

"A man trying to manage his temper doesn't leave marks like that, sweetie."

"He really isn't so bad. I should have kept my mouth shut when he got irritated. If I'd kept my own temper in check, I don't think he'd have snapped like he did. It looks terrible, but it's not. Hardly even hurts."

Sheila snorted and shook her head. "You're gonna do what you want, but I'm telling you, a man who leaves bruises like that isn't getting better. I've known some assholes in my life too. A real man doesn't hurt a woman over words. What could you have said to warrant him grabbing you hard enough to leave bruises?"

Kristina turned and Wade moved out of sight. "He was mad because I'm working here and I refused to quit when he asked me to. I could have just lied to him, and said I'd do it. Everything would have been fine. To be honest, I'm a little worried about what he'll do next. Not that he'd hurt me again, he was only trying to scare me, but he said he'd take Cadence. I know this isn't the best job for a mother to have. He's right. Would a judge take custody from someone just because they work in a bar?"

Wade had heard enough. Before Sheila could answer, he opened the door wide and poked his head out. "Hey Kris? Can you come in here?"

The women looked at each other and Sheila shrugged.

"Sure," Kristina said.

She walked around the bar and he stepped back allowing her to pass him into the office. The door closed behind him with a soft click and Kristina stood next to the desk, one hand covering the bruise, fingers tugging at her sleeve.

He walked toward her and reached out to pull her hand from her arm.

She resisted, her cheeks reddening but dropped it away.

"What's this?" he demanded.

"Nothing, I—"

"I heard you talking. Don't you dare lie to me. Not for him."

"Like I said, it's not as bad as it looks. I bruise easily."

"Maybe you do, but that bruise is as bad as it looks."

She dropped her gaze.

Wade sighed. He thought he'd seen her pride and a little self-esteem returning, but apparently her asshole ex-husband beat it out of her again.

"Really, it's nothing," she said. "It doesn't even hurt. He scared me more when he said he'd take Cadence from me. He can't, can he?" Kristina looked up at him, eyes moist with un-shed tears.

Wade wanted to take her in his arms and run off where no one could hurt her again. Instead, he smiled and shook his head. "As long as you're looking after your daughter, and you are, your job doesn't matter. Don't worry; I'll take care of him."

She frowned.

Before she could argue, Wade turned away and walked out to the bar, signaling to Sheila for a drink. Whatever argument Kristina had worked up in Daniel's defense wouldn't change his mind. It was time Daniel Riley got a dose of his own medicine and Wade couldn't wait to deliver it.

Wade closed the safe and then pocketed his keys, listening to Sheila and Kristina chatting while they waited for a cab. The door opened and closed and the bar fell silent. He reached above the safe to switch off the light. As he stepped around the boxes of booze covering the floor of his office, Wade made a mental note to get someone to clear out the storage room so he could have this room back. How the mess always managed to creep into his personal space was a mystery.

"Wade?" he jumped at Kristina's voice.

"Oh, I thought you left with Sheila."

"No, Jimmy took her home. Her car's in the shop. The cab won't be here for a while yet, they're busy I guess."

"I could drive you—"

"No, it's okay. I already called them."

Wade couldn't help smiling at how she forced a safe distance between them. Kristina stared at him now and then but as soon as he got too close, she became skittish.

"I'll walk if it's not here soon. I wanted to ask you a favor before I go." She said.

"Oh?" He knew what she planned to say. It would do her no good, but he'd pretend to consider it anyway.

"I know you think you're helping, and I really appreciate you care enough to try, but please just leave Daniel alone. I don't need you taking care of anything. I can deal with him on my own."

"Really? You've done such a wonderful job so far." He touched her arm, trailing one finger down the bruise then raised his eyebrow at the tremor in her body.

"He's working hard to control his temper. I know in his own way he loves me. He's just frightened and lonely right now. We've been through a lot, and we both have some growing up to do. I've had worse than this, believe me. It's nothing."

Wade listened to her excuses and fury erupted in his chest; rising like bile to his throat. How could she defend such a jerk? Did she truly not realize how much she was worth? God, if he had a woman like her he'd worship the ground she walked on, not throw her on it.

He reached for a stray curl, the one that always fell over her forehead at the end of the night, never staying in the ponytail. "He's as bad as he ever was, and he'll never change. Don't try to hand me bullshit. I know you're not stupid. You're smart, funny and beautiful, and you deserve to be treated with love and respect, not as a piece of garbage or as someone's property. Cadence is going to grow up seeing her mom settle for less than what she deserves, and she'll do the same. Do you want her to have the same bruises someday?"

She blushed and looked down at her feet.

Wade touched her chin, forcing her to look at him.

Kristina smiled.

His heart ached at the sadness in her eyes. "You need to find the backbone you used to have and stop allowing people like him to treat you like shit. Stop being a doormat and start standing up. You can do better than Daniel Riley and you know it."

She stepped back.

Wade crossed his arms over his chest to keep from grabbing her and making a fool of himself.

"Thank you. I do appreciate the thought, and I know you mean what you say. I'm trying to fix my life. That's why I divorced him. It doesn't change the fact I still don't want you having a talk with Daniel. Okay. Please, it will just make things worse."

"I won't talk to him, if it's what you want."

Wade didn't lie. Not technically, anyway. He didn't plan to talk.

Several men filed out of the strip club, some with a woman on their arms, most of them alone. Wade had no trouble tracking Daniel. He'd waited outside his apartment for an hour and the fool drove straight to the Peek-A-Boo Club, as he did every week. The club hosted amateur night each Monday, and Daniel occasionally left with a dancer. Wade wondered what the new girlfriend would think of that. Joe had been furious to know Daniel had done this while married to Kristina, but at the time she wouldn't listen to even her father.

The neon lights surrounding the sign out front flashed red and blue, reflecting off the puddles left behind by an early evening thunderstorm. Wade glimpsed a few familiar faces. Some he would come back to speak to later, others he would rather not see again. The popular little club didn't discriminate their clientele. The men exiting ranged from white collar to no collar. A lone figure emerged through the double doors, one of the last to exit, and Wade sat straighter in his seat.

"Well hello, Mr. Riley," he murmured as Daniel walked toward them. He was alone, the parking lot clear as he stumbled to his truck.

Laughter erupted from the backseat and Wade turned to his friends.

In the rearview Frank held his gut, laughing. "That's him? Preppy piece of shit ain't even a challenge. Jesus, come on."

Frank was used to a different kind of man, the kind that would slit your throat for looking at him the wrong way. He came along because he owed Wade a favor. Wade almost laughed along with him as he pictured Daniel's face when Frank approached him. Six foot five, bald, and pushing four hundred pounds, Frank owned a frightening picture. Because of his size, many thought they could outrun him. They'd been wrong.

"I just want to give him a warning," Wade reminded him. "He knows me, so I can't do it myself, although I'd love to rip him apart."

"Got it." John, the other man, grumbled.

John hadn't wanted to come along, but he owed Wade a lot of money and he didn't have it. Despite his grumbling, John enjoyed a good scrap, He wasn't as big as Frank, but the tattoos covering his body and the piercings in his face were as unsettling as Frank's size. According to Amy he'd pierced other parts of his body as well. Wade shuddered at the thought. Some things were not meant to have extra holes.

"So we're even after this?" John asked.

Wade grinned, to enjoy the sight of John shifting uncomfortably under his stare. He knew Wade knew about Amy and him. Idiot thought Wade gave a shit too, but it worked in his favor. "For now."

They slipped out of the car and around the building, keeping to the shadows until Daniel leaned down to unlock his truck. Wade's hands itched to knock the arrogance from his face. It radiated off him, that cocky sureness no one could touch him. Well, he was about to learn in Wade's world he was as vulnerable as Kristina.

Approaching from behind, his heavy steps remarkably silent, Frank grabbed Daniel by the throat and the moron actually tried to take a swing at the big man. Wade grinned as they put Daniel on the ground, kicking him mercilessly until all the jackass could do was cover his pretty face.

He managed to roll to his knees once but Frank wrenched his arm behind his back and continued the beating. They remained silent, despite Daniel's repeated demands to know what they wanted. Then Daniel went limp, passing out from the pain of what Wade figured was a couple of broken bones. They waited for him to come to. Then John knelt on the damp pavement, his face touching Daniel's ear, to relay Wade's warning.

Touch her again, you die.

They walked away, careful to move out of Daniel's line of sight before heading back to the car. As they got in, Daniel cowered on the ground. He didn't move for a long time. John and Frank climbed in the backseat and Wade started the car before Daniel pushed himself off the pavement and looked around.

"Not so hot now is he?" Frank murmured. "I think we cracked a few bones."

Wade shifted the car into reverse, leaving the lights off. "Good. Now we'll see if he's learned his lesson."

"I heard once a wife beater, always a wife beater," John said.

Wade turned, a frown on his face.

"Hey man, don't get pissed at me. I'm just saying it's what I heard."

"I hope for his sake it's not true," Wade mumbled.

Kristina glanced at the clock. Daniel was late. The first couple of days after her conversation with Wade she'd worried he wouldn't listen and pick a fight with Daniel. But nearly a week had passed and she hadn't heard anything from her ex-husband. Assuming Wade had left Daniel alone, she'd been relieved. The last thing she needed was someone defending her. It would only make Daniel angrier, if that was possible.

Gravel crunched outside and she looked to the window next to the couch. Finally.

She picked Cadence up from the mat on the floor where she'd placed her in an attempt to get her to crawl, but the chubby baby preferred to roll everywhere.

At the sound of the door opening, Kristina turned and braced herself for another argument. The words froze on her lips.

Daniel stood in the doorway with his arm in a cast, his face a mess of bruises and cuts. Kristina's heart tightened as guilt washed over her. Hot and prickly it traveled over her skin. Wade hadn't listened.

Daniel closed the door and walked into the room to the couch. He eased himself down, obviously in a lot of pain and then stared at her. Misery softened his gaze, the usual anger gone. He looked utterly dejected, as though he'd lost his best friend.

"Jesus, Daniel. What happened?"

He shook his head.

Kristina could have sworn his chin trembled.

"Two guys jumped me on Monday night when I came out of a bar. I don't know why, they said something about some girl, but I don't know what they were talking about. Honest to God, Kris, I thought they were going to kill me. I think I even blacked out. They didn't say anything until just before they left. They just kept kicking me and punching me and then they took off."

"You don't know who it was?" Kristina sat down on the coffee table in front of him. Cadence reached for his cast and Kristina shifted her away.

Daniel shook his head again.

She stared speechless, as he fidgeted with a loose thread on the sling. Wade wouldn't do something like this. Besides, he knew Daniel would go to the cops and he couldn't afford to go to jail. If Wade had been one of his attackers, Daniel would have recognized him.

Daniel raised head, his eyes moist with tears. "When I was on the ground, I just kept thinking about us and all I've lost. Where did we go wrong?"

"We just aren't meant to be," she didn't know what else to say. Her chest hurt. She wanted to hold him and make his pain go away.

Taking her hand in his good one, he leaned closer. "We are meant to be, Kris, I know that now. The whole time I thought they were going to kill me all I could think about was you and Cadence. I miss you so much and I've been a jackass, I know. I should have been patient with you, kinder. I just get so frustrated sometimes, and it seemed like you weren't listening to me when I tried to help you. God, I never meant to hurt Cadence, you know that. People lose control sometimes. I'm only human."

Daniel stood, pulling her with him. Kristina struggled to hold Cadence still as he drew her close. He touched her face, his gaze on her mouth.

Kristina froze, not sure if she should push him away or welcome this new Daniel. In his eyes she found the man she thought he was so long ago. She let his lips brush hers.

He smiled. "Please, can't we go back and try again?"

She said nothing. Her thoughts were a jumbled mess. This Daniel she could fall in love with. She *had* loved this man but thought he was lost forever to her.

"Let me stay the night, please."

"But what about Desiree, she—"

"You're all that matters. I don't want her."

A tear slipped down his cheek and Kristina was undone.

"Okay, just tonight," she whispered.

"You won't regret it. We're going to fix this. I want you

back so much, I don't care what you did before."

Kristina paused at his words. He didn't care what she did? She pushed it away. If they could fix this, didn't they owe it to themselves and to Cadence? Ignoring the voice in her head screaming at her to say no, Kristina allowed Daniel to stay.

CHAPTER 9

At Cadence's soft babbling, Kristina rolled over, a sigh escaping her lips. The sun wasn't up yet and her bedroom remained shadowed. She turned over and her heart fluttered. Daniel slept on the pillow next to hers, his mouth opened just a bit, soft snores issuing from his nose.

They hadn't made love the night before. He hadn't even tried to touch her in that way. Somewhat disappointed, she'd lain next to him listening as he talked until the wee hours about the future and how much he loved her. He held her close until he had nothing more to say. Then he rolled away as he always did. Kristina had lain there, staring at his back, her heart wavering between wanting him back and needing more than she knew he was able to give.

Now it was time for reality, to see if he could stay this way. Maybe the mugging, or whatever it was, had really changed his thinking. She eased off the bed holding her breath and then smiled at her silliness. He wouldn't bite her head off for making noise. Hadn't he said he was done with his tantrums?

Tiptoeing to the dresser, she opened the drawer and pulled out a t-shirt. Without thinking, she pushed it close with her usual force.

"Could you be louder? Maybe you could stomp around a bit or jump on the bed and make sure I'm up. What time is it anyway?"

"It's just after five. I have to get Cadence."

"Yeah, but I don't so try to be quiet, okay?"

"Okay," she crept down the hallway and to Cadence's room.

Cadence giggled when she saw her and pulled herself up on the rail of her crib. Kristina reached for the light and thought better of it. He hadn't freaked out, but there was no point in testing her limits quite yet.

"Hey Monkey," she whispered, and picked Cadence out of the crib. "Let's get you changed and go have some breakfast."

"Sleeping in here!" Daniel growled from her room.

Kristina closed her eyes and choked a curse; she'd forgotten to switch off the baby monitor. "Sorry."

She hurried downstairs. Daniel just wasn't a morning person. He wouldn't change overnight. He'd been so tender the night before, so unlike himself, she expected too much too soon.

In the kitchen, she fell into the routine she'd adopted since Daniel left. With Cadence in her highchair chasing Cheerios around the tray, Kristina went to the small laundry room off the kitchen—really a closet her dad had fixed up—and threw in a load of laundry, bringing out the ones she'd left in the dryer the day before to fold them. She set the basket next to the couch and went to check on Cadence.

She'd left bottles lined up along the sink, and quickly washed them, setting them on the counter to dry. While wiping the stovetop and the counter, she eyed her list from the day before posted to the fridge. She'd forgotten to clean the oven. On a page from the notebook she kept on the table Kristina added it to her list for the day, smiling as she wrote. That particular chore would see many lists before she worked up the motivation to do it. She hated cleaning the oven.

Kristina stood and went to the coffee maker. She couldn't believe she'd forgotten to make coffee, a terrible sin. Coffee was her ambrosia, a heavenly gift from the gods; one couldn't properly begin a day without it. She opened the cupboard—cringing as the rusted hinges squeaked in protest—to grab the filters and the coffee tin.

She hummed as she worked, pausing now and then to pick up Cadence's dropped keys and to wipe her messy face; pleased that for once, everything felt right with her world. No guilt over Daniel, no dread about what the future would bring, but a wide-open road filled with promise. If they could stay on track, if Daniel could really change, then they had a chance to be happy together.

She looked up at the sound of footsteps on the stairs and her body tensed. Relax. Promise, the future held hope and promise. He'd attempted to mend their relationship and she should show more faith in him. Kristina sat down, placed her coffee next to her on the little round table, and went back to her list. Her breath caught when Daniel cursed after a loud thud.

Fuck.

Daniel rubbed his knee and glared at the toppled laundry basket. Kristina had grown lazy. "Since when do you leave this shit lying around? Jesus, you're out there on your ass doing nothing when you could have had this done and I wouldn't have messed up my damn knee. I think I've got enough bruises, don't you think?"

"Sorry." Kristina stood.

And she wondered why he lost his temper with her? Stupid shit like this forced him to snap when they'd been married.

She walked to the basket.

He turned from her, disgusted with how she'd gone back to the trash she'd been after just a few months without him. The answering machine's message light blinked and Daniel walked to the end table shifting the sling on his shoulder. His neck ached from sleeping too long on one side to avoid rolling on his injured arm.

"You check this?" he asked.

"What?"

God, she was as thick as a brick sometimes. "The message, stupid. It could have been Desiree."

"I turned the phone off. I didn't want to be interrupted last night." She paused holding a pink blanket close to her chest. "I thought Desiree didn't matter."

"Shit, you know what I meant. She doesn't need to know we're trying to work things out, and I don't see any point in breaking up with her until I know we have." He wanted to slap her, but force would get him nowhere. He wouldn't convince her to let him come home if he lost it now. There would be plenty of time later to retrain her.

Kristina bit her bottom lip and her eyes welled with tears.

Daniel turned away, sick of her blubbering. Someday she'd realize life was full of shit she didn't like and she'd just have to suck it up and deal with it. He pressed the button and waited for the machine to play the message. Expecting Desiree's voice, a sharp pain knifed through his chest when a man's drawl, smooth and very familiar, addressed his wife. His face warmed and fire flared in his veins.

"Hey Kris, I know it's late. I hope I didn't wake you…"

Daniel snorted and turned to pin Kristina with an accusatory glare.

She reddened and looked down at the basket.

"Sorry I was so nosey the other night. I just worry about you. Oh, and we got some new shirts and I need to know your size. I can guess at it but I thought you'd like one that didn't ride up on you all the time, although I don't mind it one bit—"

Daniel stopped the message, punching the button so hard the machine flipped off the table and onto the floor. "Who the hell was that?"

"Just Wade. There was a problem at the bar the other night with one of the customers and he's just making sure I'm okay, I almost quit." She shrugged.

Daniel clenched his fists, taking deep breaths to stop himself from lunging at her. He knew Wade and he'd never liked the arrogant prick. Wade Bowen was dishonest and cocky, and the way he let his wife whore herself out the way she did was disgusting. Daniel had fucked her once, but only after repeated offers. He couldn't believe a man would let his wife get so nasty. The woman knew things he'd never allow Kristina to know. He paused and looked closely at her. Had Wade been teaching his wife the same things? The thought of anyone, especially Wade, putting his hands on Kristina made Daniel want to vomit. "I heard what he said. What I want to know is why he's calling you. Isn't that something he could tell you at work?"

"I guess, but he—"

"And why the fuck are you still working there? I told you to quit." He walked toward her.

She backed away, her face reddening further. "I told you I'm not quitting. I thought things were going to change, you said—"

"Shut your fucking mouth," he roared.

She lifted her chin.

A chill ran up Daniel's spine. Oh no, she wasn't going to defy him.

The room flashed red and he reached out for something, anything; his hand coming upon the phone sitting on top of the wall unit next to the stairs. His only thought to shut her up, Daniel picked up the phone and hurled it. Kristina ducked, but he watched with satisfaction as it glanced off her shoulder.

"*You* don't tell me anything. You do what I tell you and that's how things run around here. If you want to fix this shit, you're going to learn my fucking word is law and you will not have any more to do with Wade fucking Bowen. Do I make myself clear?" he clenched his jaw when she turned to glare at him as she rubbed her shoulder.

"Get out. I mean it. I'll call the cops if you don't leave right now."

"Is this how we work things out? It gets rough and you call the cops? Good thing I didn't get rid of Desiree. At least she knows who's in charge."

"You lied to me. Nothing's changed and you don't love me at all." She walked around the coffee table and to the door.

"Don't hand me your shit about wanting this to work. You're no different than the night you left, and you never will be. I'm done."

"You're done?" Daniel grinned. "Well honey I've just started."

Kristina opened the door and tried to act tough, but her chin trembled and she slouched just a little. She was scared.

He knew she would call the cops if he pushed too much, and one more run-in with them would do him no good. He walked past her, pausing to lean close to her ear. "This is a long way from over."

She closed her eyes.

He laughed and walked out the door, smiling when she slammed it shut behind him. She'd learn; whether she chose to do so the easy way or the hard way was up to her.

Kristina sank to her knees, Daniel's laughter as he walked to his truck ringing in her ears. She was an idiot, a fool, too stupid to see what she knew to be true. He played her like a violin and she'd sung the notes he wanted her to.

Cadence cried in the kitchen but she couldn't get up and go to her. She thought about Daniel's tenderness the night before, and the words he said. How could she have missed the words he didn't say? He never said he was sorry for hurting her. He never said he'd been wrong to hit her. No, he said *they* would work things out and *they* would learn how to get along. He would help her to learn what made *him* happy. What about her happiness?

Standing on shaky legs, she sniffed, If one good thing could come of last night, it was knowing she couldn't ever go back to him. It didn't matter how empty or alone she felt. They were finished.

CHAPTER 10

The following night, a busy Saturday, Kristina's heart did a little dance in her chest when she walked through the door of Dirty Truths and saw Wade behind the bar. Foolish as it was, Kristina couldn't help feeling giddy just seeing him.

He glanced up and winked.

She smiled, lowered her head and hurried into the office to grab her new shirt.

After searching the boxes that littered the floor, Kristina found the shirts, black fitted tees with a red maple leaf on the front and the bar's logo across the back. She rifled through them until she found a large one. Just looking at it, Kristina knew it would be too snug for her comfort.

"Hey, you got my message?" Wade peeked around the door.

Kristina nodded and held up the shirt. "Um, I don't think these are bigger than the old ones. This is a large?"

"Yeah, sorry."

He didn't look very sorry. Wade glanced behind him, came into the room and took the shirt from her, holding it up against her chest. "It's not too bad. Covers all the important bits."

Kristina took the shirt back. Her hand brushed his and she jerked away at the contact, as though burned.

Wade chuckled and draped one arm over her shoulder to give her a playful hug.

She smiled and slipped away from him, needing some distance between them.

"I'll go change," she mumbled and left the office.

Once inside the bathroom Kristina slid the lock in place. Wade was always touching her. He played with her hair, ran a hand over her back, or leaned in close when they talked. She didn't know what to make of it, but she had to admit she liked it, even if she shouldn't.

Pulling the old T-shirt over her head, Kristina grimaced at her desperate need to feel wanted. She had to get a grip. It wasn't as though Wade loved her. He didn't even want her. He did that with everyone. It was part of his nature, but she soaked it up like a dry old sponge. She slipped the new shirt on and tugged it over her front. It fit a little better than the old shirt, but she'd have to be careful not to shrink it.

Back in the barroom, she caught Wade's eye.

His mouth turned up slightly as his gaze traveled over the V-neck of the shirt and down to her legs.

Shivering, she walked around the bar to grab her bottle opener and her cash key from the hook above the little sink.

She managed to make it through the night, steering clear of Wade when possible and embarrassed at her stumbling efforts to remain cool when she couldn't.

Hoping to maintain what little dignity she had left, Kristina put as much distance between herself and Wade as possible, but each night she came in to work he found reasons to be close and touch her. He'd pick lint of her shirt, brush her back as he passed by, his hand lingering a moment longer than necessary; little things that shouldn't meant anything, but they rattled her nerves.

At night, his voice and the way his damn mouth tilted up on the right side when he smiled tormented her dreams. She woke each morning in a tangle of sheets, her hair hopelessly knotted from tossing about on the pillow. Sometimes she'd wake so aroused thinking about Wade and what she wanted to do to him she wanted to scream.

The following Saturday, Kristina arrived at the bar dragging her feet. She figured it would be nuts. A local band that always drew a big crowd played, and their fans had gathered once more to support them. The front of the room was a writhing mass of bodies, dancing and waving their arms to the twangy southern rock.

Exhausted, and not eager to run around the floor all night, she agreed to work the bar. Sheila bustled around the pool tables and past the packed dance floor.

Wade came in late, rare for him on a Saturday night, looking frazzled.

Kristina smiled as he passed and gave a yelp of surprise when he patted her ass before slipping by her to the office. He shut the door after turning to give her a wink.

When he emerged more than an hour later, the night was in full swing and she had too much to do to pay him any attention. Sheila had some trouble with a group at the farthest pool table and Wade left the bar to deal with them. He rounded the revelers up and escorted them out the door. The easy way he handled himself no matter what the situation impressed her. She longed to be confident enough to take control. It seemed she had little power in anything anymore, not even herself.

Pushing her self-pity aside, she smiled at the crowd lounging around the bar and grabbed bottles, shook cocktails, and took their money until Wade flashed the lights for last call. Breathing a sigh of relief—she didn't think her legs could take another moment—Kristina took the last orders, made a note to change the keg in the cooler when the tap sputtered out the last foamy beer, and worked at cleaning up the mess she'd made behind the bar.

As the band packed their gear at the front, Sheila's voice rang out over the crowd "I don't care where y'all go, but you can't stay here. Drink up or it's mine."

Kristina laughed. Sheila had nerve. In her place, Kristina

would quietly slip around the bar, taking bottles and glasses with barely a word to anyone. But not Sheila. When she worked, everyone filed out within an hour of last call or she pushed them out.

She caught Sheila's eye with a wave and pointed to the cooler. Sheila nodded, coming around to watch the bar while Kristina went to change the keg. They never left an empty one overnight. Wade said empty kegs allowed air in the lines making it a bitch to pour the first few beers from the new one.

Blinking to adjust her eyes to the dim glow, she walked to the kegs lined up on the opposite wall. A single bulb hung from the ceiling in the center of the cramped cooler, illuminating the kegs and little else. Kristina hated changing them. Heavy and awkward, she always managed to drop one on her toe, or slip on the stainless steel floor, always slick with condensation. She slid the empty keg from its position and turned to pull the full one forward. Grunting with the effort, Kristina skidded, righted herself and heaved the container up on the little ledge they sat on. She then had to push it back against the wall or the whole thing would topple over. Her fingers, slick from the wet aluminum, stung in the cold air. She hit her thumb against the valve and cursed. Unless she started bribing someone else to do this, she'd have no nails or undamaged toes left.

When the keg hit the wall with a metallic ting, Kristina straightened. She brought her hands to her mouth and blew on them to warm up her fingers so she could attach the valve to the hose leading to the tap. Numb fingers made this difficult, but she managed to snap it into place. Rubbing her frozen hands she turned to the door and touched the handle only to have it swing back in her face.

"Uh," the wind went out of her lungs as the large handle caught her stomach. She stumbled back when it swung open again.

"Oh shit, I'm sorry." Wade reached in and pulled her out of the cooler.

The hallway was narrow, too narrow for more than one

body. Kristina found herself pressed against him.

"I'm okay," she murmured.

"I wanted to tell you not to worry, but I guess you've already changed the keg." Wade didn't move, trapping her between his body and the wall. He rubbed her arms with his hands.

Kristina breathed in his scent, cigarettes and something spicy. Her head spun. She looked over his shoulder where Sheila stood at the edge of the bar, watching them while placing empty bottles along the top. "I should finish up."

"Okay, but you're all right?"

Kristina avoided his eyes, staring instead at his shoulder. "Fine, I'm fine. Sheila's waiting."

Wade turned and let her step away. He followed her to the bar and brushed her back with one hand as he slipped past her to the office to disappear inside once more.

Kristina stood, staring at the door. She jumped when a hand touched her arm.

"I'd watch it honey," Sheila muttered and bent to pick up an empty beer case behind the bar. "Wifey ain't gonna like that much, no matter how much she runs around. She don't let him too far off his leash."

"It's nothing like—he's too old for me, and I've known them since I was a kid. He's just looking out for me. Jesus, Sheila, I'd never be with a married man."

Sheila raised an eyebrow, grabbed the bottles she'd lined up along the bar and put them in the case. She sniffed and shook her head. "That's a fine looking man there, you don't know what you'd do if he turned on his charm. I can guarantee he's got the skills to go with it. Mad skills, if you know what I mean. I've been there. Just a warning because I like you and I can tell he likes you, which is dangerous... for you. I'm taking these out back; you behave while I'm gone, hmm?" She picked up the case of empties and walked to the door.

Kristina stared at her back. Had Sheila and Wade? No, he wouldn't. She walked to the bar and picked up the rag to wipe the surface, her mind reeling. What if they had? Did it change how she felt about him? She didn't know why, but it bothered her to think he would sleep around, although she didn't want to consider why it should. A lump formed in her stomach. She breathed deep and set the rag over the little sink under the bar. How could she lie to herself? She didn't like the thought of Wade sleeping with anyone, not even his wife. Kristina shook her head at her crazy feelings. She had no right to be jealous.

"Hey, dopey. You want a ride?" Sheila said, startling Kristina out of her thoughts.

"Yeah, let me get my stuff from the office. I'll tell Wade we're off."

"I'll come with you," Sheila walked across the floor, a smug grin on her face. She tossed her dark hair over her shoulder and nodded at the door. "Well?"

Kristina opened it.

Wade looked up from the cluttered desk and frowned.

Kristina felt as though she interrupted something important. "We're just going. I need to grab my purse."

Wade switched off the computer. "Wait a minute. I need to ask you about something."

"I'll wait in the car," Sheila touched her shoulder and Kristina turned.

She winked and looked pointedly at Wade.

Kristina blushed and turned her gaze to her hands.

"I just have a call to make. I'll meet you out there." Wade turned back to the papers on his desk and picked up the phone.

Dismissed, Kristina and Sheila left the office. Sheila said no more, pushing through the door and outside while Kristina sat on the closest stool toying with a coaster. At a soft click from the door she looked up.

Wade smiled, glancing around the bar before coming to sit next to her. His leg brushed hers. She inched away.

He shifted, pushing his knee against the outside of her thigh. "I was hoping you can take on a few more hours."

"Of course I can, just let me check with my mom to make sure she can handle taking Cadence more often. I think I can manage at least two more shifts." Kristina didn't know why he couldn't have asked her in front of Sheila. She stared at his hands as he took the coaster from her hands and fidgeted with the edges.

"I need you to work the closing shifts. Sheila can't do them; she's got something else going on. So you'd still have the same number of days, but you'd be here for the whole night, no leaving early."

Kristina digested this information and her heart pounded. Alone with Wade. She shivered, thinking of what could happen. If she let it. After all, he'd already been with women other than his wife, if Kristina gave him the right signs then maybe— she shook her head, silently chastising herself.

"No?" Wade frowned.

"Oh, no I was just thinking about something silly. I can do it." Blush warmed her cheeks.

"Good."

Wade reached out and picked something off her shoulder and then smoothed her shirt. He rose and walked away from her toward his office once more.

Kristina remained on the stool for a moment, collecting herself before meeting Sheila outside. She had to stop this. It would end in tears. She'd cried enough for a lifetime.

RENÉE MILLER

CHAPTER 11

As she walked down the darkened streets, Kristina mulled over the night's events. She always did this when she had to walk home. It took her mind away from the fact that she was alone, in the dark. The damp sidewalk squished under her shoes and a light mist still fell from the sky. The rain hadn't killed the humidity at all. She pulled her shirt from her sweat-soaked body.

Since she agreed to the closing shifts, Kristina no longer had Sheila to drive her home. Wade never offered, and she couldn't afford to call a cab every night, so she lied bout arranging a cab. Some nights she could barely force her aching feet to shuffle the short distance to her house. Two blocks didn't seem such a long way to walk, but when you'd raced ten miles of floor in one night, it might as well have been twenty blocks. Fatigue always plagued her, no matter how much rest she got.

Wade closed an hour early because they hadn't had a customer from ten onward. While he tallied the receipts Kristina had left. She tried not to stick around too long, afraid the temptation to give in to his subtle advances would be too strong to resist.

Turning at the stoplights, she walked out of the glow of the streetlamps toward the bridge that crossed the river in front of her house. She hated this part, and tried to keep her mind off the back streets in darkness, illuminated only by widely spaced streetlights and the moon. Wade's face floated into her mind, his smile when she peeked in and the sparkle in his dark eyes. Tonight he'd actually asked her to stay.

"You want a drink?" He'd gestured to a bottle of whiskey at his elbow.

She grimaced and shook her head.

He chuckled.

Kristina didn't care for booze. If she indulged, it was only wine and girly coolers. She'd tried whiskey during her first week at the bar and thought she would die. The fiery liquid burned a path down her throat, through her chest and into her belly. She gasped and sputtered, even gagged once, before Wade handed her a glass of water to 'chase' it down. Though she guzzled the water, her stomach burned for a long time after.

"I should get home."

"Okay, I'll see you tomorrow night."

She'd grabbed her purse and left the bar, pausing before letting the steel door close behind her. If she turned around, went back to the office and locked the door, what would he have done? Would he laugh at her? No, he'd never do that, but she didn't think she could keep up to Wade; he scared her as much as he intrigued her. Nothing she'd learned about sex could meet his needs. She'd only ever been with Daniel, and he didn't like to explore too much. When she suggested different things she'd read in her romance novels, he'd frowned and told her if he wanted a whore he'd have married one. She figured Wade would be different.

The questions she had when she left the bar plagued her still. Kristina shook her head as she came to the end of the sidewalk. There was little point in driving herself crazy over Wade, she'd never have the guts to offer him any sort of invitation. Hell, he probably wouldn't accept it anyway. She'd probably misconstrued his actions.

Before stepping onto the road, Kristina paused. No one drove the streets at this time of night but she still looked both ways before crossing, a habit ingrained from childhood. As she moved her foot to cross, her neck tingled. Were those footsteps behind her? Almost at the bridge, she lengthened her strides. No one in Laighton would be lurking in the shadows waiting to pounce on a lone woman at night. Hell, she'd walked alone in the dark for years and not once had she ever had a problem.

The footsteps were real, and quickened. Kristina turned around, her heart pounding in her chest. About ten feet away a man, tall, lanky and wearing a hooded gray sweatshirt, walked toward her. Something about him seemed familiar, but he'd pulled the hood over his head with a baseball cap on top so she couldn't make out his features. She turned and broke into a trot, instinct forcing her to move faster.

"Hey, you dropped this," he called.

She stopped, checking her shoulder to make sure her purse was still there. Kristina wondered what she'd lost and allowed him to catch up to her at the bridge. His face shadowed by the hood, he grinned as he held out his hand.

"Thanks," she started.

He lunged.

Kristina stumbled back, but he grabbed her shoulders.

She struggled to free her arms from his viselike grip.

He laughed, and then raised his hand to slap her face. His knuckles caught her cheek.

Her ears rang and stars floated before her eyes.

"Didn't your mother ever tell you not to talk to strangers?" he asked.

She tried to place his voice, but he spoke in a whisper. "Please, take my purse and I won't say a word. Just let me go home."

"Oh, we're going home, but I'm not interested in your purse."

He dragged her onto the bridge.

Kristina struggled.

He threw her down on the wooden planks.

She grunted as her knee struck the hard surface and sparks of pain shot through her legs. Kristina attempted to stand but crumpled as his foot knocked the air out of her lungs.

"I watch you in your slutty little clothes, making eyes at everyone. You think you can send the invitation and we'll be happy to leave you a nice tip? Think you're too fucking good for guys like me?" He grabbed her hair, forcing her to stand.

"I don't know what you mean."

He yanked her forward.

Kristina stumbled again, tasting blood as she bit her tongue. "Please don't hurt me."

"It doesn't have to hurt, but I'm going to get what I paid for whether you cooperate or not."

Fear froze any intelligent thoughts from her mind and she followed blindly behind him. Now and then he'd let go to push her forward. When she tried to run, he moved closer, kicking her, punching her, until Kristina couldn't breathe much less fight him. At the end of the bridge, she glanced at her house, hoping she might make the short distance before him.

He smiled and nodded to her house. "Try it. I dare you to. You think you can get inside, call the cops, and keep me out until they haul their asses away from their donuts?"

Kristina's lip trembled. She didn't want to show her fear, but didn't know how to get out of this. When Daniel attacked her, she knew how to react, how to calm him down. She also knew Daniel wouldn't kill her. This guy was a stranger and she didn't understand what he wanted. Dread settled into her belly. She pictured Cadence's smiling face and her heart twisted at the thought of never seeing her daughter again. "I'll do whatever you want. Just don't kill me."

He shoved her.

Stumbling backward, she fell on her bottom. The moisture from the wet pavement seeped through her jeans.

"Why would I kill you? I'm going to fuck you, and then I'm going to watch you again for a while. You probably like knowing I'm out there, waiting for you. Maybe when I get the urge, I'll come back and fuck you again and again. You tell anyone, or if you don't do exactly what I tell you to, then I'll kill you. Maybe I'll do your kid first."

Kristina blinked, pushing herself back.

He leaned over and grabbed the front of her shirt, ripping it as he pulled her to her feet and pressed his lips to hers. Hard and punishing, he ground his mouth against her teeth. She tasted more blood when her front teeth split the tender skin behind her upper lip. His breath reeked of booze and she gagged when he forced his tongue into her mouth. A noise to her left, near the water, made her open her eyes, but she saw nothing but a blur of grey and black. A sob lodged in her chest. Never in her worst nightmares did she think this could ever happen. Even when Daniel had raged and assaulted her, she hadn't felt this terrified and violated.

At a throat-clearing noise, her knees weakened in relief.

The man straightened, but did not turn around. His eyes bored into hers, a silent warning. "You got a problem?" he asked.

"Well, I kinda do. When I see someone treating a lady like that, I get a bit ruffled. Know what I mean?"

Wade's voice sounded like music to her ears.

The man laughed, but didn't release her. "Just me and my old lady having a little fun. Mind your business, all right?"

Wade sighed. A shuffle before he continued speaking. "Only one thing I hate more than an asshole, and that's a liar."

The man spun around.

Kristina crumpled to the sidewalk.

"You don't know what you're talking about. Fuck off before you end up at the bottom of the river," he pointed across the road.

Kristina risked a glance at Wade. Standing just a few feet away, the darkness shadowing his features, he chuckled as though the man were joking. "You think you got the parts to put me there? Bring it."

The man charged.

Wade sidestepped.

Everything happened so fast. Kristina didn't know who had the advantage. They fell to the ground, rolling around. Then Wade surfaced on top, punching the man repeatedly. She silently cheered him on as her attacker brought his arms up to ward off the blows. Wade continued undeterred. Her breath caught in her throat when she looked to Wade's face. Calm, his eyes cold and determined; he pummeled the man on the ground. He'd kill him without a qualm, she was sure of it. Then he'd go to jail. No matter the reason, the law didn't like murderers. If she allowed Wade to continue that's what he'd be. Kristina yelled for him to stop.

Standing, Wade wiped bloodied hands on his jeans before straightening his rumpled shirt.

"He deserves to fucking die." He muttered.

"You'll go to jail if you kill him." Kristina argued.

"I haven't gone yet." Wade bent and dragged the man to his feet. "Get out of here and don't let me even smell you around this town again. You got me?"

"Fuck you."

"Really? You really want to go there? You don't want trouble with me. I'm warning you, I won't be the one at the bottom of a river." Wade shoved him.

Stumbling back, the man spat on the ground, moving away but he didn't look away from Wade until he reached the other side of the bridge where he turned and jogged away.

Kristina pushed herself to her feet.

Wade rushed over to take her arm.

She looked up and frowned. "We should have called the cops. He'll just attack someone else."

"Let me worry about what he'll do." He held up his right hand.

She gasped. A brown leather wallet, held closed with a rubber band, nestled between his thumb and index finger.

"He won't do anything." Wade said.

"What are you going to do with that?"

Wade tucked the wallet into his back pocket and ran one thumb over her lip. "You're bleeding."

Kristina had no words, no thoughts, only the knowledge she was lost. No turning back or changing her mind, her heart no longer belonged to her. Even if Wade pushed her away now, she couldn't stop what she felt.

"I think you should go inside. You're shaking like a leaf and people are going to start taking their dogs out or getting up for their midnight snacks. They'll wonder what's going on," he murmured.

"I guess I'm a little shocked. I don't know what I would have done if—"

Wade shook his head.

She looked down at her feet.

"Don't. I'm sure you would have done something. You're a survivor."

"Thanks," she mumbled.

She didn't feel like a survivor. People just kept taking advantage of her and she should be getting stronger, tougher. Instead Kristina felt like a bigger target, as though she weakened with every blow life threw at her.

Wade cleared his throat. "Look, from now on you aren't walking home from work. Even if the guy never comes back—and I promise he won't—there will be others. This might be a small town but there's no invisible barrier warding off psychos. Shit, if you hadn't forgotten your tips…"

"I know, but you don't have to take me home. Dad can pick me up or I can get a cab."

"It's not open for discussion. Besides, I can't trust you to actually call Joe, can I? You lied. I don't even want to think about how many times you walked home when I thought you were safely tucked inside a cab. Now I won't sleep at night unless I see you get home. He could have killed you, or worse. That would be terrible, you know? At my age, I need my sleep. Understood?"

A finger under her chin forced her to look at him. Kristina shivered at the anger still evident in his gaze despite his little joke. "Yes," she whispered.

He lowered his hand.

"Would you like to come in for a drink? I mean, I won't be able to sleep for a while, and it would be nice to have company. That is, if you don't have to get home right away."

"What about your mom?"

"Um, she's probably not going to care. But I don't know; I could call her if you want."

Wade laughed and some of her tension slipped away. She'd just made an ass of herself and it bothered her more than her near death experience.

"I meant, what about Cadence? Isn't your mom babysitting?"

"Oh, I'm just kind of shaken up. Fear makes me stupid. Mom watches her at their place so I can get some sleep."

"So, you have all night…" Eyebrow raised, he glanced to the house and then to Kristina.

The silence grew as loud as a bomb blast.

Kristina saw the possibilities in his gaze, and in the way he twirled his wedding band around his finger.

The gold ring catching the light of the moon brought her to her senses. The idea she could go through with sleeping with a married man suddenly seemed ridiculous. No matter how much Amy and Wade hated each other, the fact remained they were married. Hadn't she vowed to herself when she'd found out about Desiree never to do the same to another woman?

Heat crept up her neck. "Well, not all night," she stuttered. "I mean, how long does it take you to drink?" Kristina shrugged and laughed, although it sounded hollow to her ears.

Wade's lip twitched, as though he might smile. "Depends on the drink."

She faltered and gave a nervous laugh. "Well I've got cheap wine and beer."

"I can't say no to cheap wine. I should stay at least long enough to be sure the fucktard doesn't come back."

"Of course," Kristina turned toward the house, his footsteps on the damp street behind her.

Kristina took her key out of her purse, but dropped it as she approached the door. She bent to retrieve it and almost collided with Wade's head. Kristina jumped back.

He picked up the key and inserted it in the lock. She murmured her thanks and stepped inside.

CHAPTER 12

Kristina reached to switch on the kitchen light. The fluorescent glow blinded her and she paused. Wade's body brushing against her back sent her scurrying into the kitchen. Inviting him in for a drink must rank the worst idea she'd ever had. He was far from stupid and she'd be willing to bet he read her every thought. Probably thought she was childish.

She gazed around the room at the crummy furniture. What she once considered cheerful and sunny yellow paint, seemed tacky now, and the chipped countertop not so charming. Wade lived in a fabulous house. How must this shitty little place look to him? He probably thought she was destitute.

Muddled and still reeling from the shock of the encounter on the bridge, Kristina walked across the small kitchen and opened the cupboard. She cringed at the squeaky hinge she intended to fix, even bought the grease for it, but never seemed to get around to doing. Kristina reached up to the top shelf for a bottle of wine that had sat there since her divorce. Though she bought it to celebrate her new life, so far she hadn't felt like drinking it. Wiping the dust from its sides she set it on the counter.

"Shit, how long have you had that?" Wade chuckled, a chair scraping the linoleum as he sat down. He was actually sitting in her kitchen and it scared her to death.

She shrugged. "A couple of months, I guess. It should be okay. Don't they charge more for the old stuff?" She twisted the top off and reached up once more to grab two glasses.

"Um, the good old stuff."

Her hands shook. Pouring the wine, she held the bottle with both hands to keep the red liquid in the glass and not spilling all over the counter. Kristina took a deep breath before turning . She took a step toward him to hand him his glass. Her fingers refused to cooperate. Suddenly she couldn't hold the glasses anymore. In slow motion, she followed their arc to the floor at her feet, red liquid splashing up on her pants and across the white linoleum. Tears burned her eyes and her cheeks warmed. With unsteady hands she grabbed a towel hanging over the sink and knelt to clean up the mess.

Wade jumped up from his chair to kneel in front of her. His breath warmed her face. "There's the clumsy girl I know and love."

Instinctively, she closed her hand, cutting her finger on a shard of glass. "Shit," she cursed. The sight of her blood sent waves of nausea through her stomach. Her head spun, heat coursed through her body, and a lump formed in her throat. Great, she'd have an all-out panic attack right in front of him. He'd be so impressed when she started crying and vomiting all over the floor. Kristina dropped the glass pieces and slumped.

Wade reached out and took her hand. He frowned as he examined the cut on her finger.

"I'm okay," she murmured and tried to pull her hand away.

Wade pulled back and raised her hand to his mouth.

Kristina knew what he was about to do, but could do nothing but stare, her chest aching.

He licked her hand, then her finger, and raised his gaze.

The warmth of his mouth, the way he dragged his tongue over her palm and up her fingers, sent tiny sparks of pleasure to her belly.

Kristina stopped breathing. She couldn't even move. Wade's gaze burned into her, so intense he might really be able to read her thoughts.

He tugged her closer and brushed his lips over hers.

How many nights had she dreamt about this moment, his

attention solely on her and his hands in her hair, pulling her into him? The way he looked at her, as though he might devour her whole, sent a shudder down her spine.

"I should go," he said against her lips.

"This is a bad idea." She agreed.

But he didn't go. Instead, he stood and pulled her with him and pressed his body against hers, his hands roaming over her back to grip her bottom.

Kristina's mind screamed for him to stop and back away. But she stood immobile as Wade ran his hands over her body. His mouth felt so much different than Daniel's, he was different. Rather than taking, his mouth gave; warmth, tenderness, and something else she didn't stop to identify. She couldn't recall ever needing Daniel this much. Why hadn't she realized this before? The thought of Daniel chilled her just a little. If he knew Wade was touching her like this, or that she welcomed it, he'd kill her.

Wade changed. His mouth hardened against hers and his teeth grazed her lips roughly before he stepped away and turned to the door.

Kristina stared after him. Emptiness replaced the warmth his hands had given and it hurt.

He turned, then smiled and opened the door. "You're not ready. I'm not about to share you. Not even with a memory." He walked out and gently closed the door behind him.

The soft click of the lock jolted her out of her stupor. Kristina crumbled to the floor, kneeling before the broken glass and spilled wine. She broke down. Hot tears soaked her cheeks. Disgusted with her weakness and for wanting a married man, she berated herself for being so stupid. She realized how unfair she'd been to Daniel, expecting him to return a love she hadn't given. She felt horrible; the lowest form of life. There was no excuse for what she almost allowed to happen, wanted to happen, no matter how lonely she felt.

Wade stood outside the door listening to Kristina's sobs, fighting the urge to go back inside and take her in his arms again. She'd let him do whatever he wanted. He knew that, but he couldn't. Not when she still had feelings for her fuck-up ex-husband. He would not fight an idiot like Daniel Riley for her affection.

The night had cooled considerably and rain fell in large drops, no longer a fine mist. Wade turned his face to the sky and let the cool water wash away the heat of Kristina's body. He spun on his heel and walked down the driveway, silently cursing when his boots sloshed in the mud. Yep, the boots were ruined. He strode to the end of the street where he parked his truck and fished the keys from his pocket.

The houses lining Kristina's street darkened long ago, with only a few porch lights lit as most of Laighton's residents felt safe enough to sleep without the added security. As he walked up the sidewalk to the slurping sounds of his tread, rain battered the tin roofs and windows of the silent homes. He bet most of the back doors in town were unlocked. Small-town folks didn't believe evil could touch them. Everyone knew everyone else, didn't they?

Wade knew better. Small towns were perfect for hiding the darkest of sins. He wiped the rain from his face as he approached his truck and thought of Kristina and how trusting she was even after being married to the most sadistic fuck he'd seen in a long time. She believed herself to be perfectly safe walking alone at night because she lived in a rural area. Naïve and foolish.

Then he remembered the wallet and the debt he owed. Smiling, Wade opened the truck and climbed in. Leaning across the seat, he opened the glove compartment and reached inside. He felt around, his hand touching cool metal before sliding to his phone, taking it out and punching in a number he'd memorized.

"Better be good," a low voice growled.

"It's W. I want to check someone." Wade read the name

and address on the driver's license in the wallet.

The sound of fingers moving rapidly over a keyboard traveled the line. This man had been a handy little contact to have, and when he'd come to them for help, Thomas, Wade's boss, made sure he took advantage of it. Wade didn't know his name, only Thomas knew that, but he knew he could hack into anyone's personal information in seconds.

"Oh, this is a naughty boy," the voice chuckled.

"What?"

"Fifteen years for rape and attempted murder. Early release six months ago. Didn't report to his probation officer last week. He has a few days before they issue a bench warrant and go arrest him for breach."

"Thanks."

Wade closed the phone and looked again at the wallet. "Well, William Allan, you won't have to worry about the probation officer anymore."

He started the truck thinking about Kristina as he pulled away from the curb and headed toward Victoria Street. The longing in her gaze nearly undid his self-control, but the naked fear dominating her being made him wary. It would have been easy to take advantage of her tonight; she desperately wanted to feel safe and loved. The shudder that wracked her body and the haunted look when he pulled away, told him she couldn't quite separate Daniel from her thoughts. Things were complicated enough without trying to get around her irrational loyalty to the idiot.

He could use her, get her out of his system and forget about her, but an affair with Kristina wouldn't satisfy him. Wade wanted more. He wanted everything. If it weren't for Amy he'd have pursued her openly, but he had to be careful. Amy could really screw him over if she chose to. So far she'd been subdued by the Brotherhood's threat but Amy often went off half-cocked and a whiff of Kristina would throw her into a proper tantrum. Although she didn't love him, Amy had always been a little jealous of Kristina, even accusing Wade years ago of having an affair with her. If Amy caught on to what was happening, she'd make them both pay. He couldn't do that to Kristina. She'd suffered enough already.

Wade turned right, crossing the little bridge on a quiet road with only a few houses stacked side by side with little space between, each one having their very own patch of grass out back. He couldn't imagine living this close to someone else, glad for his acres of property and his privacy.

The sign indicating Victoria Street was at the end of the road. He pressed the gas, eager to confront the piece of shit the legal system couldn't take care of. How many rapes, assaults and crimes against women did one guy have to commit before the law tossed him away forever? Pedophiles and rapists got less time than a thief or a drug dealer. Wade didn't understand it and he doubted he ever would. To him, it seemed they were far more interested in the minor crime of selling someone a fix—a fix they wanted and often begged for—than someone who shattered people's lives.

Wade's pulse quickened when he spotted the number he wanted. He continued driving until he reached the end of the dead-end street. He left the key in the ignition, the motor idling, and turned off the truck lights. Whistling softly he opened the glove compartment once more. He set the gun on the seat and reached in again for the cylinder that would silence the shot. As he prepared the weapon, Wade stared out the windshield.

The end of the street butted against the old Steel Works where it met with another dead end. Laighton Steel had been closed now for nearly fifteen years, although they used the building for something, Wade didn't know what. Beyond the low rambling building and opposite the narrow road, was Moira Lake, its rippling waves like black silk under the light of the full moon.

He considered finishing the job there but quickly tossed the idea aside. In the small lake, William would be found too quickly and Wade didn't want him found. Preparations finished, he opened the door and jumped down, his feet sinking in the muddy ground. Damn rain.

Gloves. He pulled the visor down, removed them from the little band holding them in place and slipped them on. The soft leather slid over his hands, caressing his skin, a feeling he always savored.

Still whistling, he walked toward the tiny duplex near the dead end. Set back from the road and surrounded by tall maple trees—the steel works on one side, an abandoned house on the other—William lived in the perfect house to remain anonymous, undiscovered... and vulnerable. Wade walked up the broken and crumbling walkway, stepping off just before he reached the door and going around to the back of the house. The grey siding had cracked in spots, fallen off altogether in others, and black shingles lifted and curled away from the roof. Wade was willing to bet it rained inside as well as out.

The light was on in the front window. William, if he paid attention, would know someone was outside. Wade wasn't trying to hide though, not from the likes of him.

He blended into the shadows of the backyard, his feet sinking into the deep mud. He'd have to get rid of his boots, Amy would question their state and he didn't need to give her more ammunition. Wade stepped up to a screen door hanging precariously by two rusted hinges. One good tug would pull it off. He rapped on its cracked glass and waited. A shadow scuttled past the door, then nothing.

He knocked once more, and the shadow grew, moving closer. "Who is it?"

"Pizza. Get the fuck out here and get it."

William pushed the door open.

Wade backed away.

He scratched his head and Wade imagined lice fleeing from the greasy brown mop. "You're joking, right? You think you're going to come here to my house and try to scare me?"

"I'm not trying to scare you."

"What then? You going to warn me to stay away from the slut? Fuck off. You made your point."

William turned sideways and reached for the door.

Wade raised the gun and released the safety, the metallic

click echoing in the silence of the night. Raindrops ran over his face and down his shirt, which had soaked through long ago.

William stopped and turned slowly, his arms rising above his head. "You don't want to do this. Fuck, I didn't do anything to her. And if you shoot me, you'll get life, no matter what I did. They'll know and they'll find you."

Wade grabbed the front of his hooded sweatshirt and dragged him from the doorway. The screen door slammed, its metallic clang like a thunderclap. William stumbled but managed to stay on his feet and backed away, circling until he stood against a large tree looming over the house. Wade followed him with the gun and smiled.

"They haven't found me yet," Wade squeezed the trigger a heartbeat before William's body slammed against the old maple.

"Fuck you, William."

Slipping the gun into the waistband of his jeans Wade squatted in front of the dead man. His forehead had caved where the bullet mushroomed and shattered the skull. The tree was now decorated with blood and bone fragments the rain had already begun to wash away. The back of William's head was a mess of matted hair and gore. Wade grabbed his shirt-front once more and hauled his body up. The head lolled forward and Wade grunted with the effort of getting under the man's arm and righting his legs. He grabbed the hood of the shirt and pulled it over his shattered head. To anyone braving the rain, it would look as though Wade was helping his buddy—who had maybe drunk a bit too much—to his truck so he could drive him home. The street had no lights and William's head slumped so his chin touched his chest. No one could see the wound.

Wade wedged the body against the truck and opened the passenger door, glancing around to make sure they were still alone. He reached behind the seat, pulled his old blue tarp and spread it over the black leather. He hated getting blood out of leather, damn near impossible. Bending down, he lifted William up and onto the seat before closing the door. As he walked around to the driver's side a thud rattled the wind-shield. William had slumped over, his bloody forehead pressed against the passenger window.

"Shit," Wade opened the door and climbed in. "You're more trouble than you're worth, William Allan."

He pulled the body back up and reached once more behind the seat. His hand brushed a roll of paper towels. Wade un-rolled a large strip and wiped the worst off the window, cursing his poor planning After tucking the bloody paper towel into the front pocket of William's shirt, Wade started the truck, backed out and turned right, toward River Street which led out of town and should be deserted this time of night. He'd drive to the highway and drop William at the old talc mines. Once William disappeared in the large pit, now full of water, they'd be a while finding him. Considering he hadn't thought it through, Wade was pretty impressed the only speed bump had been the mess on his window. So many other things could have gone wrong. Good thing he'd left the old tarp behind the seat after returning from his last job. Thomas would kill him if he knew, but Wade didn't plan on anyone knowing about William. Not even Thomas.

He whistled again as he drove through the rain, which fell from the sky in torrents now, and thanked whoever watched over him for waiting until he'd gotten out of town before opening up the heavens. Kristina's eyes floated into his mind again, haunted and longing for his touch; such a difficult com-bination to walk away from. He'd figure out a way for them to be together. If that meant another visit to the mines to get rid of an ex-husband, or a wife, then so be it.

CHAPTER 13

Giant grey clouds drifted over the sun, casting gloomy shadows and heaviness to the humid air. Rain was inevitable. Cadence squealed, crawling across the dry grass to her small green pool. She liked to lean on it and touch the water but never actually got in. Kristina leaned against the fence watching as she splashed around on the edge and giggled. Cadence loved baths but something about the pool scared her.

A drop on Kristina's shoulder and her gaze shifted to the darkening sky above. "Come on, Monkey." She knelt and picked a squirming Cadence up.

The drop multiplied and suddenly turned into a downpour as she raced toward the back of the house. When she stepped through the door and into the kitchen, they were both soaked, Cadence a slippery screaming bundle she could barely hold onto. Kristina set her on the floor and wiped hair from her eyes. Now she'd have to change before meeting her parents for dinner. Her mother had insisted to celebrate her birthday in some way and although she'd rather stay home, Kristina agreed to go.

Cadence crawled past her legs and over the step from the hallway into the kitchen. Kristina smiled, knowing where she'd go; right to the blocks she left on the living room floor. Daniel would never have allowed it, which made her enjoy leaving them out even more. She followed Cadence's progress through the living room. At the stairs, Kristina unlatched the gate, ran up to gather towels and dry clothes for both before hurrying back down to the living room. Her daughter hadn't tried the stairs yet, but Kristina wasn't about to give her enough time to consider it. Cadence had scattered her blocks in a circle around herself, picking two up and banging them together before tossing them and finding a new pair to pound.

Pulling her tank top over hear head, Kristina cursed as the tiny buttons on the straps caught in her hair. The phone rang as she tried to pull the damp, knotted mess free. She sighed, rushed to the phone and picked it up muttering a distracted greeting.

"What's wrong?" Wade's voice sent goose bumps over her skin.

"Nothing, why?"

"You sound upset."

"I just said hello. How do you get upset from that?" Kristina laughed and tugged at the shirt. It pulled free, along with a good-sized chunk of her hair.

"You're out of breath."

"I'm fine, just got my hair stuck in my shirt after getting thoroughly soaked."

Wade laughed.

Her heart beat a staccato against her chest.

"Hmm, I'd like to see that. Too bad I'm stuck over here."

Kristina opened her mouth but couldn't think of anything cool or even remotely smart to say.

Wade cleared his throat and broke the uncomfortable silence. "So, I gave you the weekend off, right?"

"Yes, you did."

"Um, about that," Wade paused.

She stifled a shiver of excitement at the possibility of working anyway. She wanted to see him.

"Can you come in tonight? You can have tomorrow off, and Monday if you need it, but Amy can't work tonight. I could force it but I don't really want to fight."

"No, it's okay. But she wasn't scheduled, was she?" The mention of Amy dampened her excitement.

"Well she wasn't, but Sheila can't come in until later and I won't be there until at least ten. I need someone here for the first half of the shift. Can you come in around eight or nine? I can probably get Lynne to stay an extra hour so you don't have to do the regular shift. If it's dead you can go when Sheila gets here."

"Yeah, I just have to call my mom."

"Okay, I really appreciate this. I'll make it up to you somehow."

Before she could argue, he hung up, leaving her staring at the receiver in her hand.

She replaced it on the base and picked the towel off the floor to dry her hair. Cadence had crawled to the once neatly folded stack of clothes Kristina had set on the floor and tossed them around.

She wrestled her shorts from Cadence's surprisingly strong grasp and pulled them on before tackling the job of changing her daughter as well.

"You want to go to Nana's?" Kristina asked as she laid her down on her back.

Cadence's eyes brightened and took a deep breath.

"Let Mommy get you changed and we'll go see Nana and Papa, okay."

Cadence stilled, as though she understood, and Kristina changed her quickly before calling her mother. So much for dinner. Maybe she could convince her mom to do it tomorrow instead.

While walking to Dirty Truths, a tiny bubble of anxiety burst in Kristina's belly. She wondered about the man from the other night, her heart racing at the memory of his threats. But she couldn't expect Wade to jump to her aid each time she felt threatened. She didn't bother to tell him her father wasn't home or he'd have come and picked her up or arranged a ride.

Wade was obviously busy, or he'd have covered the shift. It made her uncomfortable knowing he changed his plans often to accommodate hers.

Keeping his word, Wade drove her home each night before he balanced the cash and did his daily paperwork. She couldn't stand the awkward silences, but did her best to behave naturally. Now and then, Wade would stare with a strange light in his eyes that made her want to put her arms around him, forgetting everything and everyone and just losing herself in the moment. She felt the questions in his gaze, but had no answers for him. She didn't know what to do about her feelings.

Wanting someone so desperately the thought left you breathless didn't mean you just forgot about right and wrong. Did it? It was a question she couldn't answer, not with any certainty. Now and then, her grandmother's voice would echo in her mind, a voice she missed terribly. Her grandmother had been a feisty woman, outliving three husbands and, in her last years, finding the man she'd pined for since high school.

Kristina reached the end of the bridge and took a deep breath as she crossed, holding it until she stepped back into the pools of light at the end of the street. Safe once more, her thoughts went back to her grandmother.

When the family had balked at the seventy-year-old woman getting married for a fourth time, claiming he only wanted to take advantage of her, she told Kristina a wonderful story. She let the man of her dreams walk away after listening to everyone around her saying he wasn't right, and believed them when they said passion should never overrule common sense. He was younger than her and his family had money, enough so they could send him faraway so the temptation of the pretty but poor tutor he'd fallen in love with would fade.

But it never did. Through marriages and several children he'd waited, finally meeting her again at an old friend's funeral. Her grandmother laughed when she told Kristina he latched on, and refused to let go of her again despite the wrinkles and the age spots.

Kristina smiled at the memory of the light in her grandmother's eyes, a light she'd never seen before. The old woman had taken her hand and squeezed it. "Life without passion isn't life at all. You remember that. You can't experience love as it's meant to be without it."

Though Kristina promised to remember her grandmother's words, she hadn't thought of them until now, not in terms of what they meant anyway. Instead, she'd allowed Daniel to sweep her off her feet, believing the comfortable feeling of someone wanting her would be enough.

Now, as she approached the bar and walked through the parking lot full of cars, pickups and clusters of people doing God knows what in the shadows, she felt afraid. Not of Wade, but of the situation and her feelings, neither of which she could get a handle on. Excited to come to work each night, thinking of him every minute, and dreaming at the memory of his lips against hers, wore on her fragile nerves. Tempted to just cave in and do what her heart begged her to, Kristina worried one day her feelings would overrule her common sense and she'd force him into something they'd both regret. He wouldn't say no, she sensed he'd give her what she wanted, and she didn't want to end up hurt. Her grandmother didn't have to worry about that; her passion held very little risk. Aside from getting her heart broken, Kristina also feared Daniel would kill her, and possibly himself trying to get at Wade. Then Cadence would have no one.

She pushed the steel door and walked through the small hallway leading into the bar. Her eyes adjusted to the lights as the crowd inside broke into a raucous 'Happy Birthday'. She stood in the doorway, one hand on the open door, struggling to stop herself from crying. Someone grabbed her arm, and then pulled her into the room.

"You guys," she murmured and searched for him.

Familiar faces filled the bar. Staff, friends and the regular customers who she saw every night, smiled back at her, clapping their hands. Someone placed a drink in her hand, and Kristina sipped without a thought to what they'd given her as she stared, touched by the overwhelming love in the gesture from people she barely knew.

She didn't have to search for Wade's face for long. He stood next to Amy, his arm draped over her shoulders. Their eyes met, his smile faltered and he stepped forward, removing his arm from his wife.

Kristina averted her gaze.

"So? Is this worth coming into work for?" he asked when he reached her.

"Yes. Thank you."

"You've earned a celebration." Wade reached out and pulled her into a brotherly hug, releasing her at once.

"I have?"

"Of course you have, silly girl." Amy pushed Wade out of the way and embraced Kristina, the sweet smell of Poison, a scent Amy apparently felt the need to bathe in, drifted up and invaded her senses before she stepped away.

"Thank you. I don't know what else to say."

"Don't say anything, just have fun. Maybe find a nice young stud to distract you from your worries." Amy laughed.

Kristina lifted the glass to her lips and sipped again. Long Island iced tea, a drink Sheila forced her to try about a month ago. She'd said she liked it and apparently now she'd be stuck drinking it.

Amy whispered in Wade's ear, her hand possessively on his chest.

Kristina's stomach tightened and looked away.

Sheila took her arm and then dragged her to the bar. "Come on, we've got ten more where that came from. Drink."

Kristina did as she instructed, took a big gulp of the lemony drink, and smiled. She'd have fun if it killed her. "What else do we have? Shooters?"

"Now you're talking." Sheila laughed and ran behind the bar.

CHAPTER 14

Wade stared. He couldn't help it. Kristina stood out in the crowd dancing at the front of the bar. Smiling, really smiling was so rare for her that witnessing it left him breathless, although he wished it hadn't taken copious amounts of alcohol to put it there. He wanted to be the one, to light her face up like that, and damn if the blush in her cheeks didn't make him want to explore, to find out how far down her body it went.

A man about Kristina's age wrapped one arm around her waist, pulling her close. She pushed him away just a little, but allowed him to dance with her. The man's hands slipped over her ass. Bile rose in Wade's throat. She slapped him away and wagged a finger. The jerk moved on to another girl, one who welcomed his attention, while Kristina joined her group once more. Why couldn't she be as relaxed and sure of herself all the time? The way she cowered at each challenge frustrated him. She was better than that. Braver.

"Send her another one," Amy said.

Wade glared.

Amy leaned on the bar, a drink in her hand and a smirk on her face. He'd been too obvious and now Amy knew more than he wanted her to. She'd been sending Kristina doubles all night.

When Wade caught on to her, he ordered Sheila to stop, no matter what Amy said. Kristina didn't drink very often and he would not have her so wasted she couldn't speak much less make decisions. He suspected Amy hoped Kristina would get plowed, knowing he would never take advantage of any woman while she was falling down drunk. He hadn't planned to do anything, so Amy had wasted her time. Kristina wasn't ready, and he didn't know if she'd ever be. The damage Daniel had done ran deep. She had scars that would probably never heal and Wade didn't want to add to them because he couldn't give her all of himself. Yet. He eyed his wife. Not while Amy still breathed anyway.

"Sheila, take her another," Amy repeated.

"No, she's had enough," Wade said.

Amy slammed her glass on the bar. "I didn't know you were her daddy, although you are almost old enough to be, I suppose. Maybe that's it, although it's a little twisted even for you. Most daddies don't dream about fucking their daughters, honey. Shame on you."

"Just stop. She's not used to this and I won't be responsible for rushing her to the hospital when she's had so much she ends up hurting herself."

"Oh aren't you Mr. Responsible?" Amy stood and picked her purse up off the bar. "I'm going home. I guess I better not wait up, eh?"

"You never do."

Chuckling she walked away from the bar and pushed through the door.

Wade clenched his fists wishing he could wrap his hands around her bitchy little neck. She wouldn't go home. She'd been sleeping with Carl Canon for a few months. He'd seen them together in Salach having lunch at Kelsey's and had them followed to be sure. Carl's wife didn't care about her husband's activities but she wouldn't let him go without a fight either. Someday maybe he would get lucky, and Amy would fall in love with some other sucker. Then he could be rid of her for good. That is, if he could convince Thomas she wouldn't open her big mouth.

Hoots of laughter and catcalls erupted from the dance floor. Wade turned to see what the commotion was all about.

Sighing he shook his head. Someone had taken another round of shots up anyway.

Orgasms, wonderful.

Kristina and four other women leaned over the table, hands behind their backs to pick up shot glasses with their mouths. The lights flashed overhead, casting first a red, and then a white glow over her as she stood and tipped her head back to swallow the contents of the glass, stumbling slightly. She arched her neck and the creamy liquid seeped out the side of her mouth and trickled down her chin.

"Fuck me," he muttered.

He glanced at the clock behind him. Still twenty minutes, but close enough. He walked to the switch next to the bathroom and flicked it a couple of times. "Last call!" he yelled amid a chorus of groans and jeers.

Wade nodded to Sheila who ran up to shut the music off while he filled the orders the crowd yelled out across the bar. He shook his head several times when they ordered drinks for Kristina and looked pointedly at Sheila when she came back to join him. "Don't give her anymore."

"Party pooper," she grumbled, but did as he asked.

Slowly the crowd thinned out until only Kristina and a few stragglers sat at the front table, giggling and chattering as though they had all night to socialize.

"Come on ladies. Time to go," Wade called.

The girls stood and staggered to the bar. A couple asked Wade to call a cab before filing out with the rest. Kristina followed but Wade pointed and Chad, the bouncer, stopped her. She stared up at him, confusion evident on her flushed face. Chad nodded to Wade and shrugged. Kristina turned, her gaze catching Wade's and her lips curved into a slow smile.

His breath caught and he had to clear his throat before he spoke. "I'll take you home when I'm done here."

"You will? All the way home?" She raised an eyebrow and twirled a piece of hair around her finger.

"Sit down and behave until I'm finished."

"I always behave." She pouted and flounced into a nearby

chair, legs stretched in front of her. She looked up, straight at him and ran her fingers over the neckline of her shirt. "But I guess I'd like you to take me... home."

Sheila snorted.

Heat rose in Wade's belly. Kristina sounded brave, but Wade saw the flush in her cheeks and the slight tremble in her hand. She made a shitty actress. He wondered if he shouldn't call her bluff. God knew he wanted to.

Sheila busied herself behind the bar, glancing now and then but not speaking until they'd finished. "You want me to give her a ride?"

"No, go ahead. She'll probably fall asleep."

"Okay, I'm outta here."

She waved at Kristina before exiting the bar, the door slamming into the sudden silence.

Wade looked up.

Kristina leaned on the table, her chin in her hands. She smiled. "Well? Are you ready?"

"I have to balance the cash and then we can go. You want to come in with me?"

"Sure." Kristina stood.

She seemed less wobbly than she'd been an hour ago and Wade wondered if she was really as drunk as she led him to believe. He hoped perhaps it had been a show for everyone and she knew what she was doing. She walked through the door, pausing to smile at him. Drunk or not, Kristina knew exactly what she was doing and he was done acting like the good guy. He'd never played the part very well.

The clicking of the adding machine echoed in the small room. Kristina stifled a yawn and perched on the edge of Wade's desk. She glanced down at the papers that fluttered to the floor and then back to Wade.

He scowled.

"Oops, you might want to pick those up," she joked.

He ignored her, going back to his paperwork.

She heaved a loud sigh. Earlier, when Amy left, Kristina made a decision. It took courage to take what you wanted. Courageous is what she would be. She'd offer Wade what she could and consequences be damned. Maybe after they'd been together once or twice, she'd get over this infatuation, or maybe she'd find something worth fighting for. Of course, the alcohol had done a lot to help her decision along. Liquid courage. She giggled.

Wade paused, glanced at her and shook his head before going back to the computer, typing in the night's totals.

While waiting for him to finish closing, her buzz had worn off. Now, although still slightly giddy, the booze haze had cleared from her brain.

She'd noticed how he watched her all night with that look on his face, the same one he'd had at her house when she'd broken the glass. Each time their eyes met, the naked hunger in his gaze made her want to climb over the bar and drag him off somewhere private. Hell, she'd have probably settled for the alley outside. This decision was inevitable. She'd lived long enough in denial and she couldn't fight anymore. Why would any sane woman fight Wade anyway?

Leaning over the top of the computer, Kristina traced a finger across the python tattoo coiled around his right arm.

"You're asking for trouble, little girl." Wade pointed at her and cleared the cash off the desk.

"I like trouble."

He paused, his eyes darkening before turning away to lock the wads of bills in the safe. "Come on. You're drunk. I'll take you home so you can sleep it off."

Kristina gave an exaggerated sigh before slipping off the desk and following him to the door. "You're boring."

"I am?"

She leaned against the bar while he locked the door. "God, Wade. I thought you were wild, dangerous and all that stuff, but you act like my dad."

Kristina held her breath as he walked toward her, stopping just inches from where she leaned. He frowned, trailing a finger up her arm.

She smiled, catching the twitch of his lips.

"I definitely don't want to act like your father. Who would you like me to be?"

"You," she whispered.

"Hmm, I'm afraid there's a problem with that."

Kristina's gaze locked with his as he leaned close, placed his hands on her hips and pulled her away from the bar. "What problem?"

"If I act like me, you run away."

"I'm not running now."

"I'm not myself right now."

Kristina stared at his mouth, her breath hitching in her chest at his smile.

He leaned down and brushed his mouth over hers, barely touching her lips.

She ran her hands up his arms to his shoulders and then around his neck, pulling his head down to hers.

"You won't run away?" he asked against her lips.

"I'm tired of denying what I feel."

"We can't take this back."

"Good."

Wade lifted her and she wrapped her legs around his waist. He carried her down the bar to the pool tables, his lips never leaving hers. He pushed his tongue into her mouth and she groaned as he teased her, pulling away when she met him with her own.

"I didn't imagine it happening like this. Let's go to your place." He set her down in front of the table.

"Someone might see us. What's wrong with right here?" She imagined Wade and Sheila atop the pool table and her sudden bravery faltered, her mind screaming at her to stop.

Wade frowned and tugged at the button on her jeans. "You aren't running, are you?"

She shook her head, steeling her resolve. What he did before and with who didn't matter. Just once, she needed to be with him and then if he never wanted her again at least she'd have this night.

"God, I've waited years to see you like this." Wade lifted her shirt over her stomach, running his hands up her sides to her breasts.

Kristina helped him pull the shirt over her head and then pushed her jeans down over her hips. He caught her hands in his and placed them behind her on the table.

"What?" Suddenly she felt uncertain, shy.

"Let me," he lifted her onto the table, the cool wood of the rail dug into her bottom and her heart skipped at the thought of what she was doing.

Almost naked in a bar, making love to a married man on a disgusting old pool table—what the hell was she thinking?

Wade knelt in front of her, pulling her jeans down and over her legs. He kissed her ankle, trailing his tongue up her calf, over the inside of her thigh before doing the same to the other leg. Kristina gasped when he dipped his head, flicking his tongue against her before looking up with a grin.

"Want to stop?"

She shook her head and arched her back when he lowered his head once more. "Never."

His mouth roamed her body, tasting, teasing, before he stood and unbuckled his belt. She stared as he lowered his jeans, her body trembling when he stepped out of them and moved toward her to grip her waist, pulling her against him. His flushed face and the intensity of his gaze sobered Kristina, she couldn't remember anyone looking at her as Wade did.

"You're on the pill, right?" he said, trailing kisses down her neck to her shoulder.

"Yes." She hadn't even thought of that. But then, Daniel had been the only man she'd been with. She was so inexperienced and Wade had… she didn't even want to think about the experience Wade had. Embarrassed, she backed away.

He moved with her, kissing her mouth then trailing his lips to her ear and down her neck before pulling back to stare down at her. "God, I can't stop now even if you begged me to. Look at me. Don't think about anything else." His gaze bored into hers. She nodded, moving forward to press against him and running her hands over his chest.

Wade's low growl as he pushed her back onto the table, his hand moving between her thighs, sent delicious shivers through her body. Slipping his fingers inside her, his tongue darted in her mouth mimicking his hand's movements, creating a tension that built in her stomach. She'd felt something similar with Daniel, but this time it filled her heart, her mind, everything, until she thought she'd burst from the pressure. Spirals of light danced behind her eyes and Kristina cried out as waves of exquisite heat shook her body. Her voice echoed through the empty bar, returning to her ears strange, alien; not like her at all.

Wade moved his hand and pushed his hips against her. A second rush of heat overtook her as he lifted her bottom to bury himself into her with thrusts that quickened while the sound of his breathing grew ragged. He stared down at her, his face so open, without his usual control. Shocked, she clung until his body shuddered and she tightened her legs around his waist as he buried his face in her neck.

"Promise me you won't regret this," Wade murmured in her ear as he lay against her atop the pool table's rough surface.

"I won't."

"I can't let you go now. No matter what happens. You know that, right?"

She nodded and kissed him before they moved off the table.

Wade pulled on his pants and winked. "Come on, I'll take you home and we can do this properly."

CHAPTER 15

Kristina woke to a pounding in her head like a mallet making mush of her brain. She opened her eyes, groaned, and pulled the pillow over her face to block out the bright sunlight bent on tormenting her. In the corner, by the dresser, the fan hummed as loud as a jackhammer slamming into the floor. Every muscle ached and her mouth felt furry. If the awful taste on her tongue was anything to go by, her breath probably smelled like death.

She turned over and pulled the sheet up over her shoulders, wincing at the ache between her legs. A slow smile tugged the edges of her lips. Her mind drifted to the night before, to Wade and the line they'd not only crossed, but completely erased.

Shifting uncomfortably in the bed, Kristina remembered his flushed face and the way he'd stared at her, as though he'd never seen anything so beautiful. Never in her life had she felt so… cherished.

His voice had played through her dreams all night.

Promise me you won't regret this. I can't let go of you now. You know that, right?

The night before she hadn't given much thought to those words, but now, in the quiet of the morning, when she had time to filter the events through her mind and weigh everything she'd done, they haunted her.

Wade had watched her dress, his stare making her uncomfortable and self-conscious. Then he'd driven her home and followed her inside.

Heat suffused her face and she managed a shaky breath, remembering how Wade hadn't given her time to close the door before his arms circled her waist and he pushed her inside. They hadn't made it to the bedroom, falling in a tangle of arms and legs on the stairs. Kristina reached under the sheet and rubbed her back, wincing at the sting of her touch. Yep, that would hurt for a while.

Sighing, she forced herself to push the pillow away and sit up. The room spun and she rubbed her eyes before standing. On wobbly legs, she took a few tentative steps to the dresser. Her stomach seemed okay, but her head felt heavy and full of rocks. She didn't know how people drank every weekend; it would kill her if she did.

After pausing to grab some clothes, she stumbled to the bathroom. A hot shower would make everything better. The regret she promised not to feel settled in while the hot spray of water cascaded over her skin. She looked down at her body and ran her hands over the red welts left by Wade. A lump formed in her throat and nausea settled into her belly. *What have I done?*

She reached around, pushed the tap and the water stopped. Trying not to cry she reached out for her towel. When she stepped out of the shower and onto the soft mat, she choked with sobs.

She loved him, and the realization hurt worse than every blow she'd ever taken from Daniel. He would never be free to be with her and she'd never be able to wake to his face in the morning, to fall asleep in his arms at night. This is why she'd kept her distance, why she'd told herself it was a bad idea. Kristina tossed the towel aside and pulled her clothes on. Her trembling hands made it difficult and her frustration grew. A twisting, painful feeling took over her chest and she blinked to clear her eyes. She couldn't stand the thought of Wade lying next to Amy every night. He should be here with her, that's how love worked, wasn't it? Stupid. Beyond stupid.

Possessiveness was a trait she'd never have attributed to herself. She didn't recall feeling anything like this with Daniel. Even when she'd found out about Desiree, she hadn't felt the gnawing ache inside she felt now. She'd been angry, but not as though something belonging to her had been ripped away. She wanted all of Wade, not just the parts she could steal in secret. Kristina didn't know how to handle this burning jealousy.

They couldn't do it again. If she hoped to keep her sanity, and her heart, she had to tell him she'd made a mistake. She'd forget his hands, the scent of his skin and the words he'd whispered in her ear. They meant nothing. He'd done the same with a hundred other women. She wasn't special, no matter what his eyes said to her last night. What they did would be best left in the secret place deep in her soul. To be taken out now and then when she felt alone and needed to visit him again.

Her mother brought Cadence home later in the morning, and had paused for a moment, studying Kristina a little too closely for her liking.

"You okay?"

"Mom, I'm hung over. Of course I'm not okay."

"That's all?" her mother stood at the door, one hand on the knob.

Kristina forced a smile, although she knew better than to try to fool her mother. The woman could usually read every thought before Kristina knew it herself.

"I'm a little sad. Just tired of Daniel's shit… of being alone," her voice cracked and she looked away.

Footsteps on the carpet and then her mother's arms encircling her, squeezing her pain to the surface. Hot tears welled up and she swallowed the lump in her throat.

"It's going to be okay. Things will get better." Her mother whispered before stepping outside.

"Well, they can't get any worse, can they?"

Kristina stretched, moving away from Cadence's crib. Her body still ached despite sharing a nap earlier with Cadence. She felt more human though, and the headache that haunted her all morning no longer pounded her brain. She crept out of Cadence's room and down the stairs. The living room was dark, and she knelt at the bottom of the stairs to switch on the lamp next to the couch. The phone rang, startling her.

Stealing a glance toward the stairs, she rushed to answer it before it woke Cadence. "Hello?"

"Are you alone?" Wade's deep drawl filled her head.

Tightening her grip on the phone she searched for something to say, the words on the tip of her tongue just wouldn't come. She should tell him no, but her heart wouldn't allow it. "Yes, are you?"

"Not for long." He hung up.

A door slammed outside.

Kristina spun to look out the window. A shadow passed. She hung up the phone and stood frozen in place while listening to his footsteps as he ran up the walk. The knob turned and Wade stepped inside. He smiled, pushed the door closed behind him and turned the lock.

Kristina's lips curled into a grin.

He crossed the room.

She walked into his arms and he kissed her hard before lifting his head to stare at her. "God, I've missed you."

"You just saw me last night."

"Not enough of you. I think I missed a couple of inches here and there."

He pressed against her and they stumbled to the couch.

Kristina fell back to lie on the soft cushions.

He climbed over her, kissing her neck, her mouth, her ear.

She drew a shaky breath and ran impatient hands over his

back, tugging at his pants.

"I'm too old for this shit," he murmured and slid his hand under her shirt.

"Then go home, old man."

"There is not a force on this earth that would take me from you now," he whispered.

RENÉE MILLER

CHAPTER 16

Wade groaned at a vibration in his pocket. Kristina smiled and scooped Cadence into her arms, leaving him to talk with whoever the caller was. He never asked her to leave, but she did, without comments or questions. He pulled the phone out and checked the number. Flipping it open, he put it to his ear and waited.

"You called?"

"Yeah." Wade walked toward the stairs, away from the kitchen where Kristina busied herself making lunch for Cadence.

"And?" Thomas sounded annoyed, but Wade didn't care.

He could be as annoyed as he wanted, Wade needed answers. "What's the tail about?"

"The tail?"

"Fuck off, don't play dumb with me. Kristina's got a shadow. I want it gone."

"Kristina, is it? Pretty name for a pretty girl."

"You already knew her name, jackass. So stop with the games. Leave her alone, she doesn't know anything."

A sigh issued from the phone.

Wade ground his teeth. The Brotherhood had been having trouble and tightened security. He carried out delicate jobs. Profitable but dangerous, and anyone associated with him had always been closely watched. For years they'd kept one eye on Joe, Kristina's dad. He knew it and it never bothered him. Joe even messed with them a couple of times, spending the day driving all over town, down back roads or going in and out of the same stores several times. Kristina wouldn't be as understanding.

Wade had visited her practically every night the past two weeks, first making sure she was alone and then leaving early in the morning. Several times he spotted the tail, but knew better than to approach the guy. Now that he'd made him, Wade figured he'd be replaced. Had Wade tailed her, no one would have noticed. The Brotherhood had nothing but amateurs anymore.

"First, remember who you're talking to." Thomas warned. "I do what is necessary to keep our friends safe, and I don't need your permission for a damn thing. Which brings me to the reason for my second point; I can't call off the tail. If I do, I can't guarantee her safety. You were warned."

Wade closed his eyes.

Thomas continued, "Someone's been making calls and I don't mean just pain in the ass bullshit calls. This person knows details. The tail is to keep her breathing, as well as for our peace of mind. If our friends see a weakness, they'll jump all over it. You want her defenseless?"

"They don't even know about me. No one does."

Thomas laughed, a little too hard for Wade's liking. He glanced to the kitchen and caught Kristina's worried frown. She stood at the table, Cadence in her high chair. She couldn't hear him but could read his face.

"Come on W, they know you exist. Maybe not what you do *exactly*, but it's not a huge secret you're one of us."

"Okay, fine. Just make it clear to everyone she knows nothing and never will know anything. I don't want anyone touching her before you talk to me personally. I'm not making a demand. I'm asking as your friend."

"Sure and W?"

"What?"

"You might want to worry about the wife, not the girlfriend. The tail we put on her is wired. I'm sure you get my meaning. He's been ordered to take care of things the minute he smells a rat. And your wife seems fond of cheese."

The phone went dead and Wade flipped it closed. Amy? They hadn't bothered with her for years. She wouldn't snitch, she knew better. Didn't she?

A crash and a colorful curse in the kitchen. He smiled and shook his head. He should be honest with Kristina, although he suspected she knew about his connections. No, she was aware of some of it. Loving someone meant trusting them too, and Wade really wanted to trust her. But part of him screamed she would walk away if she knew all he'd done. If she turned from him, he didn't know how he'd deal with it. Kristina was such a sweet, honest person and what he did was anything but sweet or honest. He didn't regret any of his choices. The side of him that did those things enjoyed it, needed the rush and the challenge. It's not as if he'd ever taken a life that wasn't already worthless. Most of the time he did everyone a favor. Take William Allan; the world was better off without people like him. For Wade, what he did for the Brothers was as natural as breathing. He only wished she could understand.

"Do you have to go?" Kristina called from the kitchen.

Wade walked to her voice.

She was sweeping the remnants of a coffee cup into a blue dustpan. "What happened?"

"They call me Butterfingers," she joked.

"I've heard rumors."

"So? Do you have to go?"

He shook his head

Cadence banged on her chair.

Wade turned and picked her up, tossing her into the air to her slobbery delight. He glanced at Kristina, catching the wistful smile she quickly turned into a stern frown.

"You'll have her puking," she warned.

"She likes it." He lowered Cadence and bounced her on his hip just in case. Her tiny fingers traced the tattoo on his arm, her mouth forming a tiny 'o'.

"That's a python, a big strong snake," he laughed when she

raised her eyes to his and gurgled. "Maybe I'll get you one someday."

"Not likely," Kristina grumbled.

"Not a real one, just the tattoo."

"Forget it. Real or tattoo, they're both a horrible idea." Kristina pushed him aside and took Cadence from his arms.

"You don't like my tattoo?"

"That's entirely different."

Wade chuckled at her flushed cheeks. "Isn't it almost time for her nap?" He winked.

Kristina smiled. "She just got up, and you have to go home at some point you know."

"I'll be back after work."

He'd given her a night off, hoping he could regain some control. Every time he looked at her, the way her eyes changed color, darkening just at the edges of the iris, telling him just what she was thinking, he wanted to pick her up and carry her off.

Twice last week he'd left Sheila looking after the bar and snuck into the cooler behind Kristina. Later, he cursed himself for being so reckless; anyone could have walked in. Kristina had been horrified. Of course, after a few minutes, horrified wasn't what he'd have called her. He smiled and winked again.

She blushed. "I'll be here."

Listening to Wade's heartbeat, Kristina dozed. The house was silent, Cadence finally slept through the night, and she felt safe for the first time in a long time. She rubbed her cheek against his chest, the soft covering of hair tickling her skin.

His fingers touched her face. "You asleep?" He traced her jaw and then her neck.

"Sort of."

"I should go soon."

Kristina opened her eyes and looked at the clock. 2 a.m.,

yes he'd have to go soon. She never asked him to, but he always left before the sun came up to avoid gossip. He parked his truck on a different street each night and walked to her house. She loved him for that, and hated herself for not having the guts to live her life without worrying about other people. She'd resigned herself to the reality that if she wanted him, it had to be this way. It hurt to watch him leave before the sun rose, more than she'd ever admit to anyone, but as long as he remained a married man, they couldn't be open about their relationship. She'd seen enough pity in people's eyes through her life with Daniel. She didn't need their scorn too.

"I wanted to talk to you about something." He paused, ran his fingers through her hair and took a deep breath. "I just don't really know how to start."

Kristina propped her head on her elbow and stared at his face. Darkness shadowed most of his features but there was fear in his eyes, something she never thought she'd see in Wade. Was this it? Would he tell her he couldn't see her anymore? He could tell her anything but that, and she'd try to understand. She couldn't believe he didn't care. Wade rarely lied and what she felt from him had to be real. She had to stop doing this to herself and trust him. This was as hard on him as it was on her.

"I wanted to talk to you too."

"Okay, you first." He waited.

She struggled to voice her uncertainty, "I wondered about you staying here so much, all this time away from Amy can't be helping your marriage. I'm sorry it's so hard for you to be with me."

"You think I care about my marriage? It was dead long ago. I wouldn't be here if it wasn't."

"But doesn't she ask? Get upset? I'd be angry if my husband were gone nearly every night, even if we were having problems. *Especially* if we were having problems."

"And that, among other things, is the difference between you and Amy. There's no marriage left. We're done but for the paperwork. Even if she did care about me, I can't trust her, which is a deal breaker for me." Wade shifted.

Kristina rolled away, giving him room to sit up.

"Why?"

"When we were first married, Amy told me she couldn't have kids. She cried and apologized and I bought it. I was so sorry for her, I told her not to worry, we could adopt. Then, about a year later, I was going through some old papers, looking for a receipt or something and I found a letter, a reminder for a doctor's appointment Amy had. It was a follow up for her surgery."

Kristina held her breath, knowing what he was going to say, but hoping she was wrong. How could Amy do that?

Wade fidgeted with the sheet, bunching it in his fists. "She had her tubes tied; I don't know what they call it. One month after we were married. She lied, and made sure she wouldn't get pregnant. When we dated, I told her I wanted kids. I love kids, always dreamed of having two or three. She took the choice from me. Why? Because she didn't want to get fat, or some stupid shit like that. Can you believe it?"

"No," Kristina touched his hand.

He didn't look back. "At the time, I was willing to work things out. People make mistakes you know?" He glanced at her and she nodded. "Well, turns out some people just pile on mistake after mistake."

"Why not just get a divorce? Surely Amy wouldn't be stupid enough to lash out over you ending a dead marriage."

"Amy knows a lot of stuff about me, bad stuff that could put me in jail for a very long time. She likes the life she has. Money, a nice house, status.... She won't give it up. Even if she wanted to, I don't think they'd let her."

"Who?" Kristina tried to catch his gaze.

He lowered his head. "The people I work for sometimes. You know who I mean. But it doesn't matter. The point is I can't leave her. She'd blow the lid on everything. I'm not worried about going to jail; if it meant we were through, it would be worth it. I've survived it before and I can do it again. But she might die for it and I don't want that on my conscience."

"But it's not like she can prove it was just you. Unless she has evidence of what you've done, what can she really do? Jesus, she's as guilty for keeping it quiet and spending your money, isn't she?"

"I've done some bad things, and it's not drugs or guns. Those are small time." Wade ran a finger down her cheek. He stared at her for a long moment before taking a deep breath. "Amy knows where the bodies are buried. Know what I mean?"

A chill crept down her spine at the look in his eyes. She mulled over his words. Of course, he must mean metaphorical bodies, not murder. Wade wasn't capable of murder. Kristina smiled and shook her head. "I think you worry too much."

"It doesn't bother you? What I've done I mean. You don't hate me for it?"

"I could never hate you." Her heart clenched at the moisture welling in his dark eyes and she reached out to wipe the tears that formed near the corners, unable to speak.

"Promise me someday you, me and Cadence will take off together. Run away from it all," he murmured.

"I'd love to," Kristina said.

He pulled her over his chest. "And I love you."

The front door closed quietly and Kristina lay staring up at the ceiling. She thought about their conversation, how Wade worried she would hate him for selling drugs. Her chest ached as she recalled the tears in his eyes. She promised herself to never let him down. If they had to live this way forever, she'd do it. If they could get rid of Amy, things would be so much easier. The coldness of the thought troubled her. She paused. No, she didn't mean literally get rid of her, just make her go away and leave them alone. Closing her eyes Kristina pictured lying on a beach somewhere far away. She heard the surf and tasted the salt in the air. If only life were simple.

RENÉE MILLER

CHAPTER 17

Hoots and blasts of raucous laughter erupted from the dance floor.

Kristina looked up from the bar and shook her head. Jack, a local and very regular customer, attempted to smash his skull while break-dancing in the middle of the floor. She glanced at Wade, who sat at the bar speaking in hushed tones with a stranger.

As though sensing her stare, he looked up.

She nodded to the dance floor.

Wade turned and his shoulders shook in laughter. He ran a hand across his neck, the signal to cut Jack off. She nodded and he resumed his conversation.

Kristina didn't know the man Wade spoke to, she'd never seen him around before, but he stole glances at her now and then. His dark eyes staring holes through her made Kristina a little nervous. She'd probably be better off not knowing who he was. He only stared because he caught her staring at him. If she could just convince herself it was true, maybe she'd relax.

Kristina walked around the bar to gather empties from the closest tables. It had been a slow night. Sheila left an hour earlier, leaving her alone to work the bar and the floor. If it got too busy, Wade would slip behind the bar. Her thoughts drifted to the end of the night and her hand shook as she picked up the empty bottles. He'd whispered something about making dessert later when he passed her in the office, and

Kristina spied a tub of whipped cream in the cooler.

A hand on her shoulder made her jump and she dropped a bottle to the floor.

Michelle, one of her oldest friends, stood smiling. "You should cut back on the caffeine, you're pretty jumpy."

"Jesus, I was off in la-la land there." Kristina bent to pick up the bottle, glad it didn't break. She had gone almost a month without breaking anything; she'd have hated to see her streak blown.

"Are you due for a break soon?" Michelle looked nervous. She twirled her blond hair around her finger and two red spots dotted her cheeks.

"Why? What's wrong?" It had been ages since she talked to Michelle, probably a year at least. Her sudden appearance didn't feel like a good thing.

"I just want to talk to you, nothing major."

She lied. Michelle always looked embarrassed when she lied. Kristina walked around the bar and interrupted Wade.

He scowled.

She stammered, uncomfortable to be the focus of such a dark look. "Sorry to interrupt, but Michelle wanted to talk to me. Can I step outside for five minutes?"

Wade looked to where Michelle stood staring around the bar, and back to Kristina. When Wade hesitated, the man next to him nudged his arm and nodded.

Kristina frowned, since when did anyone tell Wade he could or couldn't do something?

"Sure, you've been running all night." He winked, though his face reddened.

She led Michelle through the door, grateful to be out of the other man's sight for a while. Outside they sat at one of the tables in the patio. Really, a corner of the parking lot Wade had fenced off and stuffed with a bunch of picnic tables inside.

Michelle fussed with the hem of her shirt and took a breath before speaking. "I heard some stuff I know can't be true but I didn't know if you knew about it. I thought it would really bug you if someone asked."

"What stuff?"

"That you were sleeping with Wade Bowen."

Kristina cleared her throat. Her cheeks warmed and she laughed.

Michelle smiled weakly as she searched Kristina's face.

"Come on, really? You don't believe it do you?"

"Of course I don't, I know you're better than that. But they said he goes to your house all the time and you guys are here way after closing. I mean, you're single and all, but I don't want you to get hurt. I know you'd never go for a married guy, especially an old married guy."

You're better than that.

She would have preferred her friend to believe the rumor than to put her on a pedestal she didn't belong on.

Kristina was careful not to look away, or Michelle would know she lied. "Of course I wouldn't. Look, I work at Dirty Truths. Wade drives me home sometimes, but he never comes inside. I'm sure there are worse rumors going around about me. Don't worry about it. I'm fine."

"But what about his wife? I heard she can be nasty." Michelle's eyes widened.

Kristina leaned over and hugged her. "I love you. It's nice you're so worried for me but don't be. Amy wouldn't blink if anyone said anything to her. She doesn't give a shit about Wade or what he does. Not that he's doing anything with me."

Michelle stood. "Just promise me you'll be careful, with everything. Know what I mean?"

Kristina nodded and Michelle turned away, walking across the parking lot to her car. She waved before climbing in and then drove away.

The constant 'ting-ting' of water falling into a metal pan nearly drove Kristina nuts. She called Daniel about the sudden leak in the roof, but he laughed. It was her problem; he wasn't her landlord. Cadence continued to wander over to it, scooting across the floor on her bum and overturning the pot, clapping in delight when the water from the ceiling dripped on her body.

Now she slept and Kristina waited for her dad to come over and see what he could do about it. A week of rain had made it impossible to fix the roof, but he told her he might be able to come up with a temporary solution, perhaps cover it with a tarp or a sheet of plastic until the weather was drier.

She stared at the first page of her book, not really seeing the words, and heaved a frustrated sigh. Wade had come only twice this week. He had 'other' business and couldn't make it over more than that. Kristina worried and wondered what he was doing, but she didn't dare ask. When he'd been there he'd fidgeted, avoiding walking by the windows, and only stayed a short while. It wasn't long before her imagination took hold and she began to create scenarios. He wanted out. He was no longer interested and didn't know how to tell her. The very idea made her heart ache and filled her with dread. She couldn't imagine life without him now. How would she pick up the pieces of her shattered heart if Wade changed his mind?

A knock at the door startled her out of her musings. After setting the book down, she stood and bent to look out the window next to the couch. Blurred by the water cascading down the pane, a red car sat in the driveway. *Amy*.

Kristina walked to the door, a cold, hard lump settling into her stomach. Amy had closed the bar every night this past week, saying nothing to Kristina, or anyone else for that matter. She'd come in at last call, said Wade had to go away on business, and shut herself in his office. Kristina wondered how bad the news would be. Was he in jail? Dead? Cold fingers danced on her spine as she put her hand on the knob and turned, opening the door to Amy's scowling face.

"Can I come in?" she asked, pushing past Kristina and into the living room.

"Sure." Kristina shut the door and turned.

Amy walked across the beige carpet, not bothering to take

off her wet shoes and leaving grey footprints in her wake. Kristina stifled the urge to drag her back and remove the shoes for her. Obviously she didn't consider it worth the bother to respect someone's home. She imagined how she'd get the mud out of the worn fibers, and her dread turned to irritation.

"I don't have the time or the inclination for niceties here. I want answers." Amy said as she fiddled with the small crystal elephant on the TV stand. A gift from Wade. He'd set it there saying he once heard it was good luck to keep an elephant, trunk pointing up, in your home and he figured they could use all the luck they could find.

"Okay, ask the questions." Kristina didn't have the inclination to be polite either, not when someone waltzed into her home and spoke to her as though she were a criminal. Amy was just as guilty as they were. Everyone knew about her relationship with Daniel's boss. They made no attempt to hide it.

"What's going on with you and Wade?"

"Nothing." It surprised Kristina that the lie didn't bother her.

Amy's eyes narrowed.

Kristina forced a confused frown to her face. *Let her dig. She'd get nothing.* "I'm getting tired of people asking me about this. Can't a man and a woman be friends without someone instantly assuming there is something going on?" Kristina heaved a frustrated sigh.

Amy snorted.

Kristina's struggle to work up a righteous indignation became easier. "Come on, he's old enough to be my father. You're making a mountain where there isn't even a molehill. He's been kind to me, but that's all."

"Okay, let's pretend I believe you and you haven't been stupid enough to sleep with him yet. I'm coming here as a friend, someone who actually gives a shit about you and your happiness. Wade is a master manipulator, and he's good at making people think he's a good guy. He loves younger women, because they're so much easier to play with."

Kristina's hands trembled, the urge to slap the condescending smile off her face almost too much to resist. "I told you—"

"I know what you told me, and I'm telling you what I know. He's using you to make himself feel like a big strong man, rescuing you from yourself. He likes to do that, you know? To come in like the white knight and make it all better. Then you, in your endless gratitude and admiration for his big tough guy act, are hopelessly devoted to him. That, dear Kristina is when he breaks your heart."

"Really?" Kristina turned and walked to the couch, taking deep breaths to calm herself. She sat down placing her hands in her lap and stared at Amy. "Go on."

Amy pressed her lips together, her brown eyes rolled to the ceiling as though she didn't enjoy breaking this terrible news. But Kristina knew better. She enjoyed every minute of it.

"He enjoys leading people astray. It's a game to him. You're a game."

"If you hate Wade so much and he's so awful, why are you still with him?"

Amy shrugged and gazed at her hands, fidgeting with the strings at the waist of her jacket. "He won't let me go. I've tried to leave, but his friends threatened me, told me if I left I may as well eat the bullet myself."

Kristina laughed. She had to be joking. "A woman afraid of her husband doesn't sleep with one of the biggest womanizers in town. Sorry, but if you were scared, I doubt you'd be doing things to piss him off intentionally."

Amy shook her head. She looked up at Kristina, her eyes moist with unshed tears. "Carl? I love him and I don't care if you believe me or not. Wade doesn't care about where I go or what I do. He just won't let me leave. Don't you get it? He likes to see me miserable. I have tried to force him to hate me, to push him away, but he is obsessed with controlling everything and everyone in his life and he's punishing me."

"Punishing you?" Kristina felt the fingers again, this time they waltzed slowly over her back, pausing to make her shiver before continuing their course.

Amy wiped her tears and turned to the window. "I can't have kids, never have been able to have them. I told him this and at first, I thought he was okay with it. We married and then later he changed his mind. He didn't believe me, accused me of having a surgery to do this to myself. I told him I tried to fix it. That's why I had the operation, and he said he'd never forgive me for what I'd done to his life. He promised he'd make me pay for lying to him and he has."

Wade's words fluttered around her head. Could he have been mistaken?

Amy paced the floor, her shoulders slumped, defeated.

Her heart went out to the woman and despite her resolve to hate her, Kristina recognized hopelessness and heartache. Amy was miserable. But did Wade do this intentionally? Her head ached; she didn't know what to believe.

Taking a deep breath Amy walked to the door and put her hand on the knob. She didn't open it. Instead she turned to face Kristina. "Whatever is going on, I felt the need to warn you. You're still just a kid and I think you've endured enough bullshit in your life. I'm coming to you as a friend who has seen the damage Wade can do. He's dangerous. He has friends who can get rid of someone without a trace. If Wade got tired of you, or you became a threat, they'd slit your throat and get rid of your body. No one would ever know what happened to you. He's no different than them, except maybe he's better at making people go away. In fact he is one of the best."

The tone of Amy's voice, the emotion in her words gave Kristina pause. She thought back to the man who attacked her, and wondered. Did Wade go back to visit him that night? She didn't know. Desperate to trust her heart, but remembering the look in his eyes, logic and love battled over the answers. She didn't know which to trust.

Now he knows I can find him.

Wade's words floated through her mind. Then she remembered him holding the brown wallet. The coldness in his eyes...

"Just stay away from him, for your safety, for Cadence's.

Get as far away as you can." Amy opened the door and walked out, the rain thundered in Kristina's ears before she softly closed it behind her.

She stared at the door when an engine fired up. Gravel crunched and Amy drove away.

She heard crying. Cadence was awake. Kristina stood on shaky legs and walked in a trance to the stairs. No, Amy had to be wrong. Wade loved her. She couldn't have mistaken the look in his eyes, the feeling of his hands on her body. He wouldn't hurt her. Pounding in her chest, her heart threatened to burst. She couldn't be wrong about him.

CHAPTER 18

"Me?" Cadence reached for the cookies and Kristina angled the cart away, tickling her belly. Cadence giggled.

"You have enough cookies at home."

Guiding the cart around a stack of boxes to her right, Kristina made her way to the dairy section. She eased by Mrs. Connelly, gossip extraordinaire. What made Mrs. Connelly especially wonderful was the judgment she laced into every nasty, biting word. A devout Catholic, unless you counted her three marriages and four kids whose paternity was still debated. She enjoyed nothing more than to pass out pearls of wisdom mixed with a generous helping of venom to young people like Kristina.

Hoping to avoid a conversation, Kristina averted her gaze and pretended to be extremely interested in Cadence's babbling. She almost made it to the milk cooler; all she needed to complete her shopping trip, when Mrs. Connelly cleared her throat.

"Goodness, long time no see, Mrs. Riley." The old woman pushed her cart into the aisle. To get away from her, Kristina would have to run her over. So tempting.

She gripped the cart and closed her eyes before turning around, a friendly smile planted firmly on her face. "Mrs. Connelly, nice to see you. I've been around. Just working a lot."

"Yes, I heard since you abandoned your nice husband

you'd taken to working in that place."

"The bar? I don't know any nice husband, but I have been working at Dirty Truths."

Mrs. Connelly frowned and nodded. Her silver hair, pulled murderously tight and coiled into a bun on the top of her head, looked dull and greasy. She wore a long dress that grazed her ankles with chunky white shoes. Apparently she enjoyed playing the shrew. "I really like you, and I know you're young and probably not as experienced as I am, so I'm going to give you some advice."

Kristina lost her smile and her cheeks burned, but she waited for the woman to finish. No point in causing a stir, she'd only run with it and make things worse. She didn't usually resort to profanity, not in front of people anyway, but the words 'Fuck you, you miserable old bitch' stuck in her throat.

Mrs. Connelly leaned close and patted Kristina's hand. "Married women don't work in places like that. Not respectable women anyway. If you hope to fix your marriage, you'd do well to consider what direction your life is taking."

"I don't want to fix my marriage." Kristina paused when Mrs. Connelly gasped, then she smiled. "I don't think there's any need to go back to a man who nearly cost me my life. Daniel is sick and he won't get better. And the bar, well, I enjoy it. Besides, I don't believe where I work is anyone's business but my own."

"This is your problem. People talk you know, no matter how well you think you hide it. Everyone knows what you've been up to."

Kristina pushed her cart, forcing Mrs. Connelly to back away. "What have I been up to?"

"I know about what you do at night, with that man. So does Daniel."

Kristina shivered, and then a hot, suffocating feeling of prickly heat, moved over her body. What did the old bitch do? "What are you talking about?"

"You're behaving no better than a two dollar whore, and the poor man is doing his best to repair his broken heart. I told him last week he was better off without you if you're going to act like a harlot with a married man. Poor dear still loves you, although I can't imagine why. He said he'd talk some sense into you and I suggest you give up this nonsense and listen to him. See what a good man you had."

"I don't know where you think you get off," Kristina stopped and took a breath, forcing her voice to a conversational level. "You know nothing about me or what I do in my private life. You definitely know nothing about Daniel. He is a bully and a cheat. He doesn't help to support his daughter and he still knocks me around. Did he tell you that? His kind of love left me bruised and broken, and his girlfriend was around long before I finally had enough. Not exactly what I'd call a nice boy. This talk he'll have with me will end in something bruised or broken, or worse. Does it make you happy to know what he'll do to me? Do I deserve to be beaten because I'm trying to provide for my child?"

"It's reality honey; men like to run the house. If they stray now and then, a good wife turns the other cheek. I've been married thirty years and couldn't be happier. He's strayed a time or two, but he needed to do it to see how lucky he is to have me."

"Thirty years? Is that counting all of your husbands?"

Kristina pushed away from her, milk forgotten. Her only thought was to get home and try to reach Wade. She hadn't seen Daniel in a few weeks and last night he'd left a message. He wanted to see Cadence. She should have known he didn't call her out of a sense of fatherly duty. He had a bone to pick, and it promised to be a big one.

The silence nearly drove Kristina mad as she waited for Daniel's arrival. She picked up the monitor from the coffee table and played with the volume before holding it to her ear. She set it back down after listening to Cadence's even breaths.

She'd hoped Daniel would come while she was awake, giving her a buffer between them, although Cadence's presence wouldn't stop him from doing whatever he planned to do.

She'd called Wade's pager several times but he hadn't called back. A voice in her head echoed her doubts, that he no longer wanted her. He was avoiding her. She told the voice to shut up. Wade wouldn't behave so cowardly; he would tell her. Still, she had left their code for an emergency and he hadn't replied. Either he couldn't call for some reason, or....

Kristina wrung her hands in her lap while she stared out the window at the empty driveway. The wind blew the leaves around in tiny red and yellow tornadoes. It would rain eventually, breaking the humidity of the surprise heat wave. She hated that the leaves turned so early, barely September and winter already teased her with its imminent arrival.

Daniel's truck rumbled in her ears before it turned the corner and headed toward her house. It didn't slow down, swinging into the driveway and stirring up gravel and dust as he came to a halt. The door opened and he jumped out of the cab, slamming it behind him. He'd worked up a good fury. Kristina stilled her hands. Her palms were moist, she had to remain calm or he'd have control of this in an instant.

She lifted her chin and walked to the door, opening it before he reached the top step, startling him. His brown eyes acknowledged her coolly, and he stepped up to the small stoop. "Expecting me?"

"You did say you were coming."

"You must have been sitting there waiting for me. That's a nice change."

Daniel brushed past her, his shoulder knocking her into the doorframe. Kristina closed her eyes and breathed slowly to steady her nerves before she followed him inside, closing the door behind her.

"Cadence is sleeping."

"I don't need to see her today. I can come back. It's you and I that need to have words right now."

Daniel paced the living room, kicking Cadence's blocks out

of his way with a scowl. "Did you just stop cleaning? My daughter has to live in filth now, because you don't have time for her."

"I have lots of time for Cadence. I didn't pick up her toys. I'd hardly call it filth." Kristina tried to walk casually to the window, hoping to hide the anxiety churning in her stomach.

Stuffing his hands in his jeans Daniel leaned against the wall next to the playpen. He glared at her for a long moment before his lips curved. "You aren't going to tell me are you?"

"Tell you what?" Kristina met his gaze, willing herself to stand up and not give in to her fear.

"I don't know. Maybe something I have a right to know? Come on Kris, I know you're not that stupid."

"Unless it has to do with Cadence and her wellbeing, I don't think there's anything you have a right to know."

He pushed away from the wall with such force the picture of Cadence, lying on her belly frowning out at the world, fell to the floor, the glass shattering.

Kristina jumped back cursing herself for letting him frighten her.

"You want to play games? Let's play then." Daniel reached out, grabbing her shirt in his fist and yanking her forward.

Kristina gasped, but did not struggle. Fighting him made it worse, fueled the fire raging in him. "Daniel—"

"No, not *Daniel*. Tell me about Wade. What are you doing with your so-called friend? And don't even think about lying to me. I can read it plain as day on your face."

"There's nothing to tell, my relationships are none of your business." Kristina tried to sound firm, tough, but her voice came out on a shaky breath. Even she didn't believe her words.

Pushing her forward, Daniel removed his hand from her shirt. His fingers bit into her arms instead.

She struggled then, the light in his eyes colder than she'd seen since the night she left him.

He forced her against the wall. Her head jerked back and slammed against the paneling. She gritted her teeth. The arm of the couch pressed into her leg. Kristina used it to steady herself, her gaze on Daniel's face, unable to look away.

"I've let you make a fool of me long enough, it ends today. You hear me?"

Kristina shook her head.

He punched her side, burying his fist beneath her ribs. She wanted to curl up and cry, but waited for her breath to return instead. "I told you we're done. You're making a fool of yourself."

Daniel cocked an eyebrow and smirked, leaning in so close his nose touched hers. "Done? We're a long way from done. You want to be a whore then I'll treat you like one. How's that? I bet you beg for it from him. Do you? *Please Wade, fuck me.*"

"No, Daniel."

"I'm going to make you beg me. Remember how you used to plead for me to stop? I thought you knew better than to make me look like a fool, but I guess it's time for another lesson. How would you like that?"

Pain knifed through her chest, raw terror as Kristina grasped what he intended to do. She pushed at him, bringing her knee up between them. Daniel slapped her face.

She staggered, tasting blood.

"It's good enough for Wade. I think I've earned the right to the same thing. Did I tell you I fucked his wife?"

Kristina stared. "I don't care who you slept with. You're going to regret this, please let's talk about it. I'll tell you anything you want to know."

"Oh, I'll find out what I need to know. I bet he taught you a few things. Just like he taught Amy. She's an animal. Know what she liked to do?"

"I don't want to know."

"That's a shame, because I'm going to show you." He kissed her, his lips bruising and cruel.

Kristina turned her face and he slammed her against the wall.

Stunned, her mind screamed for him to stop but she couldn't find the words.

He threw her toward the stairs. She stumbled, her gaze on the door.

"I don't think so," Daniel leaned over her and balled a fist in her hair, dragging her toward the stairs.

With no option but to follow or risk angering him to further, possibly more dangerous aggression, Kristina trailed after him.

He reached the top of the stairs and pushed her toward her bedroom.

Kristina regained her footing and turned to plead with him to stop. She opened her mouth but nothing came out.

He advanced too fast for her to think. "Did he fuck you in here? In my bed?"

"No, nothing happened. Don't do this, Daniel."

"Liar." He wagged a finger and nodded to the door. "Get in there."

Kristina backed down the small step to her bedroom, the walls shrinking around her. She realized he was really going to do this and she couldn't stop it. She could fight, but he always overpowered her. She could scream, but who would listen? How many screams had they already heard coming from this house and no one answered? Blood pounded in her ears, her vision blurred and she started to cry.

Daniel's hands went to his shorts.

She shook her head. "No, stop it. I know you don't want to do this."

"But I do. I've wanted to do this for a long time, but you don't treat your wife like a whore. That's just not done. Of course, you aren't my wife now, are you? You've made that clear to everyone. Now, I'll treat you like the slut you are. I'm sure you'll love every minute. Make sure you scream real loud, so the neighbors know it's not Wade fucking you."

Daniel let his shorts fall and he stepped out of them, advancing toward her.

Too late Kristina realized she backed into the corner next to the dresser and faced the bed. It loomed before her, mocking her. Just a week ago she had lain there, tracing Wade's mouth, mumbling nonsense about 'someday'. Then he'd pulled her in his arms and—she choked on the memory.

Daniel pressed against her, his mouth on her neck and she pushed at him. A laugh, low and menacing, rumbled in his chest sending a chill down her spine. Kristina felt his hands on her shirt, tearing it from her body and then her shorts, she resisted but still he managed to push them down to her knees. She wanted to fight him, but the last time he'd attacked her like this, he'd gone into such a rage. This time he might do worse.

His hands roamed over her, bruising, hurting, and he whispered what he would do. Kristina closed her eyes, hot tears streaming down her cheeks, their salty taste filling her mouth. Daniel pulled her from the wall and toward the bed. Forcing her to her knees at the end of it he leaned over her, his hand in her hair. Kristina stared at the bed, and felt herself slipping.

Promise me some day, you, me, and Cadence will take off together. Run away from it all.

Wade's voice whispered and she felt her mind go. Drifting between Daniel's rough hands on her and Wade's soft kisses, she struggled to hold on to reality.

Daniel moved behind her, shoving her around as though she were a rag doll but Kristina wouldn't let him have the satisfaction of seeing how he damaged her soul with his actions. She'd get away some day, but not before Daniel paid for this.

The floor suddenly slammed against in her face, the carpet scratching her cheek as Daniel forced her down, his body on top of her, then inside. Kristina squeezed her eyes tight and wished him away. She heard Wade again, laughing softly, teasing her, his hand on her hair. He wouldn't get away with this. Daniel had a weakness. She just had to find it.

Somewhere in her mind, she heard Cadence cry. Kristina forced her aching body from the floor. Daniel had left more than an hour before, promising to return. She shuddered as the feeling of his hands and his words filtered back through her mind. Nausea rose in her stomach. Her mouth filled with saliva. Lunging from the room, Kristina stumbled down the hall to the bathroom. She leaned over the bowl and retched as Cadence's cries grew louder. She had to have seen her running past her door and now she was angry. But Kristina couldn't stop now. As though a floodgate had opened, her body convulsed and she sobbed as she hung over the toilet.

Slowly it ebbed. Her stomach ached but didn't revolt. She stood. Grabbing her robe from the door she wrapped it around her, gazing longingly at the shower. She desperately needed to wash him away. The stickiness between her legs combined with a dull ache reminded her with each tiny movement of what he'd just taken from her.

Cadence had to come first and she had to pull herself together if she hoped to stand against Daniel. Kristina walked to her daughter's room, her mind attempting to push the last two hours far from her thoughts. She picked Cadence out of the crib and walked toward the stairs. She felt numb. Even her baby's cheerful grin could not shake the sense of disbelief and denial hanging over her.

Settling Cadence on the floor with her blocks, Kristina jumped when a rap sounded at the door. Her eyes darted to the window and almost fainted at the empty driveway. Not Daniel. She ran to the door.

Wade stood in the early evening shadows, his eyes weary and his mouth set into a grim frown. "Can I come in?"

"Of course you can." Her instinct was to unload and tell him everything, but something about the set of his shoulders and the tone of his voice stopped her.

"What did you tell Amy?" Wade stood next to the window, peering out at the street before turning to her. His eyes were red rimmed and he looked so tired.

"Nothing. Why?"

Wade slammed his fist against the wall, rattling the window. Kristina jumped, hugging her arms around her.

"She's a fucking bitch, that's why. You don't speak to her

anymore. Is that clear?"

Laughing, already on the edge of hysteria, Kristina shook her head unable to believe he thought it was possible. "Are you serious? First of all, she's friends with my mom, and second, you aren't at the bar, she is. How am I supposed to not talk to her?"

Wade shoved away from the window and walked toward her.

Kristina flinched when he grabbed her arms and jerked her forward. A bubble of dread burst inside her at the look in his eyes. His face flushed, he stared so intently at her she had to look away. She didn't recognize the man squeezing her arms so tight her hands tingled.

"I'm telling you to stay away from her. If I go to jail because of her, she'll regret it. You don't want to be mixed up in her shit. I don't *want* you mixed up in it." He snapped. Then the veil lifted from his face and he let go with a frown of confusion, as though not sure what he was doing.

"Why would she do that?" Kristina asked.

"There are some things going on. Things you're better off not knowing. But Amy is in deep and she's trying to bury me. She doesn't care who she shoves down there in the process. I'm sorry I got a little crazy. I just can't stand to see you hurt."

"Okay."

He ran his hands over his face.

She moved to put her arms around him, needing the embrace.

Wade welcomed her, kissing her face, her lips and running his hands over her back. "God, I wish I could hold you forever and just forget this bullshit."

Kristina remembered the bruises, the traces of Daniel littered over her body and she froze. Wade couldn't know this right now. He might do something reckless.

"I can't though, I'm sorry," he said, releasing her. "Can I bring something here? Something I don't want you to look at. Just put it away so Amy can't hand it over to the cops? I should have gotten rid of it a long time ago but there wasn't time, and now, well now they're watching me and I can't get rid of it."

"I can't look at it?"

"It's just a box of stuff, but it's something law enforcement might frown upon." He smiled.

Kristina nodded. It's not like she was hiding a body, a box of guns or drugs or whatever wasn't a big deal. She looked up at him and kissed his mouth. Wade wouldn't do anything to endanger her life and if she hoped to go to that place somewhere far away from here, she'd have to help him through this bit of trouble.

And she desperately wanted to get far away from Laighton, and from Daniel.

CHAPTER 19

In her bath seat, Cadence splashed around in the water that pooled in the bottom of the tub. Kristina scrubbed her skin vigorously, wanting to wipe the memory of Daniel from her body. She longed for scalding water, so hot it burned her skin.

How long she remained in there, her body shaking while she soaped up and rinsed off, she wasn't sure. When Cadence shivered, Kristina turned the water off and bundled the two of them in a big towel. Cadence yawned. She hurried to dress her in her pajamas before going downstairs to make something to eat.

The very idea of food made Kristina's stomach churn. She wouldn't risk eating. If Wade found her hurling into the toilet when he returned, he'd worry. Rushing around the house, Kristina set Cadence in her high chair and then heated some soup for her. Cadence clapped when she sat next to her, bowl in hand, and Kristina finally smiled. No matter what happened, she had her daughter. Daniel would have to take that gift from her cold dead hands.

She stiffened when the door opened, the spoon half way to Cadence's mouth.

Cadence banged the highchair and squealed.

Wade chuckled. "Feed that kid, would you?"

She slumped and closed her eyes in relief. Then, she moved the spoon to Cadence's mouth and turned with a smile. "You were fast. Where's the box?"

"In the living room. It can wait." Wade pulled out the chair next to her. He made a face at Cadence who rewarded him with a quick smile before banging on her tray, her signal for more food.

"Don't you have to go?"

"Tonight I am yours. After that, I'm not sure what will happen."

Kristina finished feeding Cadence the soup. When she scraped the last noodle from the bowl, she stood and walked to the sink.

Wade moved to her chair where he played Itsy Bitsy Spider with Cadence.

Leaning against the counter Kristina hated herself for doubting him when Amy spewed her venom. This wasn't a man who would use her, or who would do anything to put her in danger.

Wade made faces at Cadence and paused to glance at Kristina. "I noticed Daniel's truck here earlier."

Kristina turned to the sink. "He came to see Cadence."

He didn't need to know.

"It's been a while. Why the sudden *fatherly* instinct?"

"Who knows?" Kristina clattered the few dishes in the sink and turned on the water. Wade and Cadence made noises behind her. He sang and Cadence giggled. She hoped he'd turn from the subject of Daniel.

"Did he wake you up?" He walked behind her, and then his body warmed her back.

"No. Why?"

Wade touched her shoulder.

She sighed and turned to him.

"When I got here earlier you were in your housecoat and your eyes were red. I didn't say anything because I had to deal with the other shit, but I noticed."

"Oh," Kristina played with the cloth in her hand, winding it, twisting it, trying to form a lie he'd accept.

His hand brushed her cheek.

She closed her eyes.

"You should have looked in the mirror after your shower. I'm sure he left more than just this scrape. Actually, it looks like rug burn. What are you not telling me?"

"Nothing. I—"

"Don't. Don't ever lie to me. You're terrible at it anyway." He cradled her face in his hands and forced her to look at him.

Kristina's stomach churned, she didn't want to tell him. "He got mad. Someone told him about you and me, and he lost his temper," she murmured.

"What did he do?"

"I don't want to get into the details. Okay? I just want to enjoy what time we have and not let Daniel ruin anything else for me."

"What did he do?" he repeated.

"I can't talk about it. Please don't ask me to. It's too… I don't even know if I can find the words. I will talk about it, just not today. I'm okay."

Wade stared. A muscle twitched in his jaw but he nodded. "When this shit is settled with Amy and the cops, I'm paying him a visit. I don't care if he's Cadence's dad. You have no say in the matter. Understood?"

Kristina stared. Did she want him to do something? Yes and no… she didn't know. She wanted Daniel gone, but not if it cost Wade his freedom. His eyes bored into hers, waiting for her to do as she always did and defend Daniel. Kristina couldn't defend him anymore. Wade wouldn't do as she asked anyway.

"I could argue, but there's no point. Let's deal with this box of yours so we can do something else."

"Something else? Sounds tempting." He leaned over to kiss her cheek and then turned. "I want you to hide it somewhere no one would look for it. I thought maybe the basement. You have all kinds of boxes down there."

"How do you know?" Kristina lifted Cadence from her highchair and then followed him to the living room, relieved he let her off the hook. She couldn't even put into words what had happened with Daniel. She wanted to forget; if that were possible.

"I've been down to the basement. I had to get a flashlight. Remember when the lights went out during the storm a couple weeks ago?"

"I forgot, of course." Kristina didn't remember him going to the basement, but perhaps he did so while she slept.

Wade went to the base of the stairs, near the front door in the living room and bent to retrieve a medium sized box. Setting Cadence on her mat and moving a doll next to her she waited for Wade to bring it over. The sides were battered, and layers of tape covered it but the flaps weren't sealed, simply folded over themselves to keep it shut.

"Don't even think about it once you've put it away. If you toss it from your mind there's less chance of you slipping and mentioning it by mistake." Wade passed it over. It was surprisingly heavy.

"Okay."

Kristina carried it behind the stairs and to the small door that led to the cramped hole some nutty builder considered a basement. She waited for Wade to close it behind her. Cadence would scurry over, if she noticed the forbidden door was open. Down the small set of wooden stairs, she paused at the bottom to pull a string hanging overhead. A bare bulb lit the small space.

She chuckled softly. Wade had labeled the top of the box 'Xmas decorations' in black marker. She set it on top of a stack of other boxes marked 'Cadence Summer One Year' and next to 'Xmas Tree'. Then, worried it might be too obvious, she shifted the boxes so Wade's was nestled down the pile and moved the other Christmas stuff in front of it. Satisfied she rushed back upstairs.

As Wade weaved in and out of traffic, a horn blared behind him. He ignored it. Before he did anything else, he had a score to settle. He didn't expect to see so much traffic on the road before seven.

Kristina had been strangely quiet when he told her what he planned to do. Did she hope he'd leave Daniel alone? Did she think her quiet acceptance would make him reconsider? If so, she was wrong. This time, Daniel had gone too far.

Wade's chest tightened at the memory of her bruises, angry bluish marks along her thighs and across her arms. The welts on her stomach and breasts brought bile to his throat. The tooth marks on her back... *Motherfucker!* He hadn't wanted to touch her, he'd been so angry. But that would punish her and Wade didn't want Kristina to feel she was to blame.

His cell rang. Wade picked it off the seat to check the number. "Fuck," he opened it and drew it to his ear.

"Where are you?" Thomas sounded annoyed.

"On the road, headed to Salach. Why?"

"Fucksakes, W. You're supposed to be going the other direction."

"I have some business to attend to." Wade stepped on the brake as he approached a blue Taurus. The driver must have thought it was Sunday. The speed limit was eighty, not ten. He weaved around him and stepped on the gas as he came through an intersection, ignoring the yellow caution light.

Thomas sighed. "Is this business related to your friend?"

"What friend?"

"Come on now, don't play dumb with me. My tail saw the Dodge too. Heard some noise."

"And he just watched?" The tail and Wade would have a little talk later. He cursed.

Thomas tsked. "Now, don't get riled up. It's not worth it. You need to look at the bigger picture. Pull over."

"No, I—"

"Pull the fuck over!"

Wade ground his teeth but slowed the truck, steering until the wheels crunched the soft gravel of the shoulder. "Done."

"Now listen to me very carefully. You are out of control, and I can't have that. Got it?" Thomas sounded calm, as though talking to a wayward child. Wade didn't appreciate the patronizing tone.

"Got it." He stared out at the fields. A lone cow meandered across a muddy expanse. He wondered if it had wandered through a broken fence. Though why he cared, he didn't know.

"The business you're attending to is nothing new. He's knocked her around before, and he'll probably do it again before you can deal with him."

"He didn't just knock her around. He fucking raped her."

"I said listen, didn't I?"

Wade bit his tongue.

Thomas continued. "You can do this shit later, when the heat is off. Got it? You can't afford to raise eyebrows. He's not going anywhere."

"Later? When's that? After he kills her?"

"We're keeping a close eye on things, and we won't allow that to happen. Come on, W. Have I ever let you down?"

"No." A large transport rumbled past. The ground shook beneath him.

"Turn the truck around and do what has to be done. You won't help her from behind bars, will you?"

"No."

"Good. I'll see you in an hour." Thomas hung up.

Wade gripped the phone, the plastic dug into his palm. Glancing in the rearview, he cranked the wheel and spun out of the ditch, turning back to Laighton.

Chirping outside the window, loud and obnoxious, woke Kristina from her nap. Wade had left early and she'd stayed up long after, thinking. When Cadence yawned, ready for her nap, Kristina couldn't keep her eyes open. She laid Cadence in her crib, climbed into her own bed, and pulled Wade's pillow to her face.

He'd noticed the bruises on her thighs, his face reddening

when he'd traced them with trembling hands. Kristina waited for the explosion but it didn't come.

"No more arguments." Wade growled, leaning over to kiss the welt on her knee. "He's gone too far this time."

She had nodded.

Part of her cheered him on, but secretly hoped by the time they dealt with Amy and Wade's legal troubles he'd forget about Daniel. She didn't want to have Wade all to herself, just to lose him.

Stretching and kicking the sheet from her body, Kristina sat up. She rubbed her face and groaned when Cadence's cries erupted through the monitor. So much for relaxing on the couch for a while. She stood and walked to the doorway her gaze catching a wad of banknotes lying on her dresser. Cadence's cries turned to babbles. When Kristina picked up the money and a piece of paper fell to the floor. She picked it up, recognizing Wade's neat scrawl immediately.

I forgot to mention you're not to go into work. Please listen to me on this. Under no circumstances are you to go into the bar. I told them you took some holidays. This should cover your bills. I'll make sure I get more to you somehow.

Love you,

W.

P.S. Do not let Daniel back in the house. Call the police if you have to.

She stared at the letter, the money forgotten. Two words. Small, but powerful. Words he'd never so much as whispered last night because he'd been so angry. She'd needed to hear him say them more than anything else. *Love you.* Kristina drew a hand to her mouth and stifled a sob. She'd wanted to say so much to him before he left but she'd chickened out, worried his feelings might have changed.

Kristina stuffed the paper into her top drawer, beneath her underwear and socks. She picked up the money. Where the hell was she going to put this? Shaking her head, she wedged it with the note. She'd figure out what to do with it later.

Cadence yelled, irritated that her mother didn't rush to see to her, and clapped her hands when Kristina entered the room. She bounced, holding onto the rail of her crib.

Smiling, Kristina picked the baby up and kissed her curly head. "Want to go for a walk?"

"Ma?" Cadence cocked her head to the side.

Kristina couldn't help the laughter that bubbled to her throat. "Yes, a walk." She set Cadence in her bouncy chair and went to the basement door.

She kept the stroller at the base of the stairs, using the smaller umbrella stroller most days. But she had to pick up groceries and other odds and ends so the bigger stroller would come handy.

The steps groaned as she jogged to the bottom to collect the folded stroller. She'd forgotten to turn off the light the day before and reached to pull the string. Her gaze wandered to the boxes stacked on the right side of the room.

Shouldn't she know what she hid for him? Kristina set the stroller down and stepped to the stack of boxes, moving the upper ones until she found Wade's. Before she could change her mind she carried it upstairs, her walk forgotten.

She stared at the box on the coffee table, her fingers itching to open it, but a dull ache started in her belly. She should trust Wade and do as he asked.

Leave it alone.

Standing next to the couch Kristina argued with herself, telling her conscience she had a right to know what he asked her to hide and then telling her curiosity she'd be better off not knowing. Curiosity won out. She glanced at Cadence who bounced in her chair, gurgling to her reflection in the little mirror on the tray, and then ran to the door and slid the bolt in place before running back to sit on the couch. Her fingers flipped open the battered flaps before her butt touched the cushions.

She peered inside and a fire burned her gut, moving up to her face. Snippets of conversations between her and Wade, rumors whispered by nosy customers and friends, and finally, Amy's warnings ran through her head with the force of a freight train.

No, she had to stop overreacting and letting her imagination get carried away. Kristina pulled her sleeve over her hand and then picked up one of the items lying on top, bundled in oilcloth. The weight of the bundle filled her stomach with ice. She opened the cloth to reveal a small gun that could fit easily into her hand. Kristina wrapped the cloth around it and set it beside the box, and reached for the other bundle. She knew what to expect, but her breath caught as she peeled the cloth away. This gun was larger with a fat tube-like attachment beside it. A silencer? She never imagined she'd encounter such a thing. Swallowing the lump that had formed in her throat, she set it next to the smaller gun and turned back to the box.

Reaching inside, Kristina lifted her gaze to her daughter who bounced happily in her chair, oblivious to the can of worms her mother had just opened. Kristina's hand closed around another bag and she pulled it out, fighting the urge to just drop it and forget what she'd already seen. Inside the thin plastic was a set of keys, the ring holding them a brass P, which didn't signify they were Wade's.

Cadence squealed and Kristina jumped. She laughed, chastising herself for being so silly. She was in her own house damn it. No one could see what she was doing. Still, the guns lying on her table were enough to make her feel watched; guilty. Should she look at the rest? She had to.

Kristina turned back to the box and pulled out a half roll of duct tape, a tiny clear bag containing several dirty little pebbles, and a coiled white rope. Kristina peered at the pebbles, unable to determine what they were or why Wade would keep them. The bag shivered. She realized her hand shook and she took a breath to steady her nerves. None of this meant he'd done anything terrible. Lots of people had these items in their house. True, the guns were probably illegal and the bag of powder could be a problem, but nothing she'd found made Wade anything other than what he said he was.

The last item, wrapped in grey cloth, lay across the bottom of the box. Kristina picked it up and pulled the loose end of the rag, unrolling it until a thick plastic bag lay in her palm. Her heart pounded against her chest painfully as the sunlight from the window reflected off the blade of the knife inside. Her gaze traveled the length of it. She jumped and dropped the blade on the table.

Cadence looked up from her chair, stuffing a hand in her mouth. Kristina smiled at her and Cadence turned back to her toys.

Rust... or blood crusted the knife's tip, and next to it, lodged in the corner of the bag was a leathery looking lump. Kristina instantly thought of beef jerky, but the silver ring around the base with the emerald encrusted 'J' told her it wasn't jerky at all. Kristina sat back and stared at the table. The items in front of her, when lying together, told such an awful tale she wanted to close her eyes and pretend she'd never seen them.

What have you done, Wade?

If anyone knew about this box, Wade would be locked up forever. The question was could she ever feel the same about him now that she knew?

CHAPTER 20

Kristina closed the box. Then she stood and glanced at her daughter.

Cadence bounced in her chair, babbling to her toys.

Kristina groaned and cursed herself for opening the damn thing. Wade had told her not to look and she hadn't listened. She paced the room trying to figure out a solution, a way to get rid of the box without hurting Wade. Her heart pounded and her palms grew moist. Anxiety over what she should do built in her chest until Kristine thought she'd pass out from lack of oxygen. "Jesus, calm down," she mumbled.

Outside the sun shone bright, a slight breeze blew leaves and dust down the quiet street. She'd wanted to go for a walk but now the urge to close the curtains and lock herself inside was stronger.

She should call Wade; ask him to come get the box. Its contents could put her and Cadence in danger. Snorting, Kristina rolled her eyes; they were already in danger.

Cadence whined, tired of her chair.

Kristina leaned over to pick her up.

Cadence pointed to the box, "Ta?"

Kristina turned so neither of them could look at it. "No. Garbage."

Cadence curled her nose.

Kristina smiled. She should call Wade.

She picked the phone up, careful to hold it from her

daughters grasping hands; and then punched in the number for Wade's cell. When a canned voice answered, Kristina waited for the prompt. "Hey, it's me. I really need to talk. I'll be home all day." She pressed 'end' and set the phone back on the base.

"Ta?" Cadence reached for the phone.

Kristina shook her head. "Mommy'll get your phone, okay?"

She set Cadence down and rummaged through the laundry basket in the corner of the room that served as a toy box. Holding a blue and red phone—with Elmo's googly eyes staring out from the top—she turned to Cadence.

The baby had already found something else to occupy her. She'd crawled, or most likely rolled, to the coffee table and pulled herself up to touch the box.

Kristina rushed over, scooping her up and away from the wretched thing.

Cadence protested. "Na!" she yelled.

"New word?" Kristina chuckled. "How about 'mama'?"

"Na," Cadence reached for the Elmo phone.

Kristina flipped it open for her and pressed the buttons.

Cadence grinned when her favorite monster said hello.

Standing by the phone would only make her dread and growing panic worse, so Kristina carried on with her day. She cleaned the living room—a chore that was long overdue—and took the box back to the basement where it belonged. She didn't hide it this time, determined Wade would be picking it up soon. It had to go. She'd never sleep with it in the house.

He didn't call until she'd bathed Cadence, settled her into her crib, and ran water for her own bath. Kristina growled when the phone rang downstairs. She pulled it back on. Her irritation was short lived. As she reached the living room, the dread she'd managed to shove below the surface emerged once more. Her hands trembled.

"Hey, you called?" Wade asked.

"I did. Where are you?"

Silence. Then several male voices, low.

"I'm around. Things are a little complicated right now. I

don't know when I'll be able to see you again. I mean, I could come over if you need me too, but unless it's an emergency, it's not safe for you and Cadence."

He *had* to tell her, it couldn't be so bad he wouldn't. It *had* to be connected to what was in the box. If he came over, then someone might know she had it. But who? Surely he wasn't this afraid of the police. "What's going on? I don't like this."

"Honestly, it's best you don't know." He paused and sighed. "You didn't look in the box, did you?"

"What if I did? Would you tell me what's going on then?" her voice rose and Kristina hated the fear she heard in it.

"I know you're smarter than that. Look if you want, but I can't explain anything you find. Not over the phone anyway. I asked you to trust me. You said you'd love me no matter what. Remember? If we're going to get through this, you've got to believe I love you too." He paused, the phone sounded muffled, as though he covered it with his hand. "I have to go. Just remember, unless the police know you have it, there's nothing to worry about. I'll come by soon and pick it up."

"But what if I looked? What then? What if someone finds it and I can't lie and I tell them I looked? I'm a terrible liar, Wade. The worst."

"You're worrying about nothing. For fucksakes, just forget about the damn box," an edge sharpened his voice.

Kristina shrunk. The paint had begun to chip in the top corner. Wade had said just the other day he'd get someone in to repaint. "Okay."

The line went dead. She held the phone, startled to be cut off so quickly. She knew what was in the box and that was the problem. She couldn't forget it.

Doubt swirled in her head, about Wade, about herself, about what to do. The box housed terrible things, more than terrible.

Sinking to her knees, phone still in her right hand, Kristina stared at Cadence's bouncy chair. Her favorite keys still hung from the tray, next to a half-eaten cookie, mostly slobbered into sogginess. Torn between moral rightness, and what her heart wanted her to do, she had to think of her daughter. Cadence didn't ask for any of this. Kristine's priority was her child's safety, not what her heart pleaded with her to do. Besides, the note she'd heard in Wade's voice had terrified her, a hard edge that sent shivers down her spine and coated her stomach in ice. Loving him could be too dangerous.

The phone buzzed and the operator's tinny voice droned on to hang up or try her call again. Kristina looked absently at the phone, hit 'end,' and then turned to the basement door. The latch was in place. She'd even moved a small stand with a couple of books and her small CD collection in front of it. As long as the damn box stayed in her house, she'd know nothing but terror and dread. She couldn't do it. He asked too much.

The phone sounded again and Kristina closed her eyes to still her racing heart.

"Hello, Kristina?"

Amy? Kristina looked at the clock above the TV, just half past nine.

She took a deep breath "Hi."

Shuffling noises, the sound of a lighter and then Amy clearing her throat. "Hey, you coming back to work? I had to hire two more girls last week. With Wade taking off at all hours and your shifts to cover I've been worked to the bone."

Kristina hesitated "No, I need a few more days."

"So? Is something wrong?"

"Not really, a bad cold and then the baby caught it too.

"All this time for a cold?" Amy sounded amused and Kristina imagined her rolling her eyes and pursing her lips.

"I also needed a short vacation to straighten things out with Daniel and the house. Wade said it was okay."

A long pause traveled down the line. "Have you seen him lately?"

"Wade? On my last shift."

"I mean since," the voice changed and a feline note entered Amy's voice.

Kristina frowned. "No."

"I'm worried."

Kristine waited, Amy didn't sound worried at all.

"According to others I'm just the bitchy wife, out to ruin him. But I care, you know? I'm not the awful person he makes me out to be. I've spent hours looking for some things he's going to need. Soon."

The box. Kristine's mind reeled.

Amy sighed before continuing, her voice lowered, "He wouldn't have dropped them by you, would he?"

"Why would he bring a box of his things here?" As soon as the words left her mouth, the room spun and a sickening feeling gripped her stomach.

Silence.

"I see…" Amy's voice went from conspirator to interrogator, "sweetheart, you're too pathetic to live in Wade's world. You can't even lie properly. I never said anything about a box. Where is it?"

Kristina cringed at her tone. "I—don't know what you're talking about."

"You mentioned a box."

"I—assumed… I thought that's what you meant…a box of his things. What else to people carry their stuff in?" *Pull yourself together.* "Look, Amy, I haven't seen Wade. Really. There's nothing in this house that belongs to him either. Everything here belongs to me."

Amy chuckled. "From what I've heard, nothing in your house belongs to you. Forget it. Go out with your daughter; enjoy the break. Get your dad to take you to Wonderland or something before the season is over. Know what I mean? Just forget it."

Kristina's feeling of strangeness deepened at Amy's sudden change of tack. Had she believed her? "I don't know—"

The lighter clicked again, followed by Amy's deep inhale. "Just forget I called, honey, you've got nothing to worry about. Go on. Do something fun with the next couple of weeks. Let me know when you're ready to come back to the bar. Your job is always there, even if Wade isn't."

"Okay, thanks. I really appreciate it" Guilt washed over her.

She'd betrayed him.

"Another piece of advice; stay away from Wade. Don't answer his calls. If he comes over, tell him you're through with whatever it is you two have. I'm not saying this as his wife. I'm talking woman to woman here. You get me?"

Something in Amy's voice built a knot of apprehension in Kristina's gut, it settled into the bottom, leaving her feeling sick.

"Okay, I'll talk to you soon. Remember, go live your life, and forget about this shit."

Kristina pushed 'end' and stared at the phone.

Why had she mentioned the box? She got scared, that's what happened. But she was always scared, why did she flake out now? Kristina replayed Amy's words in her mind.

I've spent hours looking for some things he's going to need. Soon.

She moaned and stared up at the ceiling. Amy had tricked her and she'd fallen for it. Her knuckles whitened, rage replacing dismay. Wade had tried to tell her what he'd done. He said Amy knew where the bodies were buried and she'd refused to understand. She'd heard what she wanted to hear. She'd been so certain he wasn't a murderer. Cadence gurgled and Kristina straightened, suddenly alert, as if a veil of fog had lifted before her eyes. Did it matter? Did she love Wade less?

If she had a cell phone, she could send a text, although if he had the phone turned off, Wade still wouldn't know she needed to talk.

I have to warn him.

CHAPTER 21

Wade shifted the truck into park, turned the key, and pulled it from the ignition. His house sat nestled among a generous covering of pine trees, dark and barely visible from the road. From the driveway, it looked like a wide bungalow, modest and homey, but walking around to the back toward the various sheds scattered throughout the property, the house spread out in a U shape.

The basement, which Wade finished a couple of years ago, included a small home theater, weight room and sauna. In the center of the U was Amy's pride and joy: a massive hot tub ensconced in a deck that wrapped around three sides. He'd built an adjacent room connecting the house and the tub. After Amy had thrown a couple of parties where people came through the house dripping wet, ruining the expensive carpeting in the family room, Wade gave them a space to get out of their wet clothes before entering the house, although sometimes Amy's guests were too drunk to figure this simple concept out.

He opened the door and jumped down from the truck. Amy hadn't left the front light on. She'd probably left at noon and never returned. Her car wasn't out front. She could have parked it out back, where it was supposed to go. Not likely.

She spent more and more time with Carl, neither of them bothering to hide their affair anymore. Wade often wondered what Bailey, Carl's wife, thought about it all. He rarely saw her though. She didn't come into the bar as she used to, though her absence could be due to Amy's presence. He figured that's where his wife had gone tonight.

He walked to the front door and turned the knob. Unlocked. Grinding his teeth he stepped inside. He'd told Amy over and over to lock the damn thing, not just against burglars, but curious folk who wouldn't hesitate to put a bullet in her head should she catch them snooping around. Not that he cared, after the shit she'd caused, he'd be happy to be the curious shooter.

John had called him last week, urging him to set up a meeting with Bill and Thomas. They'd had several visits from a Brother within the police department warning them of an impending raid. The reason for the raid—they'd been told—was a little brunette with a big mouth. Normally a snitch would be dealt with swiftly. Anyone could disappear, and they'd planned to have her 'leave' Wade and take off somewhere sunny. They just couldn't afford for her to go missing right now. She'd done too much talking and her disappearance would raise a lot of red flags in the law-enforcement community. His wife had covered her ass very well. Now they were stuck with her and her flapping gums.

Pausing in the kitchen, he sniffed. Thick smoke and the bittersweet smell of liquor filled the air. Amy was home after all. Peeking into the den, his gaze ran over his empty leather chair, the neat desktop he rarely used displaying an overflowing ashtray and an empty glass. She must have just gone to bed. He slipped off his boots and stepped over to the fridge for a beer. The light caught something at the table to his left and he stiffened.

"Fuck, Amy. You might want to say something next time. Jesus." He slammed the fridge and stared at his wife.

Seated at the dining room table against the far wall, she smiled, a slow cocky grin, as cigarette smoke curled around her head. "Welcome home," she murmured. "Anything interesting happen while you were gone?"

Wade shook his head, eyeing her intently and wondering if she'd smoked more than cigarettes. He opened his beer and shrugged his jacket off, and tossed it over the chair next to her before he turned toward the hallway leading to the family room. He wasn't in the mood for her bullshit and wouldn't be drawn into a fight.

"Had a nice chat with Kristina," Amy said.

Wade stopped, alarm tensing every muscle in his body. What the hell was she up to?

She straightened and flipped the cigarette pack between her hands. "I think it's time you and I made a deal."

Had she gone nuts? He couldn't make any deals and she knew it. People knew she had seen too much, talked about the wrong things, he couldn't give her anything. If he could have she'd have been gone. "I don't know what you're up to, but remember who you're talking to. Although I'd love nothing more than to never look at you again, you know I can't make any deals."

Amy, still smiling, butted her cigarette and leaned forward. She wore nothing under her black satin robe. The sight of her naked body, no matter how perfectly toned she kept it, did nothing for him anymore. "I know about the box, honey. Unless you figure out something, talk to your friends and give me what I want, I'll make sure you're not the only one who goes down for what's inside. Your little girlfriend makes an excellent patsy. Well done."

"I don't know what you're talking about and neither do you." Fire spread through Wade's body, flaring in his chest.

Kristina couldn't have told. He knew she'd been scared—hell so was he—but she wouldn't have told Amy. Yet, the certainty on Amy's face, the simple fact she knew about the box confirmed it. Kristina had panicked. Shit, he should have reassured her more, told her the story of the items in the damn box, but they'd advised him to keep her in the dark. It wasn't as though he didn't trust her. God, he trusted her with his life. Not telling her what was in the damn thing was the only way to protect her—or he could have left her out of it and hidden it somewhere else. Shit, he shouldn't have let the pressure get to him. Bad shit happens when you panic. If he'd thought it through and buried the fucking thing long ago—no. If only's did nothing. He had to fix what he'd done.

"If you don't cooperate, Wade, I'll see to it little Miss Perfect sees the inside of a jail cell real fast." Amy met his gaze, her dark eyes cold and flat.

She thought she had it all figured out but Wade had a few more aces to play. "You're threatening me? Anything happens to her, you'll be the one going down. Just because I've put up with your shit up until now doesn't mean I don't have limits."

Amy's mouth curved into a thin smirk that chilled him. "We'll see." She stood and, after straightening her robe, picked up her drink and tipped the contents into her mouth, her gaze never leaving his. Slamming the glass on the table, the sound echoing through the empty house, Amy then turned away and walked to the front door to turn the lock.

Wade remained silent as she walked past him and down the hallway but his fury made it difficult not to reach out and grab her. How he longed to see the life drain from her eyes, to see her fear when she realized she'd played her cards wrong and she'd never open her lying mouth again.

He stood for a moment, taking deep breaths and forcing himself to think rationally about the situation. Kristina's face materialized in his mind, her dimpled smile and trusting eyes gazing up at him. Then it changed. Her eyes filled with tears, her chin trembled and the Kristina that haunted him only a few months ago, scared and alone, returned. Had he done that to her? Had she really betrayed him?

Wade punched the wall, his fist crumbling the drywall next to the doorframe. Pain radiated through his hand and he welcomed it. Kristina had tried to get in touch with him. Three times. He hadn't answered, afraid someone might be eavesdropping. Amy had manipulated her. She must have. She wanted them to doubt each other. Amy would have worked on Kristina first and now she toyed with him. He wouldn't let her drive a wedge between them. He trusted Kristina, loved her with every fiber of his being and he had to believe she felt the same. Unlike Amy, Kristina couldn't pretend, or hide her feelings from him. She'd do the right thing. Amy was his problem, and he would take care of it.

CHAPTER 22

The trip to Canada's Wonderland exhausted Kristina, although it had been worth it to see Cadence's eyes lit up with amazement. After Amy mentioned it, she thought it'd be a good way to clear her head. The trip only earned her a sunburn and a depleted bank account.

Once home, the reality of her situation loomed. She thought of Wade often, and the more she thought about what Amy said and how Wade had changed momentarily on the phone, the more terrified and uncertain she became.

Amy advised her to go on with her life, and that's what she'd do. She'd stay home and lay low for a while. Soon Wade would pick up his stupid box.

For a few days she did, and only went outside to cut the grass or to let Cadence play in the early fall sunshine. Her parents came to see her when she told them she felt a little under the weather and would rather not go anywhere. To her relief they didn't ask questions. She suspected her dad knew about her relationship with Wade. The way he eyed her warily, asking if she'd be returning to work at the bar and then offering her money, told her she hadn't hidden things as well as she thought. She wondered how much he knew.

Now she sat alone in the darkness, the only light flickering from the television screen, while she considered her options. Kristina wanted to run, far from Laighton, far from Daniel and Amy, even Wade; but didn't know how to do it. If she took

Cadence, Daniel could have her arrested. He would. She suspected Wade would find her no matter where she ran. The knowledge sent a shiver down her back. Would he try to bring her back because he loved her, or would he punish her for betraying him? She wasn't sure.

A sharp knock jolted her from her thoughts. Kristina stood, glancing out the window next to the couch. No vehicle, which meant Wade likely waited outside. Relieved to be able to see him but fearful of the reason for his visit, she edged toward the door taking a deep breath before turning the knob and swinging it open. Her heart skipped a beat. She froze before a man standing on her step. It wasn't Wade.

"May I come in?" he brushed past her without waiting for an answer.

Kristina shut the door, and turned.

The stranger stood in the middle of the living room, the pale light of the television casting shadows over his face.

Bald, on his neck a tattoo disappeared down the collar of his black coat. He was large. Larger than Wade even. Kristina couldn't shake the sensation she'd seen this man before, but the familiarity didn't make her feel better. She stood at the door, ready to run.

"Sorry to intrude, but I'm hoping you can help me. I'm looking for a friend of mine and I was told you may have seen him. Wade Bowen?" his voice was smooth, as though issued from a velvet-lined throat.

Under different circumstances, Kristina might have considered his voice soothing, even attractive. "No, I haven't."

He raised a thin black brow and smiled.

Kristina pushed ahead. Now that the lie was out, she might as well make it believable. "He doesn't come around here. I work at the bar, and I'm friends with him and Amy, sort of, but it's not like we hang out. Do you always walk into strangers' homes without an invitation?"

God she was such a dork. Hang out?

The man walked to the window and leaned against it. Hee ran his finger along the pane, and turned to look at her.

Kristina realized she wrung her hands in front of her, something she hadn't done in a while and quickly separated them, forcing them to her sides.

"Good answer. Or I guess I should say that's the right answer," he murmured.

He walked across the room to the door.

Kristina backed away from him, stopping against the TV stand.

His hand on the knob he paused and glanced back. "And you're not a stranger, Kristina. I know you better than you know yourself. I'll be seeing you."

He walked out, closing the door softly behind him. Kristina listened to his footsteps moving away from the house. Shaken from her shocked stillness, she ran to the door, turned the deadbolt and fastened the chain she rarely used. What the hell had Wade dragged her into?

The following morning her mother arrived early. Kristina greeted her sleepy eyed and grim.

"Honey, you look awful." Her mother walked into the house and directly to her granddaughter who played on the floor. She picked her up and kissed her messy curls.

"Thanks, you don't look so bad yourself." Kristina hadn't slept much, dreaming of Wade and of the strange man. She imagined them snatching her in the middle of the night, the man murmuring sweet nothings in her ear, his satiny voice relaxing her into submission before Wade loomed over her. The dream didn't progress. She would wake up, her heart pounding, scolding herself for harboring such thoughts. Wade would never hurt her.

Her mom bounced Cadence on her hip while masterfully dodging the baby's grasping hands as they reached for her glasses. "Your dad and I were going to the trailer. The weather is supposed to turn cold next week, so we might as well use it while we can."

"Oh, I don't think I can come."

"I know. You hate it there anyway. We wanted to take Cadence with us, as long as Daniel won't be coming to see her this week."

Kristina shook her head, she hadn't heard from Daniel in a while, not since the day he'd attacked her. She hoped he stayed away forever. "No, I haven't heard. He missed his visits last week."

"Good, I'll go pack a bag for her and you can gather up some bottles and whatever toys you think she might want." Her mother walked to the stairs, carrying Cadence with her.

Kristina, numb and unsure if she wanted her only distraction gone, went to the kitchen. She opened the door to the basement, where the diaper bag hung just inside at the top of the stairs, and remembered the box. Yes, Cadence should go for a week, she'd be safer. If anything happened Kristina would know she was okay and out of danger.

Music shook the walls of the small house and Kristina welcomed its deafening blare. She hauled the garbage bag to the door, full of old food and items she'd pulled from her cupboards. How did one get an entire cupboard full of movies, pillowcases and margarine containers? She tended to hoard, but in one cupboard?

After opening the door she turned to pick up the bag and straightened, coming against Daniel.

He stood stone-faced, eyes cold and accusing.

Kristina let go of the bag, her body trembling. Images of his last 'visit' played in her mind. She backed a step.

"I was at the bar last night. On a little holiday?" He stepped forward, closing the door behind him.

"None of your business."

"Really? None?" Daniel advanced.

Although she wanted to put up a brave front, Kristina instinctively moved away from him. "I took a leave of absence."

"Seems Wade took a leave too. According to Sheila, neither of you have been there this week."

"So?" Kristina knew where he was going with this. He thought she'd taken off with Wade. Well, she was still here, so he had nothing.

"Where's my daughter?"

"With my mom. You haven't been around so I let her go."

Daniel grabbed her shirt and jerked her forward. "So you can fuck him all you want? Tossing your kid aside so you can screw an old man isn't like the Kristina I knew. My money isn't enough? You need his blood money?"

"I'm not screwing anyone. I'd like you to leave." Kristina pushed at him, trying to extricate herself from his hands.

Daniel laughed and pushed her back, sending her stumbling against the wall. "Desiree and I are getting married. I guess you've been too busy whoring around to know that."

"Congratulations."

Daniel walked toward her.

With nowhere to go, Kristina lifted her chin, forcing herself to face him.

"I'm going to petition for custody, and I'll get it. With you acting the slut, a judge is going to look at my home, *my two-parent* home, and decide you're unfit. Just as I've told everyone from day one."

Kristina's throat went dry. He couldn't take her daughter, not once they knew what he'd done. Damn it, why didn't she go to the police? "You can't take her. I'll tell them everything."

"What have I done? I've demanded you behave as a mother should, nothing else. You have proof of these imagined wrongs?"

"Imagined? Was I the only one here the last time you came over? I imagined that? Fuck off. I'd die before I let you lay a hand on Cadence. You never loved either of us. You can't love anything. Do you rape Desiree too? Does she have bruises on her body from your love, or are you still wooing her?"

She expected the slap, but the force of it stunned her. She tasted blood and her ears rang.

Daniel grabbed her shoulders, shaking her so her head hit the wall. "Jealous? I knew you'd want it again. Last time just wasn't enough? Desiree doesn't act like a slut, but I can show you what she'd get if she did." He reached down to her pants and yanked them open.

Kristina fought him with all she had. Biting and scratching, her hands flew at him, but Daniel only grew more aggressive.

He laughed and shoved her to the floor, the back of his hand laying into her cheek.

"Stop. I'll call the cops. I'm not letting you do this anymore. I'll make sure you go to jail for it."

"I don't think you will."

He moved over her.

She recoiled at the feel of his body against hers.

"I can do whatever I want, and there's not a fucking thing you can do about it," he said.

"Please, don't do this. I'll make you pay for it this time."

"Begging? Lucky for you I'm too busy today, but I'll be back. I won't forget you."

Daniel released her. She stayed on the floor, terrified to move a muscle. The door slammed. She wouldn't forget him either. One day, Daniel would pay for it all.

Kristina rose from the floor, gathering her clothes and heading for the phone. With trembling hands she punched two numbers, nine and one, before punching 'end'. No, the police would do nothing. What did he really do this time? Threaten her? She could tell them about before. He might go to jail, but for how long? He'd just keep coming back. She wanted Daniel gone. Forever.

Wade entered her mind. He'd die before he did something like this to her. He'd make sure Daniel suffered. Punching in the cell number he'd given her ages ago, she drew the phone to her ear. It rang and rang, but no one picked up.

Shock set in. Her body shook. She had to get control over it, but nausea rose in her belly and sweat beaded her brow.

Someone should help her. If Wade wouldn't answer her calls, what choice did she have? She couldn't tell her father and she had no one else. The silence of the house was too much to bear.

Michelle. Her warnings rushed through Kristina's mind. She needed someone now and where was he? Not answering his phone.

Call her.

No, she should call the police. But what if they didn't do anything to Daniel? What if he got off again?

Michelle was her only friend. She'd always been there when Kristina needed her. Maybe she could help.

Call her.

But Wade loved her, she couldn't be wrong about that. He made a mistake with Amy and now he's paying the price. Michelle's warning echoed loudly in her mind; I don't want you to get hurt. Kristina had believed Wade would protect her. Where was he now? Her mind darted all over the place, a simple thought seemed impossible. She had to talk to someone, so she wouldn't feel so alone.

Call Michelle.

Wade didn't care about much, beyond whatever kept him away right now. But Amy was out to bury him. He had to protect himself.

Had Amy gone to the police?

The police would have come to get the box, but they didn't. Amy hadn't told. Kristina punched in Michelle's number and waited, her body shaking so badly the phone slipped from her hand.

"Hello?" Michelle answered.

"Um, I need help." Kristina crumbled, crying great choking sobs, unable to continue.

"Kristina?"

"Yes."

"I'll be right there."

Kristina let the phone slip to the floor and then lay next to it, the carpet itchy against her cheek, dampened by her tears.

CHAPTER 23

Someone knocked on the door, quiet at first and then thundering, rattling the walls. Kristina opened her eyes, immobile on the couch, and waited for them to go away. The knocking stopped and she relaxed, snuggling back into her blanket. She'd showered until the hot water ran cold and emerged shivering, her skin pink except for the bruises covering her body. Then she lay on the couch and stared at the blackened television until she drifted into a dreamless sleep.

"Kristina!" the pounding on the window and the sound of her name forced her upright. She stared an instant. Michelle. She'd called Michelle.

"Shit." Kristina ran to the door and opened it. Michelle came around the side of the house, her mouth set in a thin line. "I know I took a while, but come on." She smiled and Kristina tried to return it, though it felt weak. "Hey, what the hell happened to you?"

Kristina stepped forward, eager for friendly arms around her. She collapsed in Michelle's embrace, her chest wracked by sobs.

When she calmed down somewhat, Michelle held her at arm's length to stare at her, eyes wide, and reached out to touch the bruise on her jaw. "Did someone break in?"

"No, Daniel came over." Kristina's voice sounded small, she wanted to sound angry, but instead her voice was meek, defeated. She felt defeated.

"Did you call the cops?"

"No, the last time I called the cops they charged him, he cried and the judge ordered him to take some classes and then he put me in the hospital. The time before that, he broke my arm. They never do anything. If I called them over this he'd get a slap on the wrist, maybe some jail time, and then he'd get out and make me suffer for it."

"Did he—"

"Beat me? Yes and then he almost raped me. I should be used to it by now, I mean it's not the first time, but I'm too much of a coward to do anything about it." Kristina walked to the couch and sank down, pulling the blanket over her knees. She stared at her hands, hating the way they trembled.

"He tried to rape you?" Michelle walked over and sat on the coffee table. Her brown eyes wide, she leaned forward and reached for Kristina's hands.

"But he didn't in the end. Not this time anyway. I shouldn't have called you, I just panicked. I called Wade but he didn't answer and I had to talk to someone." She shrugged.

"So, you are involved with Wade. You silly thing. Somehow I knew it."

Kristina lowered her gaze to their piled-up hands.

"Why would you call Wade anyway? You think he'll do something about Daniel? I doubt it. Guys are guys. I bet the only thing that really matters to Wade is his hide," Michelle snorted and leaned back.

Her thoughts had been jumbled before but now that she'd gotten some sleep and calmed down, everything was clear. Calling Michelle had been a mistake. She'd panicked because of her fear and longed to unburden herself on her only friend.

"Want to tell me about it?"

Kristina cleared her throat. "I don't know where to start."

Michelle's mouth twitched. "Try at the beginning."

Over the next two hours, Kristina opened her heart to Michelle, telling her about her trepidations about Wade and the snatches of happiness she'd enjoyed with him. She told Michelle about Wade bringing the box for safekeeping in the basement, but didn't elaborate about its contents.

Michelle sighed and Kristina looked up, following her gaze to the window. The sun was setting, splashes of lavender and orange filled the sky beyond the green bridge. Light reflected off the water, the colors rippling on its black surface. She used to love watching the way the colors melted into one another but couldn't remember the last time she took a moment to see it. At least, not since she married Daniel. She made a note to sit with Cadence and enjoy as many sunsets as she could once this shit was over. The three of them, Kristina, Cadence and Wade, would enjoy every single one forever. Her chest tightened as she thought of Wade. She hoped he would be there with them, but nothing seemed certain anymore.

Michelle cleared her throat, bringing Kristina's thoughts back to the present. "So, did Wade pick up the box?"

"No, it's still here."

"Do you want me to take care of it? I could dump it somewhere," Michelle laid one hand on Kristina's knee as she spoke. "You can't trust them, honey. I know what they're like. Amy pretended to be my friend once, and that got me into some hot water. Wade's no different."

Kristina smiled at her friend's offer, suddenly feeling less lonely. "No, I'll wait for him to come and get it. I told him I'd keep it and I will. You could be in trouble too and that's not fair. You're the only other person who knows about it anyway," she bit her lip, thinking of Amy. "It's fine where it is."

Michelle leaned forward and ran her fingers through Kristina's. "You're being silly and naïve. What if he doesn't come back? What if Amy finds out about you guys?"

"He'd be here if he could. I know he would. And Amy already knows."

"I would hate to think he's feeding you bullshit and you're eating it right up. Perhaps you should get with reality, Kristina."

"I think you're wrong." Kristina crossed her arms over her chest.

"Did you even look inside the box?"

"No, I didn't," she lied, suddenly wondering about Michelle's interest. Most of her questions had something to do with the damn box. Curiosity?

"There may be important things inside. Maybe illegal things. Doesn't it bother you he didn't want it at his home?"

In her friend's eyes, she found an ocean of concern. Michelle was worried, and the realization dispelled her fears. Kristina leaned over and hugged her. "No, and I'm not going to look either. I trust him."

CHAPTER 24

Amy paced the length of the patio doors, ignoring the sunset and its glorious display of color. She pulled on her cigarette and flicked the ash on Wade's favorite rug. After darting a glance at the silent phone, she crossed over to the built-in bar in the corner of the living room, dropped a few ice cubes into her glass and drowned them in gin.

The telephone rang.

Amy jerked, the cherry of her cigarette grazing the hand holding the glass.

"Fuck!" She jumped back as the heavy cut glass shattered on the floor, liquid splattering her jeans. Giving wide berth to the glass shards, she hurried to catch the phone after its third ring. "Hello?"

"She has the box," the voice sounded ragged, as if its owner had been running.

"Are you sure?"

"Of course I am. She's just told me."

"You've seen it?" Amy opened a small drawer on the telephone stand and rummaged for cigarettes and a lighter.

"No, but she says Wade left it in her basement."

Amy watched a catlike smile on the face reflected on the pane of glass. "Thanks. I owe you, Michelle."

Silence.

"Yes?"

"What about our deal?"

"Ah, that—you're right, consider your debt settled." Amy ended the call. Instead of replacing the receiver in its cradle, she took a deep drag of her cigarette, flicked ash on the rug and punched a local number.

Sleep proved elusive for Kristina. She spent the night dozing at intervals—but waking with a start as dreams tormented her—and gave up when the sun brightened the living room, teasing her eyelids until the headache that threatened most of the night finally exploded.

She groaned and sat up, rubbing her eyes and then stretching. Good thing she'd agreed to let her parents take Cadence, the thought of having to do all the things her daughter would demand made her cringe. Besides, she didn't want her daughter around the mess she'd created. She stumbled to the kitchen to make a pot of coffee. Welcoming the dim light of the small room, her headache subsiding just a little, she padded to the counter and pulled the coffee maker from the wall. As she turned to the sink, something caught her eye. She paused, leaning toward the door she squinted at it. Mud?

Kristina set the coffee pot on the counter and walked across the kitchen for a closer look. Definitely mud, but just a clump of it, no tracks across the room, and dark like the dirt in her backyard. She frowned and checked the door. It swung open. Hadn't she locked it?

Her gaze went around the room, settling on the blue recycling container next to the door. She laughed at herself. Of course, before Daniel's visit, she'd brought the box in from the curb yesterday. Heat crept up her neck and into her cheeks as she thought of him. Shaking her head, she forced the dark memories away. There would be time to deal with them later.

The mud must have fallen from the container when she brought it in. She hadn't noticed and then she forgot to lock the stupid door. Smiling, Kristina turned back to the sink to finish making the coffee.

Either relax a little or suffer a nervous breakdown.

She also had to mop her floors again.

Puttering around the kitchen, making coffee and wiping off the counter and stove, Kristina hummed to herself. She'd stop this doubting; stop being afraid and move on. If Wade wanted her, he'd come back.

Shuffling to the sink to rinse the dishcloth, Kristina realized the past hours had triggered an epiphany. Her doubts and fears happened because she didn't believe in herself. It had nothing to do with Daniel or with Wade and whether he'd told her the truth or not, but her ability to let someone love her.

Amy could rant and rave all she wanted; Kristina wouldn't give her anything else. She had enough worries without adding someone who was simply bitter and angry to add to them. Wade would come and get the box when he could. Amy couldn't touch them

The satisfying aroma of coffee brewing filled the room. She turned to the cupboard, and reached for a cup when the phone rang. Closing her eyes, she set the mug next to the coffee pot, and ran to answer the phone.

The brightness of the living room—after spending so much time in the dull kitchen—startled her. She blinked. The ache in her head returned. Brilliant morning sunshine blazed through the window next to the couch. She made a note to get some blinds.

She picked up the phone. Wade's voice barked in her ear before he had the chance to say hello. "Go and make sure the decorations I gave you are where you left them."

"What?"

"The decorations. Make sure they're still there."

"Okay, just a minute." Kristina set the phone on the stand and turned to the basement door.

The latch was still in place and she wondered why he suddenly thought it might not be there. If he cared so much, maybe he should come and get it. She opened the door, reached to switch on the light and her gaze fastened to a clump of dark mud on the second stair from the top.

"No," she whimpered and hurried down the stairs. It wasn't possible. I barely slept last night. Surely she would have heard if someone came in, especially if they'd gone down here.

The stairs creaked and groaned. The box should be…right on top. Shit. Stepping slowly, afraid of what she would discover, but not wanting to prove it, she walked down the stairs. He would hate her. He would hate her and then his friends would kill her.

Kristina reached the bottom and glanced to where she'd left the box. It wasn't there. Hoping she'd remembered wrong, that she'd buried it, she moved boxes and bags tossing them across the dirt floor uncaring of where they landed or what was inside.

Her heart pounded against her chest and an ache ate away at her stomach. She turned, her eyes searching the cramped space, praying she overlooked it somehow. Her breath came in short gasps, suddenly she couldn't get enough air and sweat trickled down her back despite the damp chill of the room.

Stilling her raging mind, she tried to think the situation through. She'd blurted about the box to Amy but didn't give up its location. No, the idea was ridiculous. She wouldn't have known where to look anyway. The dirt on the stairs could have come from her own feet she may not have noticed it before because she tended to clean in a haze. Who else could have taken it?

Daniel hadn't come down to the basement, not since he'd lived with her, and she would have heard someone come into the house last night. So where the hell did it go?

A light went on in Kristina's head. She forgot the trip to Toronto, when she took Cadence to Wonderland. She'd been gone overnight. Did she look down here after she returned? No, she didn't. She'd come home and everything had gone ballistic on her. Daniel went nuts, the man…the man.

Would he have come back? She'd been certain he and Wade were friends or at least 'associates' after he left. He wouldn't take it without telling Wade. Would he? A thought hit

Kristina suddenly, one that angered and relieved her at once. What if it was all a setup? Did Wade come and get it or send the stranger here to pick it up? He must have. He was testing her.

Furious at him for stressing her out, but relieved to have figured out where the box was, Kristina ran upstairs and picked up the phone.

"When did you come get it?"

"I didn't. Are you telling me it's not there?" Wade growled and the menace in his tone irritated her.

"Wade, this isn't funny."

"Christ, I did not pick it up. I'm not joking. I told you to lock the damn doors. What is it with women? Do you have an allergy to fucking deadbolts?"

Kristina's throat burned, her eyes moistened with tears. He had to have picked it up. It was the only thing that made sense, the only thing that didn't imply she was a fool. The room spun, the walls bending and shifting toward her, and Kristina stared at the basement door, still ajar and the light blaring at her. She didn't want to admit she forgot to lock the back door. He'd be furious, although he was pretty pissed already.

"I…uh, shit." Kristina paused struggling to find a way to tell him about the door without sounding like an idiot. Wade said nothing, but she heard his breathing, heavy and angry. "I forgot to lock the door yesterday, and usually I'm so careful, but Daniel came over and he was angry and then I didn't know what to do, so I called you, but you didn't answer and I panicked."

"What happened?" Wade's voice sounded calm, but she knew better.

"I panicked. I'm so sorry, Wade."

"What happened when Daniel came over?"

"N-nothing, he just got mad and—"

"Damn it Kristina! Stop covering for him. Did he fucking rape you again? I suppose you didn't call the cops either. Jesus Christ, I go away for a couple of days and everything falls apart."

"He didn't—I'm sorry," she murmured, not knowing what else to say. Guilt pressed hard against her heart. If she'd just trusted him, Daniel would have been gone long ago.

"Don't apologize for that prick. I'll take care of him. What about after I didn't answer? Did you call the cops at all?"

"I—I called my friend."

"Which friend," ice crept into Wade's voice.

"Michelle."

"And?"

"I needed to talk to someone, you didn't answer and—"

"Did you tell her about the box?"

A blinding light exploded in Kristina's mind and she had to lean against the wall to stop crumpling down. "Well, yes but—"

"Shit. Shit. Shit." The line sounded muffled.

Kristina held her breath as the silence lengthened.

"Go and check again. Maybe you panicked and overlooked it."

"No, it's not there. I'm sorry. I haven't even gone down there since I put it there."

"Okay, we need to think about this logically. It's not your fault, honey. I'm sorry I got mad. I shouldn't have asked you to do this. It was unfair."

"No, I should have trusted you," Kristina murmured. Wade was silent for a moment and she wondered if he heard her.

"The decorations are clean, do you understand? No one knows who they belonged to and they won't be able to find out. Of course if you're careful, you can deny ever having them. Unless you looked, and then it's likely your prints are all over the bags. No, don't deny you had them. Maybe you could say Amy brought it over or something and it said decorations so you opened it and... Shit, I don't know. If this is Amy's work, you can claim she's lying and shift the blame to her but you have to make sure you don't trip up. If it's your word against hers, they have to prove otherwise."

"Why Amy?" She clung to her last shred of hope, praying the name screaming in her head was only a figment of her imagination. It couldn't be. "She didn't know where to look."

"Didn't she? Don't be so fucking naïve. You told Michelle. They've been friends, more than friends now that I think of it, for years."

Kristina cringed at his words. *Michelle...* She really was naïve. Until now it hadn't seemed like such a terrible thing.

"You don't have to talk to anyone, got it? Just lay low while I figure out how to fix this."

"Okay." Kristina gripped the phone and closed her eyes. This had spiraled out of control and fast. She'd betrayed Wade, one tiny little doubt could send them both to jail and it was all her fault. And Michelle had betrayed her. Why? Tears burned her eyes and she sniffed.

"I love you. You know I wouldn't let anyone hurt you, right?"

Her hands trembled and she nodded. "Yes, I know."

Wade sighed and she felt his frustration in every muscle of her body. He still loved her despite this huge fuck up. Guilt gnawed at her belly for ever thinking he didn't care.

Wade cursed again.

She flinched.

"This is Amy's doing. She must have bribed Michelle to do it. Stupid bitch. Look, don't worry. Who am I kidding? You're freaking out. Just let me handle it. Everything will work out in the end. Okay? I'll be in touch. I love you." The line went dead.

Kristina stood, the phone to her ear and Wade's words running through her head. *I love you.*

It was time she earned his love.

"Bitch." Wade cursed, running a trembling hand through his hair. He paced the small office and considered his options.

Sheila was due to open the bar any minute and he wanted to be out of there as soon as he handed her the keys. The

Brothers had told him to lay low, to disappear until they'd solved their *little* problem. That had been his intention—after he picked up the box. Now what? He couldn't disappear but how did he tell them? They had no clue how far out of control this thing had gotten. If Thomas knew how badly he'd fucked things up, he'd be in a landfill before next sunup.

Amy had stepped up her game; it had to be her. No doubt she had something big planned. Somehow she'd fooled Kristina and he'd bet money she had the box, but he couldn't be sure what she'd do with it. Going to the police meant exposing her role in the Brotherhood over the years. Would she risk it?

"Of course she would," he muttered.

He'd tried to protect Kristina but hadn't thought about how much pressure he put on her by asking her to keep the damn box. She worried about everything and with that asshole Riley in her life, she second guessed every thought she had. He should have realized it. Then to top it off, he told her not to look. He was a fool and deserved the bullet he was sure would be in his brain very soon.

Wade cursed. She would have been fine and she definitely wouldn't have freaked out if Daniel hadn't been around. He should have known the jackass would throw a goddamn wrench into things. It infuriated him Daniel could still hurt Kristina. What good was he to her when someone like Daniel could walk in and rape her any time he wanted? He should have taken care of him at the Peek-a-Boo Club, no matter what Kristina's feelings were. Then he found those bruises all over her body. When he'd realized that as he had driven by the house that day and kept going because of the black Dodge in the driveway, Daniel had been inside brutalizing her, he went berserk. He should have gotten rid of him. She'd never have known if the bastard were dead or had just disappeared. He'd been too wrapped up in his own problems.

Stupid decisions. The only thing he cared about at the time was winning Kristina over. Worried she'd hate him for what he'd done for the Brothers, he tried to do things differently than he always had. Well, now she knew what he was and she still loved him. All this time he'd cursed her for her inability to trust. *What have I done?*

Wade turned, his gaze on the phone. He could call Thomas and tell him what happened and how Amy had fucked him over royally. Thomas might see things rationally and help him out of this pile of shit he'd buried himself under. The box was partly Thomas's responsibility. If he'd taken the damn thing like he said he would—fuck, they were in deep. But the particulars of who should have done what wouldn't matter to Thomas. He cared about results. And the result here was Wade had fucked up. Now he had to own up to it and hope their friendship meant more than 'business'. Friends or not, Thomas would only consider keeping Wade alive if he had a solution to the problem. And Wade didn't have any.

Kristina told him she hadn't looked in the box, but the poor girl couldn't lie if her life depended on it and it might. Her prints would be all over the stuff. Wade had cleaned everything else. The knife, the bags, the guns, all of them had nothing on them except Kristina's prints. If she stuck to the story he'd suggested, there might be a chance, but Amy could fuck it all up.

Amy had to go. That much he knew. He'd battled Thomas on this for a long time, each of them teetering on either side of the decision at different times. Amy was the only one who could link Kristina to the box, and she would sink Kristina to get at him. No matter what happened, he wouldn't let Kristina suffer anymore.

Wade grabbed the phone and turned it over in his hands. He pictured Kristina, her eyes heavy with sleep their last morning together as she smiled. A rush of emotion he'd never imagined he'd be capable of feeling rushed over him.

He punched the numbers into the phone.

Hearing Thomas's voice, a voice that could sound velvety smooth one moment and cold as ice the next, he took a deep breath and considered his words.

"It's me."

Thomas was silent.

Wade continued. "We have a problem."

"Yes, we do."

"Let's get rid of it."

"Are we talking about the same problem?" Thomas's voice dropped to a whisper.

Wade faltered, unsure if he should do it. What if it made things worse? Would Kristina hate him if she knew? She'd figure it out. He closed his eyes, nodding to himself. He'd killed for money and revenge, why not love? "Yeah, I need a divorce."

CHAPTER 25

Grunting, uttering a muffled curse, Kristina reached into the closet and pushed the clothes aside. She'd cleared out everything earlier that morning and spent three solid hours tossing old clothes, separating what she planned to keep. Idleness gave her time to think, to focus on negative things she had no control over. She could have gone back to work but Wade advised against it and she didn't want her decisions to hurt him again; he'd suffered enough because of her mistakes.

The pile of clothes Kristina would donate to the local thrift store seemed mountainous. She eyed it warily. *I need some bags.* There was no way she could carry the pile in her arms. Sighing, she left her room and wished she'd thought of that when she started. But then, she hadn't planned to do quite so much, only to straighten out the mess of clothes she'd jammed on the shelves and in the corners.

As she stepped off the bottom step, the phone rang. Her mother said they'd call when they were on the road home, but she didn't expect them to leave today. Her dad hadn't even dragged the boat in or packed the trailer when they called yesterday. She hoped it wasn't her parents, and they were already on the road bringing Cadence home. After the past week's events, she yearned for her old boring, empty life. It was easier to deal with than with the roller coaster of emotion that came along with Wade.

Kristina answered, and phone in hand continued to the

kitchen to search for some garbage bags.

"Mrs. Riley?" a male voice, very serious.

She halted in her tracks. "Yes,"

"I'm Sergeant Jacobs. I wonder if you could come to the police station and answer some questions."

Her mouth went dry. Kristina moved to sit at the table. "What's this about?"

"We'll be happy to fill you in when you get here. This is a very urgent matter though, I can send a car to pick you up if you'd like."

Kristina bit her lip. It had to be about the box. Could she lie to the police? They'd see right through her, wouldn't they? Isn't that what they were trained to do? "No, that's not necessary. Can I ask if I'm in any sort of trouble?"

"Not at this point."

Not at this point? She closed her eyes to collect her thoughts. This didn't have to end badly; she just had to figure out how to deal with it. Could she refuse to go down to the police station? No, they'd come get her if it was about the box. That kind of evidence would make them very eager to speak to her. Maybe they thought it was hers. Kristina opened her eyes and gazed at the clear sky outside the window and the green bridge, such a familiar sight she rarely noticed the way it seemed to reach up into the clouds. Birds perched atop, flapping and squawking, each battling for the prime position in the center so they could easily swoop down over the falls to grasp the fish that leapt out of the water below. She felt like the fish, swimming against the current so close to freedom, yet knowing the predators that loomed above could snatch her life away at any moment.

She frowned and cleared her throat. No, she was done waiting for someone to take everything from her. No one had the power to run her life. This had gone on long enough. She was only a victim as long as she allowed it. "Sure I'll come down. Is an hour okay? I'd like to shower and change and I'll have to call a cab."

"Sounds fine, and thank you for your cooperation."

"Of course, whatever it is, I hope I can help or at least clear things up for you."

"Yes, me too." The line went dead.

She walked to the stairs, her mind reeling. One hour to figure out this mess, to decide how to deal with the questions they'd ask. In the bathroom she pulled her shirt over her head, crinkling her nose at the scent of her own sweat. Kristina glanced in the mirror.

The image before her wasn't startling, but encouraging. For the first time in months, her eyes sparkled with fire, determination. Color blossomed in her cheeks and she stood straighter, shoulders back, chin up. Wade loved her, and she loved him. She didn't just want him or needed him; she loved him more than anything she'd loved in her life. Cadence meant the world to her and she'd always come first in her heart, but this feeling for Wade was different than a mother's love for her child, and just as consuming.

Staring in wonder at the way her features had changed, Kristina's resolve strengthened. Her eyes narrowed and her mouth thinned to a determined line. She wouldn't just coast along anymore, taking each bump life threw in her road, meekly accepting her fate as though she was powerless.

Kristina turned on the shower and discarded the rest of her clothes as she thought of ways to handle the police. They'd ask her about what was in it but she'd tell them she didn't know. She'd—her prints! Kristina shuddered, her body chilled despite the steamy warmth of the shower's spray. What did she actually touch? Could they find fingerprints on cloth? Jesus, she didn't know about this stuff. Kristina took a breath and tried to still her racing thoughts.

First she had to figure out how they'd gotten the box. Wade said Amy must have taken it. She could tell them the story he'd suggested. That Amy brought it over... but then it was Kristina's word against Amy's. Other than Wade, Michelle was the only one who knew Kristina had it. And Michelle had been friends with Amy, though Wade never elaborated. It had to be Amy. But why? Just to be free? She could have walked out any time she wanted. Couldn't she? The question flipped around her brain as she soaped her hair and leaned into the hot spray. Amy didn't care about being free. She hated Wade and wanted him to suffer. That's why she stayed and that's why she stole the box. She wanted to ruin him.

Well, it wouldn't happen. Amy would pay for manipulating Kristina and for all she'd done to Wade. She'd love to see Daniel paid as well. Daniel. Kristina turned the tap off and stepped out of the shower, a plan forming in her mind.

At the police station, Kristina faced a hive of activity when she walked through the door. People in uniform rushed back and forth while people in 'regular' clothes moved faster. She paused to watch the bustle before turning to a window near the door where a uniformed man sat punching at his keyboard, his brow furrowed in concentration.

Reluctant to interrupt him, she stood quietly and hoped he noticed her so she wouldn't have to.

To Kristina's relief Sergeant Jacobs spotted her and introduced himself. She didn't know what she expected but it wasn't what she found. Jacobs looked close to her age, his face kind and his hand warm when he shook hers. She would have found him attractive, if he wasn't a police officer who wanted to put her or Wade behind bars.

Jacobs led her to a small room with a table and two chairs. Another officer waited, leaning on the wall opposite, a manila folder tucked under his arm. This one looked older and not so nice. Under the too-bright lights, they appraised her with eyes full of pity. Her hackles rose. They thought she was some stupid girlfriend who had no clue what was happening. Either that or they thought she was desperate and content to take the fall for a man who had used her. They thought wrong.

"I'm glad you could talk to us." Sergeant Jacobs smiled.

"I bet," she mumbled.

"I know this is scary. I'm sorry I couldn't give you more information, but this is a very sensitive matter. I couldn't share anything that may skew what you're able to tell us. We're not against you. We want to help."

"I don't know what kind of help you think I need, but yes, I'm scared. I don't usually get called in for questioning. I don't get called in at all."

"Of course, and it's not what you think. Right now, we just want to talk."

Sergeant Jacobs looked to his partner who sat in the chair opposite Kristina, rubbing his temple as though thinking about something that pained him.

He cleared his throat and picked up the folder that now sat on the table between them. Opening it, he perused its contents before training cold eyes on hers. "We've been given of a box containing some rather alarming things. This box has enough evidence to put its owner in prison for a very long time." He paused, a trick used to allow the information to sink in.

Kristina widened her eyes.

"The problem we have, and the issue we need you to clear up, is how the box came to be at your house. Care to explain?"

Fidgeting with the hem of her shirt, Kristina looked at both officers, hoping her face appeared sufficiently puzzled and confused. She didn't have to feign fear; she was terrified. Worried she couldn't pull off the charade and forced to turn Wade over.

"I'm not sure." She frowned and ran a trembling hand through her hair, choosing her words with care. "I have a lot of boxes at my house. Jeeze, the basement is a nightmare."

The officers exchanged a glance.

Kristina wondered who would be good cop and who would be bad cop, so far they'd both played it pretty evenly. Did they do that in real life? If they did, she thought the older one would make the better bad cop. His stare was unnerving.

He didn't disappoint her.

He stood abruptly, a frown on his face. "You know what box we're talking about. I'm not fooled by this little act you're giving us. The box you had in your basement, marked as Christmas decorations. The one you hid for Wade Bowen and the one you'll go to jail for if you don't tell me the truth. The box that will cause you to lose your daughter."

Heat filled her cheeks. Kristina took a shaky breath. To think, she worried about how she'd act terrified. Her nerves frayed as she weighed her reply and forced her hands to be still in her lap, although the urge to fidget was strong. Taking a deep breath, she looked bad cop in the eye.

"Wade? I barely know him, and I certainly wouldn't hide anything for him." The lie rolled off her tongue easily enough but both men looked doubtful.

Not yet. Wait a little longer.

"You work for him, don't you?" Sergeant Jacobs asked.

"Yes, but we aren't close or anything. He's friends with my dad, but even Dad hasn't really talked to him in a while." She shrugged, her mind working furiously to ready her bomb.

Bad cop sat back and glanced at the file.

Kristina imagined he was working out a way to trap her, to get her to say something that would make her look guilty. That was Daniel's favorite trick, and then he could turn everything around on her. But she'd learned, boy she'd learned. Her belly fluttered. Yes. Finally, Daniel could do something useful. *Payback time.* Staring at Bad Cop, she took another breath and folded her hands on the table in front of her.

He leaned forward, a smirk playing on his lips. He thought he had her.

She would disappoint him. "Okay, I need you to promise if I tell you what I know, you can protect me. I was afraid, and that's the only reason I didn't come to you a long time ago. I'm still afraid. He's done such awful things to me. If he knows I told…"

"Of course we'll protect you," Sergeant Jacobs took the chair next to his partner and sat down. Both men were all ears.

Kristina bit her lip to stop a grin. "Daniel left a box of his stuff downstairs and he told me not to touch it."

Their faces paled.

Not the answer you expected?

Kristina lowered her voice. "It was marked Christmas, but I don't think there's anything to do with Christmas in there."

RENÉE MILLER

CHAPTER 26

Silence filled the little room but for the hum from the bright fluorescent light hanging over the metal table.

Kristina looked away as they collected their thoughts.

Sergeant Jacobs did a better job of hiding his shock, but Bad Cop stared at her open-mouthed. They exchanged glances and then back at her.

Kristina offered a nervous smile. Again, she didn't have to act, scared they'd smell the lie. Now that she'd made the leap, she wouldn't be tipped over by guilt. Daniel deserved the grave she was about to dig for him.

Sergeant Jacobs pulled a little notebook from his shirt pocket and clicked his pen. "You know what's in it? Did you look inside?"

"Sort of. I mean— I opened it and shifted things around a little. Underneath a bunch of stuff wrapped in dirty old cloths, there was an old knife. I thought it was weird and got a little scared to be honest. I put everything back and closed the box right away. It's his stuff. I told him to come get it after that. I guess I'm probably guilty of something. I mean, I went through the box and I should have told someone what I saw. I'm not stupid. I know it means something bad. God, I've been so scared." Kristina paused.

A skeptical look passed between them. They didn't believe her.

Sergeant Jacob's face reddened and frowned. "So, you don't

have a relationship with Wade Bowen? Is that what you're saying?"

"No, I don't have a relationship, not beyond friendship and that's pretty casual."

"I'm sorry, forgive my bluntness." Sergeant Jacobs rubbed his chin, as though uncomfortable with what he was about to ask. "Are you and Wade Bowen not lovers? This is the information we've received from more than one source. Reliable sources."

Blushing, she looked away. *Shit*. She'd weighed her lying; figuring a bit of the truth would satisfy them. If their source had evidence, her deposition would amount to nothing. "I'm—shit, I'm so embarrassed. A while ago, when he and Amy were having problems, we did sleep together. It was just a couple of times. They worked out their issues and he went back to her. I felt so awful about it. I don't do things like that normally. I kind of hoped no one had to know about it."

Bad Cop snorted. "You call that barely knowing someone?"

"Sorry, I guess I'm confusing things more. We really don't talk a lot and those times we were… intimate, I was pretty drunk and messed up. I'd just left Daniel and he was still coming to the house and threatening me. I just gave in to the stress I suppose. I'm not proud of what I did, and I'm sorry I lied to you about it. I just—it's not a shining moment in my life. I wanted to forget about it. Wade and I haven't spoken for a while. I took a leave of absence from work because it's gotten rather uncomfortable. Amy found out and I felt so guilty. I found out she and Daniel had been messing around, I don't think it was more than a few times, but I know they still talk. I was so confused then. I hate that I did it, but I did. She said a lot of mean things, and I understand she was hurt. Mostly I worried because she promised to make my life hell. I just thought it would be best to stay away from both of them. Wade and Amy. God, this sounds like some awful soap opera, doesn't it?" Kristina wiped an imaginary tear from her eye and bit her lip.

Sergeant Jacobs smiled and his eyes softened. He leaned

over to his partner and whispered something in his ear. Bad Cop shrugged, and then nodded. They compared their notes.

Kristina relaxed, slumping into the uncomfortable chair. They'd bought it. She waited for the rest of their questions, trying to remain calm. Now that they swallowed the bait, she wanted to run. She didn't want to risk stumbling and losing her advantage.

"You understand how we might be a little skeptical knowing you lied about this relationship. But I do get why you hesitated."

Kristina nodded.

Bad Cop continued. "I need honesty here. Understand? You lie to us now and it will come back to haunt you. Everything comes out in the wash one way or another. None of the information you give us is going to be broadcasted anywhere. We are investigating some very serious crimes and I'm sure you want to see justice served."

Indeed, she did. And justice would definitely be served. To Daniel. "I'm sorry. I was too embarrassed to tell you about me and Wade. I don't want to obstruct justice or whatever it's called. Please, ask me anything and I'll answer the best I can."

Sergeant Jacobs stood and walked around the table. "Tell us about your ex-husband. What was your relationship like?"

This is an easy one. "Oh, well I suppose you'd have the police reports. Daniel was very abusive, that's why I filed for divorce. I was afraid for my life at the end."

"And now?" Jacobs asked.

"Now? I'm still afraid of him. He's hurt me a few times and he's done things, terrible things. He raped me, but I can't prove it because I didn't report it. He said he'd kill me if I told anyone. I—I saw the knife and... he's a scary person. I didn't even think about why he had it there. I didn't want to. I try to keep him happy. Then he has no reason to hurt me. So when he told me to keep the box I didn't question it. I did wonder why he didn't just take it with him. I mean, he took everything else that wasn't nailed down. I noticed it was gone and I assumed he came and got it while I was away. To be honest, I was glad to see it gone."

They made notes. Bad Cop looked up and raised an eyebrow. "Anything else? What about his job? Friends?"

"Oh, I don't know much about that. Daniel was always very secretive and it's not like I could ask anything. I mentioned one of his friends once. I think I said the guy made me nervous and he sprained my arm when he wrenched it behind my back. He told me to mind my own business and I did." She shrugged and took a shaky breath. "He's engaged to someone else now. I suspected he was seeing her during our marriage. I found out he had rented her an apartment. I can give you her work number if you want to talk to her. I don't think she'll be willing to talk to you anywhere else but here. She's pretty timid and does whatever he tells her to do. I think he hits her too."

Bad Cop chewed his pen and stared.

She'd been honest for much of the discussion about her marriage. She didn't have to paint Daniel as a bad person. He really was.

They continued to pepper her with questions, often repeating them more than once; when did Daniel leave the box and what exactly did he tell her about it? Kristina kept her answers vague. She knew she was terrible at lying and didn't want to have to remember too many details.

Her stomach rolled. A faint twinge of guilt tugged at the edges of her mind but then thought of Wade. She imagined him smiling down at her, moonlight streaming through the bedroom window illuminating his crooked smile and the dimple in his cheek. Her guilt disappeared. She felt his breath on her neck as though he were behind her right then, whispering into her ear, promising forever. Kristina sat straighter in the chair. She'd do anything for that promise.

CHAPTER 27

Something was wrong. He'd drawn the curtains to block out the brightness of the full moon and the bedroom was still shrouded in darkness, but something was amiss. Slowly Wade sat up, his gaze moving to the empty pillow next to his. Amy had got up at some point and he hadn't heard her. Not unusual, but given recent events he cursed himself for falling into such a deep sleep.

He lay back against the pillow and stared up at the ceiling. A shuffling noise drifted up from the rooms below. She must have gone downstairs. Maybe she planned to go see Carl. Then another noise brought him suddenly alert again. A heavy tread on the stairs. A pause. Wade sighed. It was time.

The bedroom door swung open. Two police officers, in vests and helmets, charged through with their guns drawn. Wade smiled and sat up, carefully arranging the blankets around his waist before folding both arms behind his head.

The officers exchanged glances.

Wade suppressed a chuckle. "Let me guess, you have a warrant and you are now searching my house. Is this a social visit? It makes my heart all fluttery knowing you guys missed me so much you had to break in. You're so sweet."

"Very funny," the officer on the right motioned with his gun. "Stand up slowly, hands where we can see them."

"All right. But, I don't usually get company in the middle of the night, so I'm afraid I'm not exactly dressed for the occasion." Wade kept his hands high and threw his legs over the edge of the bed. He kept his gaze on the officers, grinning as he stood. "Guess there's no need to search me."

Wade caught the look that passed between them. He vaguely recognized one, but the room was too dark to be sure. Thomas said they'd try to make sure their guy was in on the bust when it happened, to ensure they found what they should.

"Get dressed," the officer on the left ordered. "Where's the light switch?"

"Next to the door. On the right."

Wade blinked. He knelt down, keeping one hand high and picked up the jeans he'd discarded next to the bed only hours earlier.

"Can I lower my hands to put these on, or would someone like to help me? I must ask you to be careful with the zipper."

The officer on the right walked over, his gun pointed at Wade's chest, and took the pants from him. He shook them and, satisfied they contained nothing dangerous, he handed them back. "Put them on so we can get this over with."

Wade pulled his jeans on and they escorted him downstairs. He wondered why they didn't cuff him. The last time they'd raided the house he'd been cuffed and hauled out the door before he even knew what was happening. The hallway remained dark but the lights in the kitchen spilled over the stairs. Where was Amy?

As he rounded the bottom of the stairs, a flush of anger heated his skin. They had torn the house apart. At least a dozen officers roamed the lower level, searching every nook and cranny. The freezer stood wide open, its contents on the floor.

He shook his head and glanced at the officer who appeared to be in charge, the only one who stood still, talking on a cell phone. "I hardly think it's necessary to destroy my home. I would have been quite willing to help you find whatever it is you're searching for."

The officer flipped the phone shut and smiled back. His dark hair curled at his collar, the vest made his chest look enormous. He stood about Wade's height and his dark eyes leveled him with a gaze that dared him to get cocky. Wade never could resist a dare. In fact, he planned to make sure they put him in jail; it was the only way his plan would work.

"I'd like you to sit right there." He pointed to the table. "Keep your hands where we can see them and your mouth shut."

"Sure, but can I ask what it is I've done?"

"We have reason to believe—in fact we're certain—you and your associates have been in the business of selling illegal drugs and weapons, among other things."

Wade snorted and allowed the officer behind him to nudge him toward the table. He walked around to sit on a chair positioned against the wall. "My associates? Boy, I'm an important man."

"You were." The officer turned and clasped his hands behind his back, his gaze on the activity around them. But he remained tense, as though expecting Wade to do something shady any moment.

Wade sat back, careful to keep his hands on the table, while the police searched his home. He knew they'd find something. He'd planted it, hoping Amy would seize the chance to set him up. Tempted to tell them where they could find it, he bit his tongue as they dumped cabinets and removed cushions from the L-shaped sofa in the family room. Several officers moved upstairs, boxes and bags ready for any evidence that might pop up. They had turned on every light in the house. Wade wondered where Amy had gotten to. He hoped they'd found her a safe house. It would make things easier. They wouldn't have to search for her. One carefully set fire and bye-bye Amy.

They wouldn't actually slap the cuffs on him until they found what they needed. The last time they searched his house they went ahead and shackled him. Boy, were there a lot of red faces and disciplinary actions for the officers involved, when they found nothing to pin on him. It was taking them an obscenely long time to do their search. Their guy on the inside knew where to look, but he'd been instructed only to go for it if his peers drew a blank.

Voices from upstairs, loud and excited. The man in charge glanced at Wade and raised a brow. "Let's see what we've found," he murmured and walked to the stairs.

Another officer walked to stand over him, his gun drawn. He waited until his superior had disappeared upstairs before turning his gaze. The slight nod told Wade all he needed to know. This was his man. Wade looked away and to the front door. Two cruisers and a wagon waited outside. Shoot, they'd called out the Calvary just for him. He felt honored. Amy had really outdone herself. Strange she hadn't stuck around to gloat.

His thoughts drifted to Kristina, and an icy hand clutched his gut. Had they searched her house too? He looked to the officer next to him, but the man stared straight ahead. Wade couldn't ask him anything anyway. If Kristina were in trouble there was little he could do, except hope she didn't panic.

The bustle of activity in the rooms above him increased.

Wade fidgeted.

The officer glanced at him.

He smiled. "So, nice night, eh?"

The man's gaze darted around the room before he spoke. "It is, a shame we couldn't be near the water where there's at least a breeze instead of out here in the middle of nowhere. I know a great spot, a bridge in town where you can sit and feel the wind on your face. Haven't been there in a while."

"Yeah, I like the water but Amy hates the bugs. I had to stop going so often."

The officer nodded. He looked too young to wear the uniform but Wade knew from what Thomas told him he was wise beyond his years. If he wasn't, the Brotherhood wouldn't have paid his way into Law Enforcement. Wade's eyes drifted to the nameplate below his badge. Jacobs.

"Not fond of bugs either. Where you're going there won't be nothing like that, maybe a rat or two. No lovely ladies either. I bet you're going miss those."

Wade nodded. "I bet I will too. But then, you guys have to

pin something on me first."

"Oh we will," he smiled and looked to the door. "You know what's strange about this place? I never hear the birds. I see lots of them, but they never sing. I'm not from around here, transferred in from Toronto."

"Hmm."

"I hear birds singing all day long down there, even with all the traffic and sirens, but here, they don't seem so chatty. I thought you'd hear more wildlife in the sticks."

"I guess they're shy."

"I saw one today that seemed pretty rare. It had the prettiest green eyes. Red feathers too. Gorgeous bird. Thought for sure it'd start squawking any minute, but it didn't chirp at all."

"Maybe it had nothing to say."

"Maybe I asked it to sing the wrong tune." The officer shrugged.

Relief flowed through Wade. They'd tried Kristina and she didn't give them a thing. He smiled at the comparison of her to a bird and thought she might not like it. He wondered what this guy would consider Amy to be, and snorted as he imagined a crow. Yes, that would be Amy.

Wade turned to footsteps on the stairs. Four officers rounded the bottom with boxes in their arms, avoiding his gaze. The last to descend was the man in charge, the cocky prick. Wade nodded as he stepped off the last stair and into the kitchen, cuffs in hand. "I see you've found what you were looking for."

He nodded and motioned to the officer who'd stood next to Wade. The man took Wade's arm and pulled him up. "Hands."

They cuffed him. He listened silently as they read his rights. The officer rattled off the charges and Wade did his best too look disappointed. Darn, he'd be spending some time in jail. In fact, he expected to serve a couple of years before they were done, but any amount of time would be worth the reward. Freedom and Kristina.

They nudged him forward and Wade followed without resisting. An officer waited at the door, opening it as they approached. Amy stood in front of the porch, two officers at her side. Their eyes locked.

"Sorry, I had to do it. I just can't live like this anymore," she said, wringing her hands.

The sun had begun to rise, and over the empty field bordering the left side of the property a pink fog drifted. Wade smiled and looked back to his wife as they urged him to the waiting cruiser.

"Bye Amy, say hello to Karma for me, will you?" he murmured.

Her eyes widened and she paled.

Wade turned. Chuckling he let them lead him to the cruiser. He didn't look back. He wanted to remember his wife as she was at that moment, as reality hit her like a brick.

CHAPTER 28

Cadence's soft snore against her chest forced a smile from Kristina, although she had little to smile about. Her father told her Wade had been arrested. They'd heard it on their way home from the cottage. That had been two days ago and she'd heard nothing more about him or the box. She wondered if they had arrested him anyway, despite what she'd told them, and considered the possibility they let him believe she ratted him out. Would he believe it? She hoped she was wrong but her instinct told her not to hope for too much.

Standing, she picked Cadence up, tiptoed from the couch to the stairs and then up to Cadence's room. Since returning from the cottage her daughter refused to let Kristina out of her sight, and the only way to get her to sleep was to let her lay with her. Although glad she was missed, Kristina hoped she got over it soon. She couldn't get much done when she had to sit for an hour waiting for her to drift off.

After laying Cadence in her crib and waiting a moment to make sure she'd stay asleep, Kristina crept downstairs to tidy up. She'd have to go back to work soon, but not to the bar. She couldn't bear working there without Wade. She would go see John and ask for her old job back at Mac's. She hoped he hadn't filled it.

The phone startled her. She paused, one hand over her heart. The damn thing hadn't rang all day. Rushing to pick it up she murmured a quick hello, listening with her other ear for

Cadence's cry.

"Kris?"

Wade. Her heart skipped and she almost sank to the floor when her knees weakened in relief. "Where are you?"

"Jail."

"Oh."

"I'm okay. It's not the first time I've been a guest of this fine establishment. It's not exactly five star—not even one star—but I'll make do. I just wanted to check on you. My lawyer told me the police questioned you."

"Yes but I—"

"I don't have time much time. I just wanted to tell you I'm okay. I heard you had some trouble and wanted to make sure you didn't pack everything up and move away."

"I—no I'm still here," she realized what he was doing and tried to think of an answer that would tell him everything and absolutely nothing to the people listening. "The police were just doing their job. Amy told them I had something that belonged to you, but I told them she was mistaken. It was Daniel's. I had to tell them about her and Daniel and what he'd done."

"Oh honey, I'm so sorry. I know you didn't want to anger him, but you're better off with him locked away."

She heard the smile in his voice.

"I think so. He won't bother me anymore now that the police know everything. It's nice not being scared all the time. And I've met someone special."

"You have?"

"Yes, he's quite a catch. Seems everyone wants to keep him away from me, though."

"People should leave you two alone."

"I miss him."

"I'm sure he misses you too."

Tears burned her eyes, and despite her happiness, despair clutched her heart. "I don't care how long it takes; I'll be here waiting for him."

"He's a lucky man."

A murmured voice in the background.

"Hey kid, I gotta go. Chin up, okay. If the guy's smart, he'll do whatever it takes to see you again."

"I know. Thank you, Wade."

The line went silent and Kristina set the phone on its base.

She didn't have time to mull over her mixed emotions as Cadence's cries erupted from upstairs. Sighing she rushed up to get her. Cadence stood in her crib, screaming into the darkness. She paused when Kristina stepped inside the room but only for a moment.

"Okay, I get it." Kristina picked her up and turned to go downstairs.

A knock at the door and she froze. Part of her dreaded answering it; the thought of Daniel confronting her was more than she could bear. But he'd just break the door down if she didn't answer.

Bracing herself for the worst, Kristina rushed down the stairs and to the door. She slid the deadbolt opened it and came face to face with the stranger.

"Mind if I come in?" he asked, pushing past her.

Kristina didn't know who this man was, but he terrified and fascinated her at once. His presence brought tension into the room. He emanated a quiet power, one that anyone with a brain in their head wouldn't cross.

Cadence had stopped crying, her eyes widened at the interesting stranger.

He turned and held his arms out; a frisson of fear ran down Kristina's back as her daughter happily leaned toward him. She pulled back but he took Cadence from her arms as though it were the most natural thing in the world for him to do.

"Please put her down. I want you to leave," she said stepping toward him.

"Going to call the cops?" he asked, stroking Cadence's brown curls.

Her daughter gazed up at him, raising a tiny hand to trace the lines on his neck.

Kristina stood close enough to see the tattoo clearly. The

scales of justice wrapped around his neck, black ink depicted a feather on one side of the scale, a smoking gun on the other. She frowned, unable to decipher its meaning. Although clearly it was related to justice, the feather made little sense to her.

"You like it?" he asked and chuckled when she didn't reply. "The scales stand for justice, the legal kind anyway, and the gun is obviously the proper way to see justice served. Street Justice, if you will. Of course, that's just my humble opinion. I do believe in an eye for an eye. Too cliché?"

"And the feather?" Kristina couldn't help herself. Curiosity overwhelmed her desire for him to leave.

"Ah, the feather. Are you familiar with Egyptian mythology? No? I am well versed in it. As a young woman, my grandmother came to Canada from Egypt. She told me many tales. This one is my favorite though. The feather is the symbol of the Egyptian Goddess, Maat. The Feather of Truth and Justice. It's a long history, changed over the centuries, adapted to fit the times, but I'll give you the condensed version.

"Maat stands at the entrance to the Halls of Two Truths— that's in the underworld—ready to place her feather on the scales. If it were you standing there, you would wait with bated breath to see what happened as she placed your heart on the other side. If your heart balanced with the feather, you would have eternal life. If not..." He smiled, pausing to touch her chest briefly.

Her heart pounded and she knew he felt it. The light in his dark gaze sent a tremor down Kristina's spine.

"The waiting monster, Amemait, would eat your heart and your life; your soul would be gone."

Speechless she stared up at him.

Cadence squealed in his arms.

Kristina's gaze dropped to her daughter who played with the collar of his leather jacket. She longed to rip her from his arms, but something in his eyes told her it would be a stupid move. The way to deal with this man was to remain calm. He wouldn't strike unless she gave him reason.

"Know who Amemait is?" he asked.

She shook her head.

"She is known by many names; 'The Bone Eater,' 'she who destroys the wicked,' or simply 'The Devourer'. Part lioness, part hippopotamus, and part crocodile; she is not a pretty creature. Her function is to devour the hearts of the dead who did not pass judgment, thus destroying their soul or extinguishing their 'light'. Tell me, would your heart balance? Have you led a life that has been true and just?"

"If you don't leave, I'll go straight to the police."

His words troubled her, but not because she believed them. Myths were silly nonsense made up by old people to scare small children into behaving. It was the way he said them, as though he knew the turmoil raging in her heart over what she'd done to keep Wade.

He set Cadence on the floor, and then gave her a couple of blocks from the toy box next to the wall. Kristina stiffened as he straightened and then walked toward her. He stopped inches from her face.

"I know what you've done. You're lucky Wade is so taken by you, or I'd have exacted the punishment any other rat would receive. I'm not fooled by a pretty face, and he'll realize the truth before long."

The hairs on her neck stood on end but Kristina raised her chin and met his gaze. His dark eyes gave her chills, so dead and cold, but she would not be intimidated, she'd done nothing wrong. "I asked you to leave."

He smiled and leaned forward, his lips pressed against her ear. She resisted the urge to pull away, clenching her fists at her sides in order to stand her ground.

"I'll be watching. No one crosses me. But Wade has made it clear you are not to be touched, for now. If his arrest opens a can of worms for the rest of us though, it won't matter how much he begs; you will pay."

"I didn't do anything. You should be visiting his wife. I've talked to the cops and they aren't looking at Wade for anything but what they found at his house. Maybe you should talk to him before you go around making threats."

"Maybe I will," he said brushed past her and out to the door. He opened it without looking back and walked down the steps.

She rushed to close it.

Outside, a black car pulled up and the man climb inside. He disappeared behind its tinted windows and the car sped away.

CHAPTER 29

The sky darkened as dusk approached, casting a grey pall over the town. Amy pulled out of the parking lot of the bar, pleased with herself for orchestrating Wade's arrest. Wade probably figured he'd get a slap on the wrist from law enforcement, get away with a two-year-sentence and be out in half the time for good behavior. Not when they had the box. He'd go away forever once the police pulled that little bomb out. Amy snorted, reaching down to turn up the air. Christ it was humid.

The questions they'd peppered her with after Wade's arrest left her a little disappointed. They hadn't once mentioned the box and she didn't want to bring it up in case he'd managed to turn it around. She didn't trust him. But really, how could he turn this around? Amy had peeked inside the box and its contents would put him away for a long time. That it implicated Thomas only made it sweeter. Thomas couldn't let Wade hang around for too long, not when he might slip and mention the Brotherhood. The cops could be very convincing and although Amy doubted Wade would rat, they couldn't be sure the pressure wouldn't get to him. Amy smiled as she stared out at the empty highway. Wade might last a week, perhaps even a month before the Brotherhood took care of him.

She'd already cleaned out the safe at the bar and their bank accounts, and wouldn't stick around much longer. Amy wasn't stupid. The Brotherhood would be after her once they put the puzzle together. When she arrived home, she'd grab her jew-elry, all the pretty little trinkets Wade had given her over the years to shut her up. God, he was stupid. She'd watched him set a few items in his safe in the den as well. She'd been careful not to tell the cops about those. She'd be able to disappear with her small fortune.

Pressing down on the accelerator as she left town, Amy sped past the few cars meandering down the main street. She drove past Tim Horton's and onto the highway, her heart rac-ing in anticipation. The prosecutor would definitely want to speak to her. When he did, she would tell him a whole ream of stories. She'd bury Wade and his spineless little bitch. A real woman would have known how to protect her man. If it were Amy, and if she gave a shit about Wade, she'd have taken the box and tossed it into the deepest darkest hole she could find. But Miss Pathetic couldn't handle the pressure. As soon as Wade put the damn thing in her hands, she'd sung like a fuck-ing canary. Amy almost felt sorry for Kristina—almost, but not quite. She deserved everything she had coming to her.

Approaching the junction where the main highway ended and the road leading to her home began Amy stepped on the brake and frowned. It felt stiff. She slammed her foot down to get the car to slow. "Fucking idiots," she muttered.

She'd taken the car in to the mechanic's the day before to make sure everything was in working order; not dumb enough to trust Wade's friends before leaving town. It would be just like them to mess with her car or something. Everything was fine, "in perfect condition," the guy said. He even filled the tank for her. Fuck, he probably hoped she'd be so pleased not to have to pump gas that she wouldn't notice he didn't know how to replace brake pads.

The highway was empty, not a car in either direction. Amy turned left, the address of the safe house the cops had arranged clear in her mind. She could hardly wait. Once Wade was con-victed, Carl had arranged a condo in Key West and would join her there within the month to celebrate her freedom. He made excuses about why he couldn't leave his douchebag wife, but

Amy no longer cared. Once she got out of this shit hole, she'd be getting rid of Carl too. She had enough of Wade's money, besides her private stash, to keep her until she found someone else. Carl was small potatoes; a pain in the ass really, with his over inflated ego and his loser wife. She could do better than Carl.

The sky had darkened to a deep inky blue. Amy couldn't see the moon if there was one, but stars dotted the dark expanse. Her mind filled with the fireflies she used to chase while camping as a child. A sense of triumph filled Amy's chest. She'd beaten him. Finally, after all the time she'd spent building up to this moment, she had ruined Wade. All he had, all he'd lied, cheated and killed for, was hers. Men were idiots.

Ahead, the road traced a slight bend, a section she hated because of the high jagged rock cuts along either side of it. She pressed the brake, her foot meeting some resistance before recalling the damn thing was stiff. Not that she had much to worry about; there was no one else on the road. She shifted her foot back to the gas pedal and absently tapped her finger on the steering wheel.

As she turned into the bend Amy eased off the gas just a little, but the car didn't slow. "Fucking pricks. What the hell?"

Amy muttered curses against inept mechanics and shifted her foot onto the brake pedal one more time. It resisted. Panic bubbled in her chest. She pumped the brake pedal, relief washing over her as the car finally slowed a fraction. To her right, the wall of rock loomed close. Amy jerked the wheel and drew in a deep breath when the car eased away from it. That was better.

Her gaze back to the road, she blinked to blinding lights directly in her path. She was on the right side, wasn't she? Suddenly disoriented, Amy did nothing to move from the incoming car's path. He had to see her, obviously. If she saw him, he'd see her and move over. She couldn't go anywhere, not with the rocks.

She contemplated waiting him out but her gut took over. As the last section of rock disappeared, her hands tightened on the wheel, swerving to the right and away from the lights.

Closing her eyes for a moment, Amy breathed a sigh of relief. She opened her eyes to peer in the rearview and frowned. Behind her, the car had pulled off the road. Why did he stop? Did he think she was going to pull over for a chat? He was fucking crazy, obviously. No woman in her right mind would pull over to talk to a strange man, a jackass who couldn't keep to his side of the road, although she'd have loved to give him a piece of her mind.

A bump sent her against the wheel. Amy grimaced, lowering her gaze to the road. A large tree loomed ahead.

"Shit," she breathed.

Amy braked, or she thought she did, but the tree kept coming. The car careened into the ditch toward the giant oak tree and Amy braced herself for the impact. The rocks and the fucking car lights had caused her to panic and lose control. All along, she should have worried about staying on the road. Everything moved as if in slow motion, even her thoughts. The car kissed the tree, glass shattered, and then everything went dark.

Thomas watched the impact and got out to lean against the hood of his car. The plan had been to run her off the road, but as he passed her and turned his car around, he realized she'd do the job for him.

When Amy's car bumped over the edge of the ditch, his pulse skyrocketed and his hands clenched. The screeching sound of metal folding against wood echoed in the still night, and a flash lit up the embankment.

Billy worried that if the plan didn't work, they'd have to pay Wade's wife a visit, but Thomas knew he could pull it off. Normally he'd give a job like this to a subordinate, but with so much riding on it being done right, he chose to do it himself. God, he missed this feeling. Blood pounded in his veins and his legs trembled just a little as adrenaline rushed through his body. From the moment Wade introduced her, he'd wanted to wring the skinny bitch's neck. Thomas knew a piece of shit when he saw one and could smell a liar a mile away. Amy was both.

He waited, his eyes on the road as he lit a cigarette and inhaled before blowing small rings into the air. Nothing moved at the site of the crash, but then he didn't expect anything to.

He hoped the front end hadn't crumpled too badly else it would be rather difficult to remove the strip of rubber his man had placed under her brake pedal. Wade said she'd keep driving. She did. The rubber caused just enough of a malfunction to make her panic. Again, as Wade said she would. Even if they couldn't remove it, Thomas wouldn't worry. His guy was long gone. If the cops discovered a piece of charred rubber they might question the shop, to find they got nowhere fast. Wade sat in jail, so his alibi would be solid.

The road remained silent, empty. Thomas tossed his cigarette away and pushed off the hood of his car. Time to fix the scene. He fished his keys from his pocket and pushed the button on the black remote. The trunk opened with a soft click. Thomas rounded the back of the vehicle and peered inside. After removing his gloves and cell phone from a black duffel bag, he paused to scan the road once more. It was as though Lady Justice were looking out for them, giving him ample time to ensure Amy kept her meeting with Maat. Smiling at the thought, Thomas walked to the crash site. Unhurried, he whistled as he approached. The car smoked, but only a small flame flickered beneath, near the driver's seat.

Mrs. Bowen never remembered to fill her tank but tonight the mechanic had gone to the station and filled it to the brim before she picked it up. Shame. Had she done her usual shit and left it for others to fill, she might have lived long enough for the ambulance to arrive. Her husband was in jail, thanks to her big mouth, but Karma was a funny thing.

He stopped next to the car and peered inside. The front had crumpled into nothing against the tree and the dash looked at least a good six inches too far back. Amy's head lay against the seat, a mess of blood and shards of glass.

He let out a low whistle. That wouldn't heal well. No, not at all. Far better to end it than to continue her life as a disfigured freak. Amy wouldn't like that. Her chest rose and fell in shallow breaths as though she had trouble getting air. The air bag had deployed, probably broken some ribs, and definitely her nose.

Thomas slipped his hands into the supple leather, his favorite pair of gloves worn smooth from years of use, then he knelt down to inspect the damage. Clear fluid trickled to the ground below, he wouldn't have to puncture the tank.

Eying the small flame at the front of the car, he frowned. He couldn't be sure the damn thing wouldn't blow before he finished. He didn't know where the small fire came from. Thomas moved to the front to check his friend's wife. Her eyelids flickered and his groin tightened. He hadn't counted on being able to speak to her.

This just gets better and better.

Thomas pulled at the door. It creaked on its bent hinges, opening just enough for him to lean over Amy's inert body and reach for the gas pedal. It was a bit of a struggle, but he managed to shift her foot and slip his hand under the brake pedal. When his fingers touched the edge of the rubber—a dangling strip left by his guy so it would be easy to pull off—he yanked. Thomas grunted in satisfaction as it pulled away. Straightening, he stepped back and closed the door. Amy stirred. Tucking the rubber into his pocket, he grinned down at her.

"Shit," she slurred.

He could tell by the sibilance in her voice that the poor girl no longer had most of her teeth. Part of him was tempted to let her live, to face the horror that was her once beautiful face, but no, Maat shouldn't be kept waiting.

"Can you move?" he asked, touching her shoulder.

"My legs...stuck." She didn't open her eyes.

He leaned closer so she could see him clearly when she did. "Look at me?"

Amy's eyes fluttered and she gazed around her for a moment, unfocused. She turned her head toward him, wincing in pain. "Help, please. Can't move my legs."

"I'd like to help you, Amy, but I can't." he smiled as her eyes focused on his face, lowering to his neck.

Recognition froze her features. "Thomas," she breathed.

"Yes, I hoped we'd get to say farewell, but I hadn't counted on being so lucky. You remember the last time we spoke, don't you?"

She gazed up at him, her mouth open but silent. Yes, she remembered, he could tell by the way her jaw clenched when she pressed her lips together. Thomas would never forget the last time he'd been so close to Amy Bowen. She'd just ruined his life, her big mouth taking apart all he'd built that was good and real.

"I remember," he said running a gloved finger down her cheek. "Diane left me the same day. Took my daughter and everything that meant anything to me and left. I was devastated."

"You lied."

"For her own good, but you didn't care about that, did you? No, you wanted to see me suffer because I wouldn't play your games. Wade just didn't see what you were. I did. When I told him he was pissed, wasn't he? Oh, I remember the way he'd lost it, actually punched me in the mouth for my kind words of warning."

"Fuck you." Amy's chin trembled.

For all her bravado she was scared. Thomas loved it.

"You wanted to, didn't you? Too bad my wife meant more to me than that. So did my friendship with Wade."

"A real man wouldn't have let her go."

"Really? I beg to differ. When you love something enough, you're willing to let it spread its wings. Diane is a good person, the most beautiful soul anyone will ever meet, and you were jealous of that. She couldn't live with what I was and I knew she couldn't. Forcing her to stay would have broken her soul and I loved her too much to do that. You know nothing about such things, given the black hole you have inside."

"This is stupid. Someone will see you." Amy shifted in the seat and gasped. "Please, I won't tell anyone."

"I'm supposed to believe that from you? I don't think so."

Thomas leaned forward and brushed his lips over hers, tasting her blood and smiling at the shiver that coursed through her and vibrated against his mouth.

"Farewell, Amy. I hope you rot in Hell."

He backed away from the car; the sound of her screams a sweet symphony to his ears. Reaching into his pocket, he pulled out a long slim barbeque lighter and clicked it a couple of times until a small flame glowed at the end. Thomas turned the dial. The flame danced and grew to a long flickering tongue. He walked to the back of her car, pausing when she dissolved from murderous screams to a pathetic whimper. Shaking his head, Thomas knelt next to the rear tire and tipped the flame into the moist earth behind it. For a moment only a faint spark caught the gas-soaked grass but slowly it grew, eating the gas as it licked across the ground and up toward the tank.

He backed away. The flame below lit up the belly of the small car, the one Wade had bought for Amy's thirtieth birthday, the one she had to have or else. As he edged toward his vehicle, he gazed at the blue-orange glow willing it to ignite the tank before he moved on to the final step. It danced along the underside of the vehicle, reaching around to caress the wheels and then the doors. A crack and then a hissing sound.

Amy's screams sounded again and grew and grew.

Thomas waved. "That's for me, and everyone else you've fucked."

The car ignited. Flames burst beneath and up over the crushed hood. Amy's voice drowned out by the sudden roar of fire that enveloped her. Thomas took the phone from his pocket and flipped it open, punching in the number he'd memorized. It rang three times and he hung up. The person on the other end, the one waiting outside the Mac's Milk store in Laighton, would call 911, and inform them of a crash on Highway 7. Too bad the call would be anonymous, and too late. The informant panicked and ran upon seeing the crash. Then, feeling guilty, he had stopped at a payphone and done the right thing. Odd though, the payphone the police would trace the call to—if in fact they managed to do that—would be wiped clean, the cleanest payphone on the damn planet.

Thomas flipped the phone around in his hand before letting it fall on the ground. A booted foot on top, he twisted his heel to a satisfying crunching sound. Bending over he picked up the mess of plastic and wires, slipped it into his pocket and walked to his car.

Flames lit the night sky as he eased onto the road, black smoke billowed up, disappearing into the darkness above. Thomas glanced in the rearview. Headlights flashed in the distance. He pressed his foot down on the gas.

RENÉE MILLER

CHAPTER 30

Several cars inched along ahead of Daniel's. He tapped the wheel as they moved forward and stopped again. Seething, he punched the button on the radio. The static in his favorite station wore on his already frayed nerves.

What the hell was wrong with people? He didn't understand how they managed to pack this particular section of the highway every single day. It didn't matter what time he left work, an hour early or an hour late, he managed to catch the snarl of traffic at the same time, just as his exit came into view. He'd considered taking the main road out of Salach, past the hospital to the highway and then driving through the Indian reservation to get to Laighton. God knows he would have saved a lot of time. But the damn road was covered in gravel and littered with ruts big enough to lose a small child in. The rocks never failed to scratch his truck. No way.

He hated that he had to go to Laighton in the first place, but that's where Carl kept the main office and he had to check in every goddamn day before going home. Their business was in Salach, even the showroom was there, and Daniel couldn't figure out why the stupid prick insisted on keeping anything in the shitty little town. Probably so his wife would have something to do that kept her out of his hair.

Large grey clouds rolled in as evening approached. It looked like it might rain, which pissed him off even more. Daniel hated driving in the rain, especially with all the fuckups on the road panicking because the roads were a little slick and increasing the risk one of them might slam into him.

He'd been stuck on the same twenty or so feet of highway for almost one hour. At this rate he wouldn't make it home until well after dark. Normally he didn't give a shit, but he hadn't been able to get Desiree on the phone all day. She'd had a doctor's appointment in the morning, to confirm what they already knew. She was pregnant. It shouldn't have taken all day. She didn't have the damn thing turned on; it went straight to voicemail each time he tried to call.

Running one hand over his face, Daniel leaned his head back on the seat and counted to ten, as they'd taught in the class he'd been forced to take after divorcing Kristina. He told them he didn't have an anger problem, he could deal with his emotions just as well as anyone. What was he doing right now? A man out of control would have jumped out of his car, walked up the road to figure out who was causing the delay and dealt with them. Not Daniel Riley. He patiently waited with the rest of the suckers, counting to ten and resisting the urge to break someone's nose.

They didn't understand the actions he'd taken when dealing with his ex-wife had nothing to do with anger. No one did, it seemed. It was about her refusal to see his way on things, and her determination to ruin what he'd worked hard to build. It was about showing her the way he expected her to behave. A smile tugged the edges of his lips and he rolled his window down, thinking of the last time he'd stopped by his old house. She learned a thing or two that day. At the time, he'd been frustrated because she didn't react as she always had—with apologies and pleas for mercy—but he figured she'd realized she had done wrong and he'd finally gotten through her thick skull.

Still, Daniel stayed away, allowing her time to think about things, to want to make amends. That she didn't call the cops said everything. She loved him, no matter what she said to the contrary. Kristina needed someone strong, someone not afraid to take charge, and that someone was him. Too bad Desiree got herself pregnant; it complicated things a little, but he saw no reason why he couldn't go back to his wife and take care of Desiree.

The car ahead moved forward more than just a few feet and Daniel let out a sigh of relief. Finally, whoever clogged the damn road had gotten their shit together. Probably some dickhead truck driver who couldn't stay awake. The line progressed faster until up ahead, about four cars from Daniel, blue lights flashed and two police officers peeked in windows before waving the vehicles through.

"Fucking cops and their drunk driving campaigns. Brilliant," Daniel grumbled.

What the hell did they think they'd find on a Wednesday evening? The cops seriously needed to find better ways to spend their time. Is this what his tax dollars paid for?

He inched forward. The cop in front glanced at his plates then spoke into the radio on his collar. Why were they calling in plates? Stolen car? Daniel tapped the wheel as the two cops conferred with each other. He pressed the gas lightly and attempted to follow the other cars out of the blockade but the cop closest to him, a fat pig who probably sat around all day eating donuts rather than catching criminals, held up his hand.

"Jesus," Daniel muttered and stopped.

Fat Cop walked to Daniel's car and leaned in the window, shining his light over the interior of the truck and then in Daniel's face.

"Problem?"

"License and registration please," the cop said.

Daniel reached up to the visor, pulled a little wallet down and handed it over. If he shined the light in his eyes one more time, he might give them a reason to take him in. Fucking jerk.

The cop walked away, Daniel's license in his hand and motioned for another cop to join him. Daniel slammed a fist on the wheel. *This is ridiculous.* They had no reason to treat him like this. His license was valid, he didn't get traffic tickets, and he'd certainly never stolen a car. His truck lit up from behind, blue and red flashed in the rearview and a sickening chill coated his gut. Two more cruisers pulled up behind him.

Kristina. Had she called the cops after all? Why not just go to his house? Of course, he had no known address, the apartment was listed in Desiree's name and he hadn't told Kristina where it was. But Carl knew. Why wouldn't they call his work if something was up? Carl would have given them the address and Desiree would have told them—Daniel paused. Unless...

"Miserable lying bitch," he cursed. Desiree had turned her phone off. Had they gone to his place after all? What did Kristina tell them?

The fat cop came back and opened Daniel's door. "Step out of the vehicle please."

"What's going on?"

"I said step out of the vehicle please, sir."

"Okay, I just don't understand what the problem is." Daniel climbed out of his seat and stood.

"Hands above your head."

Bitch. Daniel raised his hands, his gaze roaming over the scene before him. One cop leaned into his truck his flashlight searching the glove compartment, under the seats, and behind the visors. Two more spoke in hushed tones behind them, more than once they bent their heads to murmur into their radios.

The fat cop nudged Daniel to the side of the road and ran his hands down his sides and up his legs. Why were they searching him? "If you could just—"

"Mr. Riley, you have the right to remain silent," the cop recited his rights.

Daniel's mind reeled.

She really did it. The fucking slut had called the damn cops on him. When he was through with her, they'd have to call the morgue.

Three hours. Long, wasted hours where Daniel sat in the tiny room alone. Now and then, a cop would come in and offer him coffee, water, a smoke, but Daniel refused. They could get him a goddamn lawyer, that's what he wanted. They arrested him for murder, possession of something or other and drug trafficking. He'd told them how ridiculous all of it was and demanded to know where they'd gotten their information but they weren't forthcoming. If he agreed to an *interview* then they'd explain, but he'd asked for a lawyer. Until he talked, apparently they weren't offering him anything except beverages and cancer.

He'd called Carl after they booked him, but he was a blubbering mess. Something about Amy, Daniel stopped listening after Carl said he couldn't help him. After all he'd done for that man, when Daniel needed help the asshole didn't come through. Cheap bastard.

The steel door opened. Daniel looked up, his position relaxed, lounging in the uncomfortable chair. The table, a cheap Formica topped nightmare, filled most of the room. Shit, it couldn't really be called a room. They probably cleared out a broom closet or something.

"Mr. Riley?" a small man in blue suit asked.

Daniel nodded and prayed this was not his lawyer.

"I'm Timothy Chambers. I'll be your Duty Council for now. If you wish to retain your own attorney you may, but I'm under the impression you don't wish to proceed without representation and have not been able to secure your own."

"I can get my own lawyer. These pricks won't let me call anyone."

Timothy nodded, his curly black mop bouncing as he did so. He looked intelligent, and if Daniel didn't have to pay a lawyer for this bullshit it would be better. The small man opened his briefcase and pulled out a yellow legal pad and a pen. Also in the case was a file, which he opened and glanced through while biting his lower lip.

Daniel gritted his teeth and looked away. If he could stop that nasty habit then maybe he'd consider giving him some work. "So, what if I accept you as my lawyer? Do I have to pay you?"

"I work for the Crown, sort of. I provide free council to those who can't afford it otherwise. In cases like yours, I am sort of an emergency contact, here for you until you retain your own council. The government pays me in most cases. We'd straighten out the money issue before this goes to trial anyway."

"Okay, fine. Let's see what you can do."

"Good, shall we begin?" Timothy clicked his pen and sat down.

"First, I didn't do any of what they say I did. I know everyone says that, but I'm telling the truth. I don't even know where they got the idea I could kill someone."

"Possibly from the assault charges filed against you by your wife?" Timothy didn't look up as he spoke. Instead, he continued to read the documents in the file.

"Those were lies. She exaggerates."

"Hmm, there are pictures."

"Fuck off, I don't need you." Daniel crossed his arms and glared at Timothy, wondering how the idiot thought accusing him of this shit helped at all.

"I'm not against you, Mr. Riley but you have to be honest with me. If this goes to trial, and judging by the evidence it just might, I need to know what the Crown Attorney is going to pull out in order to build his case against you so I can defend you accordingly."

Timothy met his gaze, his face serious and calm, as though he were talking about the weather or something. The fluorescent light hanging over the table did nothing for his pasty complexion. His skin looked downright green. Daniel looked to the door. Two officers stood outside, probably listening to every word.

"Okay, we had some problems but we're working them out. I love Kristina very much."

"Indeed? Well, that's not for me to judge. The evidence they have was given to them by a friend of yours, an Amy Bowen. She claimed your ex-wife hid it for Wade Bowen, her husband. When questioned about it, your ex-wife claimed it belongs to you. It's a sordid mess, but your wife also led the police to believe you and Mrs. Bowen had an affair."

"What evidence?" Daniel couldn't imagine what she could have given them to justify these charges. Murder? Did she kill someone just to fuck him over? He snorted. The idea that Kristina could hurt anything was too much. She could barely wipe her own ass, let alone construct such a complicated plot to trap him. But Amy and Wade...

"Apparently there is a box containing evidence linking you to two murders, possibly more if they dig, and two illegal weapons. I have a list here." Timothy passed a paper to Daniel and waited.

Daniel read the list, his chest tightening as his eyes ran down the items. A finger? A fucking finger? Jesus Christ, where would Kristina get a finger? What the hell was happening?

"That's not my shit, none of it. I swear to God, it isn't mine. Amy gave it to them? Fuck, I haven't had anything to do with that slut in a while. Once, just once, I slept with her and that was enough. I don't know where either of them got this stuff but it is definitely not mine." His voice rose, and he knew he sounded hysterical. Hell he was hysterical.

Timothy nodded and took the page back, replacing it in his file. "So, here's what we do now. You need an alibi, at least three, the week of August 19, 2003, the week of December 12, 2005, and the last week of July this year. If you can give them this, then they will have little to discuss with you."

"I didn't do anything, so I hardly established alibis. Fuck, three whole weeks? Isn't it supposed to be a night or something? Can't they narrow it down a little?"

"Think on it for a bit. We can come back to it later."

"You're obviously misunderstanding me. How am I supposed to remember where I was for three fucking weeks? Two of them were more than five fucking years ago, for crying out loud. Who can remember what they did that long ago?" Daniel raked the fingers of one hand through his hair. Fuck, he could use Desiree, maybe. If they'd let him call her then he might be able to get something worked out. But he hadn't known Desiree for the first two dates. Shit.

Timothy cleared his throat and continued. "The police will question you. I advise you to answer the questions they ask, and only that. Don't elaborate, don't ramble, and above all remain calm. You tell them the truth and we'll work out the rest later. Answer the questions, and if they don't believe you that's fine. You don't have to convince them, you have to convince a jury."

"A jury? If I convince them then there won't be a jury."

"Mr. Riley, let's get one thing clear right now, so you don't feel I've let you down in any way. It is likely this will go to court. They have enough evidence to make it happen no matter what you say right now."

"I don't have much choice, do I? Fine, I'll answer their questions and I'll tell the truth because the truth is this is bullshit. I didn't kill anyone, I don't have any drugs, and I definitely don't own a weapon."

"Good, I'll let them know we're ready to proceed."

"Wait—why didn't they just come to my house or my work? Why the fancy roadblock?"

Timothy cleared his throat. "Apparently your wife... er, your current one, thought you might resort to violence and they didn't want to have a hostage situation."

Daniel felt sick. Desiree fucked him too?

Timothy walked to the door and waved. The cops opened it and filed in.

Thus began the nightmare, at the hands of the one person he would never have imagined would have the balls to do it.

CHAPTER 31

She stood on the edge of the cliff, watching the waves crash against the rocks below; caught on the wind white foam sprayed and misted her face. Kristina breathed in the scent of the ocean, tasted the salty air and smiled. The sky was a brilliant blue. In the distance a bird soared, turning in her direction. The gull neared and opened its beak, but it didn't make the cawing sound she expected, instead a shrill ring erupted from its throat.

Frowning, Kristina stepped forward and lost her footing, the grassy edge of the cliff crumbled away. Suddenly she was weightless, freefalling to the rocks below, the shrill ringing of the gull echoing in her ears.

The blue sky vanished and Kristina smelled potpourri, like the stuff she used to clean the carpets. The gull still rang... she paused and listened before sitting up and gazing around her. She had been dreaming. The gull hadn't been ringing. Her phone had, and still was.

She groaned and stood. Obviously, her drop had been off the couch where she'd fallen asleep last night and onto the floor. Rubbing her eyes she walked across the room to pick up the screaming phone, amazed Cadence hadn't woke as well.

"Hello," her voice sounded groggy even to her ears.

"Kris, you're still in bed. I'm so sorry," her mother sounded excited.

"It's okay. What time is it?"

"Just a bit after eight, I thought Cadence would have had you up long before now."

"She woke up for a while around midnight. She must have worn herself out."

"Well, at least you had more than just a couple of hours of rest. You need it."

"Yeah," Kristina stretched as she waited for her mother to share whatever it was that had her so riled up. She didn't often get worked up.

"I've got some bad news, and I didn't want you to go out and hear it somewhere else."

Kristina's breath caught, her throat suddenly dried and she waited. Something happened to Wade. Please don't let it be Wade.

"Amy had an accident last night." Her mother paused and Kristina nearly cried in relief. "She didn't make it, the car burned up and they couldn't even identify her without dental records."

"Oh no," Kristina breathed. She hadn't imagined Amy would ever die, just disappear. Although shocked, part of her rejoiced. Finally she could be with Wade, guilt free.

"I think after Wade got arrested those friends of his were on her. They aren't a nice bunch, you know, and she must have been trying to run, disappear so they couldn't get her."

"Why would they want to hurt her?" Kristina hated lying to her mother, even this little pretense felt wrong.

"Your dad said they think she's the one who sent Wade to jail, she went to the cops with some information or evidence. I mean, how else did she manage to stay out of jail too?"

Closing her eyes Kristina listened to her mother ramble on about the gossip. Her knees felt like rubber. She stumbled to the couch. Wade was okay, still in jail but okay. The one person who could have pointed the finger at both of them, ruining her story about Daniel, died in that car. How lucky was that? No, luck had nothing to do with it. A shiver shook her body and she paused, staring at the stained coffee table, her gaze traveling over the scars and coffee rings that littered the top.

Kristina recalled the day she sat in the same spot—the box on the same table—and learned things about Wade she never imagined. Had Wade's friends caused the crash? Of course they had.

She blinked when her mother's voice continued, "there wasn't even a problem with the car. She was going too fast, must have looked away for a minute and slammed into the tree. They said she might have lived if it hadn't caught fire."

"How could they know that?"

"Someone told your dad they heard there was smoke in her lungs. She died from smoke inhalation, not the crash. Terrible."

"Hey, I gotta go, Mom. Can I call you later?" Kristina could barely speak.

"Sure honey, Dad and I are going to Salach to do some shopping later. You'll be okay?"

"Oh, I'm fine. It is really sad, but I wasn't ever very close to Amy. I'm shaken up, I mean to know it happened here, in Laighton, but I'll be okay."

"No, I can't believe it either. Hopefully it was all just an accident like the police said. You get some rest and we'll talk later."

Kristina set the phone down and put her face in her trembling hands. She should feel guilty or horrified; something other than excited. But she wasn't. She was thrilled about the future, about Wade and about eliminating something standing in the way of all of that. Even if Wade had orchestrated Amy's accident, she didn't care. Amy got what she deserved. A woman should never plot against her husband, not when he is as kind and sweet as Wade. He could have gotten rid of her long ago but a sense of loyalty and his innate goodness wouldn't let him do it. She'd drawn first blood by going to the cops. He drew last.

Cadence cried. Kristina pulled herself together, shaking away her unsettling thoughts. She had only one more obstacle. Daniel.

The ringing of the phone startled Kristina, loosening her fingers and causing her to drop the pan she'd been carrying to the sink. She growled, glaring at the greasy mess on the kitchen floor. Never in her life had the damn thing rung so often as it had since she left Daniel. That would have been fine, if the calls didn't usually herald bad news.

Cadence played in the living room, seated in her bouncy chair while Barney sang his stupid love song. He sounded just a little maniacal, as though the purple beast knew he drove parents bonkers with his annoying and flamboyant personality.

She rushed to the living room. "Hello?"

"Kris? How are you?" Michael, Daniel's brother. He sounded upset.

"Good, I'm good. You?"

Silence and then a shaky breath before Michael continued, "To be honest, I've been better. Have you seen the news?"

Kristina's gaze went to the TV screen, the purple blob bounced across while a gaggle of kids followed behind him cheering. "No, I don't watch much TV. Why?"

"Dan's been arrested for murder and a bunch of other shit. It's not looking good."

She curled her lips in a smile and took deep breaths to calm herself. The bastard would finally pay and it was her hand that had hammered the first nails into his coffin. If she could, she'd be the one to make sure the damn thing stayed sealed for eternity.

"Are you still there?" Michael asked.

"What? Oh, yes I'm sorry. This is so shocking. What happened?"

"I don't know. They won't let me talk to him. He's been crazy since they locked him up and now they've got him separated from the other inmates and he's not allowed seeing anyone but his lawyer."

"Oh." She hadn't imagined he'd react like this. Daniel usually turned on the charm in situations that involved his own ass. She never expected him to act like a maniac. How perfect was that?

"You knew he was with someone, right?" he asked.

"Yes, but I didn't know her." Lies, more lies.

"Did you know they were married a couple of weeks ago? She's pregnant."

Floored, Kristina sat on the edge of the coffee table and digested this information. She shouldn't care, but couldn't help the sickening pain that burned her chest. A couple of weeks ago, Daniel had visited her, raped her and accused her of all sorts of things. He even claimed to love her while he did it. He should have been on his honeymoon, with his new pregnant wife.

Kristina glanced at her reflection in the darkened window, her eyes were moist, her face pale. It felt like a betrayal, but she didn't understand why. She hated him, that's what she had to remember. He betrayed her and Desiree. Now she'd see he paid the ultimate price. "I knew they were engaged, but I haven't seen him in a while."

"Oh, well you guys weren't meant for each other anyway, both of you are better off."

"I know."

"The cops questioned her and she told them he beat her. I just can't believe it."

Was he serious? Kristina had really liked Michael, missed seeing him since she'd divorced Daniel but this was the side of him that frustrated her. She'd told him several times about Daniel and how he 'trained' her to be the perfect wife, but Michael refused to believe his baby brother could do anything so horrible. Kristina gave up trying to convince him.

"The things she said," Michael voice broke. "That he locked her in a room—kicked her and punched her—I'm just so shocked. Did he do that to you? Did he really hurt you like that?"

"Michael, I've told you this before. He hurt me daily, for infractions like turning on the vacuum when he was trying to hear the TV, and I was terrified. I should have left sooner but I was so scared."

"I'm sorry I didn't believe you. It's just not like him, when we were kids he was such a goofy sweet guy. He never got mad."

"Well he changed." She wouldn't get into this discussion and refused to imagine Daniel as a boy, with so much promise within him. Thinking like that is what made her stay for so long, she could see the boy in his eyes, and longed to make him emerge, to stifle the other one; the evil and hateful one.

"Dan says he's innocent though, that's what the news said. I managed to get his lawyer to fill me in a little, and he thinks it's definitely a setup."

Her heart pounded and blood roared in her ears. Shit, the lawyer could ruin it all. If she hoped to bury Daniel she had to convince his own brother of his guilt. If she couldn't do that, how would she convince a jury?

"I didn't want to tell you this because I value your friendship and I'd hate to lose that." She paused, taking a breath. "But I might be the reason they arrested him. I don't know, but I had to tell them. I'm sorry."

"Tell them what? You're not making any sense. If he's done something then I need to know, I won't hate you for telling me the truth, Kristina."

She almost laughed. The truth was something that hadn't left her lips in a while. "I found a box in the basement, one he left here after we separated. I told him to take it several times and he said to just leave it, he'd get it when he could. He forbade me to look inside, and one day I just got curious. I saw a knife and closed it. I didn't look at anything else, so I can't tell you what else was in there."

"Shit," Michael drew a ragged breath.

He'd bought it.

"I didn't give it to them, though. I wouldn't do that. He's Cadence's dad, I don't want him in jail. Someone took it and I don't know who or how or why, just that someone broke into my house and took it and they gave it to the police."

"Someone broke into your house?"

"Yes, and I didn't report it because Daniel had done it before to scare me, and that's what I thought happened. I didn't even look for the box until the police called me."

Michael cursed and Kristina let silence fill the line.

The phone sounded muffled for a moment. *Is someone else listening to this conversation?* When the noise cleared, Kristina pushed ahead more determined than ever "they told me they'd arrest me for it and I'd lose Cadence. I didn't want to tell them."

"I believe you, and he should never have put you in such a position. He's not a man. He's a coward."

Her heart soared.

Cadence cried from her chair. "Up!"

Kristina stood and walked to her daughter, bending to pick her up while Michael digested all she'd fed him. Cadence grabbed at the phone, her gaze intent on the power light on it. "No." Kristina pulled back, so her clutching fingers couldn't reach the phone.

"What?"

"Not you, Michael. Cadence keeps trying to take the phone."

"She must be so big," his voice broke again.

"She is. You should come by and see her some time."

"I should, instead of being such a shitty uncle. You're sure you don't mind?"

"Not at all. I'd love to see you, and so would Cadence."

"I will and you do what you have to do. Hear me?"

Kristina pressed her lips together before answering, he was a good man and she despised lying to him, but it had to be done. He couldn't see what his brother was before. Daniel was a monster. This would save him some heartache later. It was just a matter of time before Daniel did kill someone and her lies might have saved that girl. "Yes, I hear you."

"He's a big boy, and he's done some terrible things. He should pay the consequences."

"Yes he should."

RENÉE MILLER

CHAPTER 32

Shivering as the cool breeze that had taken over the once pleasant evening chilled her to the bone, Kristina tucked her chin into her coat. Dinner at her parents had been an ordeal. She'd never lied to them before and each lie that passed her lips made her feel further away from them. Telling herself she had to do it, and she couldn't drag them into her mess, made her feel a little better.

The clanking sound of a pop can rolling across the pavement sent the hair on her neck on end. She glanced up. Her body tensed when a man crossed the street by the post office, about ten feet from her. She resisted the urge to turn back and take the long way down the main street home. Instead she continued toward Colborne Street, one of the darkest in town. Only a few streetlights blessed it with illumination.

The man, tall and built like a linebacker if the way his jacket hugged his shoulders was anything to go by, turned right at the funeral home. She breathed a sigh of relief. She hated walking alone at night. Since the attack she'd avoided it. But her dad drank far too much at dinner to drive her and she hadn't told them about the incident, hadn't wanted to worry them. Her mom demanded she leave Cadence for the night. Kristina had left alone.

A sense of exhilaration filled her at her little show of bravery. The stranger hadn't forced her to take the long way home as his presence would have only yesterday. It made her feel strong, as though she'd reached another milestone in her journey to becoming independent. She turned left, toward the green bridge and home. If she had a life, Kristina might have called up a friend and gone out, but she didn't want to. Besides, with Wade in jail and Amy dead, Dirty Truths had been closed. What did the regulars do when the only watering hole in town closed? Kristina smiled at the thought. The Beer Store would be doing a booming business.

She'd been so wrapped up in her thoughts she didn't notice him until he fell into step beside her. Kristina opened her mouth to scream, but his hand slapped over her face before she could utter a sound. She trembled in fear, her eyes burning with tears. It took her a moment to realize who it was before her. The stranger.

"We need to talk," he said.

Kristina nodded.

He smiled and relaxed the hand clutching her hair, but didn't remove the other from her mouth. "First, promise not to scream. You do, you're in that river... after I snap your neck."

Her gaze darted to the water, settling on the falls rushing down into a shallow but rocky bed below. Kristina hated this part of the river, had hated it since going over the falls as a child. The bottom, where the water was shallow and safe, didn't bother her but the rushing flow over the falls always made her nervous. His threat would have been enough to silence her even without the added terror of having her neck broken.

He moved his hand from her mouth and lowered it to her back, then he nudged her toward the bridge.

Kristina obeyed, not wanting to anger him until they moved far enough so the water wouldn't be an option.

"You've been a busy girl. I'm impressed," he said.

Kristina glanced up, and relaxed a little when she caught the grin on his face. His dark eyes had softened. The coolness she'd seen in his previous visits had vanished, replaced by a friendly warmth. She stumbled as they came to the end of the bridge and her foot hit the curb that separated the boards from the road. Catching herself, she turned as they continued across the road to her house. She risked a smile. "Is that all you came to say?"

"No, but I don't think it's wise to discuss what I have to say out here, where anyone can hear us. It's about a mutual friend, one who saved me from making a huge mistake the last time we spoke. I'm sorry I misjudged you."

They'd reached the end of her driveway and Kristina considered running, but her gut told her she had nothing to fear from this man. Something in his eyes as he grinned, the way she didn't shudder when his hand pressed against her back. If Wade trusted him, then she would.

She pulled her key out of her coat and led him to the door. Inserting it in the lock, she fumbled with the simple effort as she remembered the last time a man stood watching her open it.

"I won't bite," the stranger said.

Kristina glanced back. The top of his bald head reflected the glow of the streetlight and the glare shadowed his features. "I didn't think you would."

She took a breath to calm herself, forcing the memory of Wade's mouth on hers, the warmth of his tongue as he licked her finger, from her mind. Kristina opened the door. The stranger walked in. In her mind, her mother's voice reprimanded her for being so stupid. Despite the certainty she wasn't in any danger with this man, she offered up a silent prayer.

He'd switched the kitchen light on but as she entered, he was nowhere to be seen. Her gaze darted to the darkened living room and a flutter of dismay tickled her stomach. Brave or not, she wasn't going into a dark room with him. Relief made her dizzy when the living room flooded with light.

He moved to the center of the room, an eyebrow raised in question.

Kristina walked toward him and stopped near the television, a few feet away from where he stood.

"You'll testify?" he asked.

"About what?"

The stranger reached to touch the picture of Cadence that hung on the wall next to the stairs. He ran a finger over her face, and a sad smile played on his lips. "I have a daughter."

"Really, you don't seem the fatherly type."

"There's a type? Your Daniel is a father. You'd call him a fatherly type?" Lowering his arm he turned to look at her, his eyes cold once more.

"No, I suppose not. I just don't see you with a child. But I don't know you either, aside from the fact that you like barging into strange women's homes and your grandmother is from Egypt."

He smiled and stuffed his hands in the pockets of his coat. "True. I meant Daniel. You'll help bury him? Make sure he takes the wrap?"

"Of course, he's guilty, isn't he?"

The man's gaze held hers for a moment before nodding.

Was that respect in his eyes? Kristina looked away first, turning to remove her coat and set her purse on the coffee table. "Is that all?"

"We'll help make sure he goes under, but you'll have to disappear. In my experience, if you stick around people you know, things have a way of coming out; things you think you can keep to yourself. There's also the little problem of some friends of ours who aren't exactly friendly. They know about you, and that's not good. The Brotherhood has decided it would be best for all of us if you take a holiday."

"I can't leave. People will think I'm hiding. I have no reason to hide." Goosebumps erupted over her skin, and she recognized the rolling sensation in her stomach as panic threatened to overwhelm her.

She couldn't disappear; her parents would be terrified. And what about Cadence? She couldn't take their granddaughter away from them. No, she'd testify against Daniel and everything would be fine. She could keep a secret. Hadn't she covered what Daniel was so well that when she asked for help, no one believed her?

"You need to be realistic, sweetheart." He advanced slowly.

The nearness of his body when he stopped made Kristina uncomfortable. "I am being realistic. I have a child and my family is here. I can't take her away from them. They'd never understand."

"We'll figure out something. Your dad has proven very loyal to Wade. I think we could let him in on some of it."

Let her dad in? No way. "No. Absolutely not. My parents can't know anything about what's going on here."

"We'll work it out, as I said. Look, you can go anywhere you want and the Brothers will make sure you're looked after. Money, a house, you name it and it's yours. You scratched our backs and we'll scratch yours. You can tell people whatever you want. I don't care. But the important thing, the thing that should make you want to do this, is you can take your daughter and start over again. Forget all of this. After a decent amount of time, you can let your mom and dad know where you are and sort of hide in the open. You don't have to disappear forever."

Kristina chewed her lip, wondering if he really gave her a choice. If she refused, what would he do? Kill her too? Her gaze moved to his neck, to the tattoo representing justice, his justice. He would do what he felt he had to.

"And Wade? I won't leave him."

The stranger studied her for a moment then nodded. "He'll have to do a couple of years at least. They don't let you off light for possession and trafficking you know. But I'm sure he'd find you, wherever you went. Do you want to be found?"

"Yes, that's the only reason I've done all of this. If not for Wade I wouldn't have lied to anyone."

"You love him?"

"More than you could ever understand."

"I doubt that."

The man turned, walking past her to the back door. Without looking back, he left.

Kristina stood staring at the empty room, her heart aching

for the sorrow she glimpsed in his dark eyes. Not everyone was as lucky as she'd been. She hadn't considered that. Maybe the stranger had a reason for his moody darkness beyond the *coolness* factor. After all, everyone had a story.

CHAPTER 33

The room hummed with excited murmurs, conspiratorial whispers and the annoying buzz of fluorescent lights.

As the Crown Attorney called her name, Kristina rose.

Richard Long, a man in his fifties who looked remarkably well preserved—though she would lay a bet Grecian Formula and Botox helped him along—smiled.

She smoothed her skirt, a soft black A-line that fell demurely to her knees, and composed her thoughts. Kristina walked to the front of the room, ignoring the stares of reporters and locals from Laighton who had traveled to see the trial. Only a few managed to get in, the media filled most of the seats. Daniel's brother and friends occupied the entire row behind the defense table. Desiree was noticeably absent.

She stepped up into the little box next to the judge and raised her right hand as the bailiff instructed. After swearing in, she sat in the chair, surprised at its comfort but unable to relax into it as she was sure the manufacturer intended.

"State your name for the court please," Richard instructed.

"Kristina Lynn Riley."

"Thank you, and do you know the defendant?"

"Yes."

"How do you know him?"

"He's my ex-husband."

The crowd murmured again and Kristina fought to keep her gaze on the lawyer as instructed. She knew the questions he'd ask, most of them anyway, but a lump formed in her throat.

"We have a statement from you where you claim a box which was brought to the attention of authorities recently was left at your house by your ex-husband, Daniel Riley. Is this correct?"

"Yes." Kristina's gaze moved to Daniel.

He stared, his mouth pressed in a firm line, his lawyer reached over to place a hand on his arm. Daniel shrugged him off.

Richard passed copies of Kristina's statement to the judge and then to her. He read it over, adjusting his glasses on his rather large, red nose. She averted her gaze to the paper in her hands and waited for the next questions. A shuffling from the prosecution's table brought her eyes up to see what was happening.

A long table sat in front. Richard pulled various items from a bin beneath, laying them on the table next to yellow cards. Her breath caught as Kristina recognized many of the items. He pulled out a few things she hadn't seen before. Her gaze fell on a bloody shirt and tarp. Amy must have added to it. She turned her gaze to Daniel.

He frowned, raised an eyebrow and then looked at the items as well.

She wanted him to look scared, to know she'd done this to pay him back for all he'd put her through; the abuse, the misery and for nearly shattering her soul.

He didn't seem very worried, leaning over to whisper something to his attorney, a smile playing on his lips.

Richard walked toward Kristina. She forced herself to look away from Daniel.

"Do you recognize any of these items?" he asked, waving toward the table.

"The box."

"The box? How do you recognize the box?"

"That's the box Daniel told me to leave alone. He said he'd pick it up later."

"You lying fucking bitch!" the courtroom erupted as Daniel sprang from his chair.

Two police officers swept down on him, pulled his arms behind his back and forced him to sit back in his chair.

"Mr. Riley," the judge's deep voice carried over the noise of the crowd. "One more outburst and you will be held in contempt."

"But she's lying—"

"Mrs. Riley has sworn an oath, and she has the right to speak. If you'd like to counter any of her statements or prove your claims, then you will have an opportunity to do so. But until then you will let her answer the questions without comment. Are we clear?"

Daniel nodded, his face reddened. His brown eyes blazed with hatred and although her initial reaction to his outburst was fear, it quickly changed to satisfaction. He would not get out of this, if it was the last thing she did.

Richard waited for silence and continued his questions. Kristina answered each one, keeping her eyes on him, only meeting Daniel's gaze when she answered questions about him.

The judge motioned for Daniel's attorney to proceed with his cross-examination.

Kristina stiffened.

Richard had warned the defense would try to tear apart her testimony and stressed she must keep to the facts, an easy thing to do when speaking the truth. The trouble was, Kristina lied through her teeth and she trembled just a little when Daniel's lawyer approached her.

"We've established your story about the box," he said and paused, running a thumb over his chin. "But I'm wondering why it is you didn't turn it in to police."

"I didn't know what was in it."

"You didn't look?"

"I did, but I saw the knife and I closed it without looking at the rest. I didn't want to know what else was in there." Kristina twisted her hands in her lap.

Daniel's attorney walked to the defense table and flipped

through his notepad.

She wished he'd just ask his damn questions and let her go.

"Okay, let me tell you a little story, if the court will allow it?" He looked at the judge who nodded. "This box was brought to the attention of law enforcement officials by an Amy Bowen, is that right?"

"I don't know—I think that's what they told me. I don't recall." She tried to remember the discussion she'd had with the police, but couldn't.

"It was. She claimed you told an unnamed friend of hers the box was left by her husband, Wade Bowen who, I'd like to add, is already imprisoned on charges of drug trafficking and possession of illegal weapons. Isn't it true you and this Wade Bowen were having an affair?"

"Objection! Irrelevant, your honor." Richard stood, his face flushed.

The judge looked to the Defense, raising an eyebrow.

"I'm hoping to show Mrs. Riley has reason to lie about the box."

"I'll allow it, but be careful. You're treading a thin line here."

Richard sat as the judge spoke and Kristina swallowed as her throat went dry.

Daniel's attorney continued. "Could you answer the question please?"

"No, I did not have an affair with Wade Bowen."

"In your statement you said you and Wade did sleep together."

"It wasn't an affair. It was a couple of times and that's all. I explained what happened to the police."

"Interesting. His wife's statement claims you did and you confessed the two of you were in love."

"She lied."

"Well, considering she's not around any longer to confirm or deny that accusation, I guess we'll have to let it rest."

"Please stick to the questions, Mr. Chambers," the judge admonished.

Running a hand through his dark curls, which sprang back into place immediately after, Daniel's attorney continued, although Kristina thought he looked frustrated, unable to find a way to trap her.

"Why did you tell Amy Bowen her husband left the box at your house if it in fact belonged to your ex-husband, Mr. Riley?"

"I didn't tell her anything. I didn't speak with her about any box. She must have been confused." Kristina clenched her teeth. Did he not understand English?

"Oh, yes… the unnamed friend. Who may that be, I wonder? Care to enlighten us?

"I don't know. I might have mentioned it to a few friends but… I was going through a difficult patch. I was scared, hurt…"

"Hurt, Mrs. Riley?"

She turned her gaze to Daniel.

"He raped me—"

"Objection! Your honor." Daniel's lawyer turned to the judge.

"But… he asked…m—"

The judge nodded. "That he did." He then turned to the jury. "The witness's allegations fall outside the matters tried in this court. You will disregard her last statement."

For another thirty minutes, Daniel's lawyer battered her with the same questions, wording them differently each time, but Kristina stuck to her story. He didn't mention the abuse, or that Desiree had also claimed to be fearful of him, but relentlessly pursued his questioning of Wade and their relationship.

At 12:45, the Defense finally rested.

Kristina collapsed in her chair when the judge called a break. She left the stand, careful to keep her chin high as she passed Daniel. Her eyes remained on the large doors at the end of the room. Cameras flashed as she walked through. She lowered her head and forced her way through the crush of people and media swarming the hallways of the courthouse. Shocked at the attention the case was getting, the stranger's words came back to her. *If you stick around people you know, things have a way of coming out; things you think you can keep to yourself.*

As Kristina opened the doors, blinking at the brilliant sunshine that blinded her, she realized why he advised her to disappear. If Daniel was convicted—when Daniel was convicted, she corrected—the media would go into a tailspin. They'd nag her as much as they did now, possibly more. She couldn't remain in Laighton, not if she wanted any sense of normalcy for Cadence, and definitely not if she hoped to be with Wade. They'd jump all over that.

The room buzzed with activity, every bench packed with people.

Kristina sat behind the Crown Attorney's table, her emotions in turmoil. She feared they'd let Daniel go and yet she felt vaguely worried they wouldn't. All week she'd flip-flopped through extremes, one minute hating him and confident she'd done the right thing, the next uncertain she could live with the guilt of what she'd done.

The doors to the court opened and Daniel entered escorted by two police officers. He wore a dark grey suit, his blond hair freshly cut and his face clean-shaven. He turned to look at her before he sat down, a smirk playing on his lips. He winked.

Kristina frowned. The bastard actually believed they wouldn't convict him. His arrogance astounded her even after all he'd put her through.

A shuffling behind. She turned. The stranger sat two rows back to her right. No longer in his regular leather jacket and jeans, he wore a black turtleneck sweater and dress pants.

His gaze met Kristina's. He nodded.

She turned back to face the front as the bailiff ordered everyone to rise. Standing, she wondered if he had been there for her testimony. She didn't remember seeing him, but then, she'd avoided looking out into the sea of faces that witnessed

Daniel's attorney try to paint her as a vindictive slut. Was he pleased with her testimony? Did she screw it up? Ice coated her gut as another thought occurred to her. Was he there to 'take care of her' if Daniel got off?

As the judge entered and took his place at the front, he ordered the court to be seated. He motioned to the bailiff who walked to the far side of the room and opened a small door to allow the jury back into the room. The men and women who Kristina had carefully avoided looking at until now filed in and took their seats. She gazed at them, each face unreadable and wondered what they thought about her testimony. Did they believe her?

Her eyes paused on a face in the small group. Blood drained from her cheeks and a chill shook her frame. The man Wade spoke to months ago in the bar, the one that made her so nervous and who Wade seemed to be afraid of, stared back at her. The judge spoke, but Kristina heard none of what he said, her gaze riveted on this man who until now she'd forgotten. Blood roared in her ears and the room swayed. They'd had the jury fixed all along. Why hadn't they told her?

The man stood, held out a piece of paper and passed it to the bailiff. Was he the foreman? Kristina suddenly felt giddy, almost to the point of laughter. The stranger told her they'd help see that Daniel went down, but she never imagined they had this much power. She resisted the urge to turn and look at him, although it took great effort. Instead, she leaned forward. Her breath caught in her throat as the judge asked the jury to read its verdict.

A hush fell over the courtroom.

She glanced at Daniel who stood next to his lawyer waiting to hear his fate.

He didn't look at the jury though, his gaze rested firmly on Kristina, the smile still teasing his lips.

She looked away, focusing on the words of the foreman as he read off the charges and then their verdict.

"Guilty."

"What?" Daniel asked.

The judge turned to him and frowned.

Kristina heard the word over and over and then the room erupted once more. She turned to Daniel slumped in his chair shaking his head, his eyes wide.

The judge ordered him to stand and his lawyer touched his shoulder.

Daniel rose, turning to pin his accusing glare on her.

She listened as the judge made the verdict official and reminded the courtroom that sentencing would convene in the morning.

The officers pulled Daniel's hands behind his back and cuffed him.

Kristina dreamed she heard the satisfying click over the hum of voices.

His eyes darted around, coming to rest on her face as she stood to watch them escort him out. He shook his head. The realization he hadn't gotten his way and she'd been the one to ruin him, was evident in his eyes and the way his shoulders slumped. "Why?" he mouthed as they pulled him to the door.

Kristina smiled, and shrugged. She placed a hand to her mouth and blew a kiss as he stumbled to the door and then turned to smile at the stranger. After scanning the seats behind her, she couldn't find him. When had he left?

The Crown Attorney spoke.

Kristina turned.

His hand outstretched, clasping hers, he smiled. She returned the smile, still reeling over what had happened and allowed him to lead her out of the room.

Daniel would never be able to hurt her again, the knowledge lifted a weight from her shoulders that until now, she hadn't realized was there. She'd done it, he would rot in jail for those murders and she'd been the one to put him there. She murmured a saying she'd heard often, though it hadn't held much meaning until this moment. "An eye for an eye."

"Pardon?" Richard asked, pushing the doors open and placing a hand on her arm.

"Nothing," she smiled.

CHAPTER 34

The steel door opened and Daniel straightened.

She walked through, hesitant at first, the guard behind her.

He stood, wishing the damn cuffs didn't restrain his hands so he could wring her neck.

She moved forward and sat in the chair, the guard stayed by the door.

"Kristina, nice of you to come."

"You wouldn't stop calling, so I really had no choice." She smiled.

His gut hardened. She thought she'd get away with this. "I'll be out soon," he said.

"No, you won't."

"I've filed an appeal and the judge will have to look at the evidence again. It's bullshit and they know it."

"Hmm. Maybe. But you have to make it out of here first. Don't you?"

Daniel stared. Was this his wife, his Kristina, threatening him? How did she figure she could hurt him in here?

"I'll make it out. Don't you worry. You better be ready too, you've got some explaining to do if you want to keep your pretty face."

"Are you threatening me, Daniel?" her voice rose and the guard turned, hand on his belt.

"No, I'm not." He smiled at the guard who relaxed a fraction.

"Listen, I don't have time for your usual crap, okay. I have a child to raise and a life to go on with. You've said all you had to say to the media. Loved the tears in your last interview. Priceless. But if you have nothing new to say to me, this is goodbye." Kristina stood.

He gritted his teeth to keep from screaming. Cocky little slut. She thought she had it all figured out. He'd relish every minute of his revenge. She'd be begging him for mercy when the light went from her eyes. He'd fuck her the way she fucked him and then he'd kill her with his bare hands.

"We're going to miss you so much," Kristina's mother choked as she hugged her close. "Call us as soon as you land, okay?"

"I will, and you guys are coming out next month, remember?"

Her mother nodded and picked up Cadence, squeezing her until the baby grunted in protest.

She wished she could have stayed, that her life didn't have to be turned upside down, but the reality was she couldn't. After Daniel's conviction she couldn't even go out to cut the grass without someone stopping or flashing a camera. The stranger, whose name she knew now to be Thomas, had arranged for her to relocate to Mexico. Not a bad place to hide out.

"I wish those pricks would just leave you alone," her dad muttered.

Sunlight streaming in through the large windows opening onto the airport runways behind him cast shadows over his sullen features. He had aged in the past few months, but the worry that clouded his features for years had vanished and Kristina was glad to see it gone.

"It's their job, Dad, and Daniel's been giving so many interviews that they expect me to do the same. Don't worry. It will die down. I'm just lucky I got this job offer."

"Don't you think it's kind of strange someone would offer you a job out of the blue like this? Someone who doesn't even know you?" her mother frowned, adjusting Cadence onto her hip.

"I checked it out, and they really are just nice, honest people who felt sorry for us. Besides, a housekeeper is not an illustrious position."

"But you'll have your own house and—"

"It's a cottage, and I'll be fine. It's not forever." Kristina reached to take her daughter and kiss her mother's head.

A tinny voice announced her flight. She hugged her parents one more time before joining the crowd that milled about the gate. Wade had called her several times from jail, urging her to take whatever offers came her way; his way of telling her that this job wasn't really what she told her parents it was. She would have a little cottage to live in, and work cleaning a house for a while. The Brothers had arranged it all, and she didn't think too long over just how far their power reached. Once Wade was released, in two more years—if Thomas was right about good behavior and his early release—they'd move again.

The line shifted and Kristina looked back to her parents who stood together, her father's arm draped over her mother's shoulder as they waved. Her mother wiped a tear on the collar of her bulky old jacket and her dad shook his head. Kristina had bought her a new one, an early Christmas gift, but her mom hadn't worn it yet, preferring the quilted pink coat she'd worn for years. Her mom hated change. Kristina used to, but now she welcomed it.

She waved back and turned, blinking away the tears that filled her eyes. She'd miss them terribly but it was time she stood on her own, made a life she could be proud of and Cadence would be happy with. A life that included a passionate love and devotion she'd never known. Until Wade.

Daniel lay on the cot, his back to the cell doors and he stared at the hole the previous tenant chipped into the grey wall. Two months he'd sat in this damn cell. Alone. Sixty days without anything but this sorry excuse for a bed, a toilet that rarely flushed, and a tiny window to let in the sunlight. He was only allowed out onto a tiny patio for thirty minutes each day.

He supposed he should be thankful they hadn't let him in with the rest of the prisoners. Bunch of losers. He'd made enough stink his first week they stuck him here. Isolation, they called it. Although, his new attorney warned him if he wanted the judge to see things his way, he had to start showing he wasn't a murderer; that he really was a nice guy.

This afternoon he went back to the regular population, with the real murderers and crack heads. Daniel didn't look forward to that, but he figured if he kept his head down and avoided too much contact they'd leave him alone.

Fucking bitches. Both of them, Desiree and Kristina, turned on him and after all he'd done to make them what they were today. He'd improved their position in life, supported them financially, and taught them what made a good woman.

His new lawyer, one who could scratch his own ass and try a case, would see he got out of this hole. They'd appealed immediately after the last disaster. Daniel awaited an answer from the Superior court. He'd blow the bitch out of the water when they freed him. She'd pay for all of the time he wasted in this shithole. When he was finished, then he really would be guilty of murder, but he didn't intend to get caught.

Keys jingled outside his cell. Daniel rolled over and sat up. It was time to go. He hoped they had better control over the rat population in the main block of cells. Up here, the damn things had formed an army, one that preferred to come out in the cover of darkness and jump on his bed. The first night he recalled the guard's chuckles when he'd freaked out. He didn't allow them to enjoy the spectacle again. Instead, they found a special treat in the mornings if Daniel caught the little bastards. Snapping a rat's neck was pretty easy, as long as the fucker didn't bite you first.

"Come on, Riley. Time to meet your new roommate."

The fat one, Solmes, opened his cell and stood back. Daniel rose and stepped through the open door. "So, who's my new roommate?"

"Not sure. I just move you. I don't make the room assignments."

He nudged Daniel's shoulder. They walked through the security door at the end of the long hallway and down the stairs to another security door. In there, they handed him new bedding and pushed him through once more.

As he passed the cells, he kept his eyes trained forward, refusing to acknowledge the idiots who taunted him. Catcalls and jeers echoed across the cement walls, "fresh meat" and "sweet cheeks" the most disturbing of them all.

A couple of guards stood near the far end, on either side of an open cell. They paused just before it. Daniel turned while Solmes walked inside and did whatever it was he felt necessary to do in there. He ignored a clicking to his left. Some prick trying to get his attention, probably hoping to scare him. Daniel Riley didn't scare easily. These jackasses were in for a shock.

"Aw, you're pretending you don't know me. I'm hurt."

Tiny fingers ran over Daniel's spine. Cold fingers that crept up his back and traveled straight to his heart. He turned, his gaze meeting the one person he didn't want to see in here. Wade Bowen.

"Hey buddy," Wade smiled.

"Fuck off."

"Oh, now is that any way to treat an old friend?"

"We aren't friends." Daniel turned back to the guards, wondering what the hell was taking them so long.

"I hoped we could kiss and make up, Danny. You don't want to make up? Kristina would want you to have a friend or two in here. You know the nights are long, and painful, when you don't have the right friends."

Daniel stiffened at Kristina's name and turned back to Wade.

The jerk grinned and leaned on the bars. With his head shaved his eyes stood out, colder than Daniel remembered even with the wide smile.

"Kristina is going to pay for this. I promise you," Daniel said.

"I don't think so. You'd have to make it out of here alive to see it happen."

"Riley!" the guard called.

Daniel didn't move. His body remained frozen in place at Wade's words.

Wade laughed and retreated into his cell.

Someone touched Daniel's arm. He turned. Solmes nodded to the cell ahead.

"I want a different cell," Daniel said.

"Oh? Well let's see if we can find one with a view then, shall we? Wouldn't want you to be unhappy with your accommodations." The guard shoved him forward.

Daniel resisted. "That asshole just threatened me. Didn't you hear him?"

"Who? Bowen? Don't worry about him. He's moving soon. Besides, he wouldn't mess up his good behavior. He's hoping to get out early. I heard he has a fine piece of ass waiting on the outside for him."

"What?"

"Oh, that's right I forgot. You and Wade go way back don't you?"

"How do you—"

"How do I know that? I go way back with Wade too." Solmes winked and pushed him forward.

Daniel walked to the cell, his mind reeling. What the hell? They were fucking with him, because he was the new guy. Stupid asses. "I'll call my lawyer and I'll make sure you lose your job. This is unprofessional," he warned.

"Oh now honey, you won't be making any phone calls." Solmes moved closer, pretending to mess around with the mattress on the lower bunk. "Last I checked, dead men can't use telephones." He laughed and straightened to nod toward the shadows before exiting the cell.

Daniel glanced to the right, where a large man stood next to the cell doors grinning at them.

He waved and then blew a kiss in Daniel's direction.

Daniel shuddered. This wasn't right. They couldn't do this to him. "I demand to speak with someone in charge."

"Sorry, it's his day off. Maybe tomorrow. I'll see you in the yard, Riley." Solmes waved, winking as the other two guards pulled the doors closed.

The echoing clank as the lock slid into place sent a chill up Daniel's spine.

The man advanced, brushing against Daniel's shoulder as he climbed onto the top bunk.

"Hey Chunk," Wade's voice called from his cell.

Chunk?

"Yeah?" the man replied. His dark gaze on Daniel.

"You make sure my friend gets real comfortable. I want him to feel like he was at home."

"Oh, I'll make sure he feels real welcome."

Daniel moved to the far side of the cell, his back to the wall.

The man—Chunk—grinned and rolled onto his side. He ran a finger over the rough wool blanket and raised an eyebrow.

"Stay away from me." Daniel warned. His voice sounded shaky and he thought he might vomit.

"Don't worry, Sugar. We won't get acquainted till the lights go out."

RENÉE MILLER

CHAPTER 35

"What's that, Mama?" Cadence pointed to the wall that stretched high above them, the top lined in barbed wire.

"Wire," she replied, urging the toddler forward.

"Ugly. Don't like it."

Smiling, Kristina ran a hand over her daughter's dark curls, and adjusted the little bow that held her ponytail in place. The damp spring morning had grown into a beautiful afternoon. She looked up to the sky, breathing in the warm air. The clouds rolled lazily across the sun. She could hardly believe the day had come.

Cars whizzed past them, many paying no heed to the yellow caution light that hung overhead or the orange signs indicating men at work a few blocks ahead, warning them to slow down. The last time she'd visited the penitentiary had been shortly after Daniel's conviction. He had requested she speak to him, and to stop the relentless calls from the press and the nagging curiosity in her gut, she'd gone. He had little new to say, other than his vow to prove she was lying. Strangely he didn't mention Wade, and Kristina wondered at the time if Wade had been moved to another facility to avoid contact with Daniel. She had no way to find out though.

Another inmate, a terrifying man serving two life sentences already, took exception to Daniel's attitude just a few months later and had stabbed him several times with some kind of tool while working out in the yard. He'd succumbed to his injuries days later. She didn't shed a tear.

Before the prison, Kristina stopped and checked her watch. Almost time. She'd been told to wait across the street. Thomas told her to try to blend in. She chuckled and looked around. Pretty hard to blend into nothing.

Cadence bent to pick up something from the sidewalk and Kristina opened her mouth to admonish her, but the little girl beamed up at her before the words left her mouth. "Look, a pinny."

"A penny," Kristina corrected. "It means good luck."

A thud and voices across the street. Kristina turned. She took Cadence's hand in hers, and pointed to the steps of the prison, where a lone figure stood.

He walked down the steps slowly, shielding his eyes from the sun.

Wade.

Kristina longed to run into his arms, but remained rooted to the sidewalk, her heart pounding faster with each step he took.

He stopped at the edge of the steps, his gaze locked with hers.

She covered her mouth as a sob escaped.

He grinned.

Time stood still as Wade ran the rest of the way, sweeping her off her feet as his arms closed around her so tight she lost her breath. He released her only to kneel down and touch Cadence's cheek. Her daughter smiled up at him and leaned closer to Kristina.

Wade stood and turned back, his eyes brimming with tears. He took her face in his hands and kissed her hard.

She laughed as he hugged her.

"God, I've missed you," he murmured against her lips.

THE END

Other books by

Renée miller

Welcome to Albertsville: Population 397 and falling.

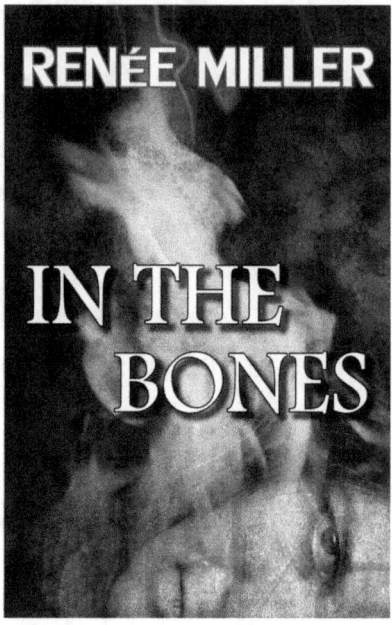

When Ryan Cassidy claims a house left to him by his estranged grandparents, he becomes tangled in the mystery of a town crushed by a deadly secret spanning generations.

The town's power core, which includes the reeve, his council members, and the local police, smother opposition with deceit, brutality and fear. They will stop at nothing to keep the horror they've committed buried.

A severe winter storm leaves Albertsville snowbound—a trap only the dead can hope to flee—and Ryan becomes a liability that must be silenced at any cost.

The answers to the town's mystery and its salvation are hidden...In the Bones.

Jackson Murphy wants, freedom… at any price.

Murphy wants to end his marriage and keep his money. There are many ways out of a bad marriage but Jack chooses the most expedient one.

He commits the perfect murder but his brilliance leads to trouble. Soon, his business partner wants out, his mistress insists on a wedding ring, his blackmailing cousin comes back for more, and an enterprising competitor tries trying to squeeze Jack out of business.

Each problem he eliminates creates two more. Jack ends up on the run from the Mob and a tenacious police detective.

What they don't yet know is this: what Jackson Murphy wants, Jackson Murphy gets.

Coming in 2014 from
Crescent Moon Press

Lucky

Everything Caerus Thornton touches turns to gold... or dies.

Thanatos, god of death, has an almost flawless record until he encounters Caerus. For some reason, he can't fulfill the simple task of delivering death to the tiny blonde fated to die in the delivery room.

Furious at his failure, the Fates exile Thanatos on Earth, where he must remain until he redeems himself in the eyes of his fellow gods.

Somewhere along the way Thanatos finds himself falling for the woman he's spent more than two decades trying to kill.

ABOUT THE AUTHOR

Renee Miller lives in Tweed, Ontario. Books have always been a treasured item in Renee's home, and she reads all genres, preferring strong character-driven plots. She's also a big fan of humor and tends to root for the bad guys.

Reneemiller@bell.net
www.twitter.com/ReneeMJ
www.facebook.com/pages/Renee-Miller/548882035137022
Blog: www.authorreneemiller.com

You've been enjoying a DeadPixel Publications Book.

DeadPixel Publications is a group of people with day jobs, writing for the pure love of the craft and hoping for a little success along the way. By joining forces we help promote each other and create a community of sharing and collaboration with one goal in mind: Helping the public find some kick ass books to read (if we do say so ourselves).
Please visit our website.
www.deadpixelpublications.com